THESE TRESPASSES

BOOK ONE OF THE INFINITE CYCLE

by Kenneth W. Cain

Macabre Ink

-For Heather

The drug store door banged, the corpse of the woman keeping it from opening. She heard a whomp-whomp-whomp as if something were batting against the door, pushing to get inside. And she heard the woman's body give. One of the woman's arms slapped against the floor as the door forced her to roll to one side. Whoever was outside pushed harder, the door ramming against the woman's weight, sliding her a little more out of the way. Sheila heard it all, the corpse knocking into several small boxes scattered across the floor. Then, they pushed in through the opening, scattering several boxes of medicine across the tile floor. She heard their feet moving through them for a split second, as they seemed to stop and take in the store.

A second later, there was nothing but dead calm, similar to the moment that no doubt came right before a rattlesnake struck. She considered her options, thinking it might be best to thrust herself up, whip out an Uzi and blow her intruder away. The problem with that was Sheila didn't have a gun, and she wasn't even sure she'd know how to use one if she did. She considered throwing some boxes of condoms at her intruder, maybe she'd get lucky and poke an eye out. Perhaps that would give her enough time to run away.

Who are you kidding?

She'd never been the violent sort, let alone athletic. She was fit and had a decent body, but she rarely even used the hardcore vocabulary that went along with any of this action hero stuff. If this ended up being one of those soldiers, and they were looking for her, she'd be better off using charm over fisticuffs. And she didn't like trying to charm anyone given what they'd done to some of the citizens. So instead of being reactionary, she kept her face plastered to the floor hoping whoever or whatever had come inside wouldn't discover her.

Chapter 1

Sheila picked herself up from the ground among a cloud of dust and debris, ears ringing. Around her, chaos ensued, people running down the street with bloodied faces, their clothes in tatters, some of them screaming, and others looking only afraid. They scattered like cockroaches, all except Sheila, who felt too dazed to see straight. She thought to call her parents, to let them know she was all right, but couldn't find her purse or phone.

After steadying herself on a nearby wall, she scanned the ground, searching for either. She observed the horizon, seeing the result of the bombing spread across the bruised evening sky.

"Why would they do this?" a man said, talking to no one as he limped down the street, his voice muted to her ears.

But he'd asked the right question. Who had done this, and why?

Regaining some of her senses, she stumbled down Main Street of the small town of Elks Grove. The haze surrounding her seemed to intensify, making the dark seem darker, and she wondered when it would disperse. She heard things, too, strange unrecognizable sounds. Those sounds were getting louder and closer.

The resulting dust cloud had engulfed the entire area, making it difficult to see. She could feel particles landing on her skin, getting in her eyes, making them tear up. Still, she forged ahead, her hands up, as she tried to maneuver her way down the street, with no idea where she was going.

Something in the murk moved, and her eyes went to it, struggling to recognize anything through her welling tears. She wiped her eyes with balled-up fists, surprised when she pulled them away and saw blood. Gathering up her shirt, she dabbed at her face, trying to wipe it away. A fresh warm bead trickled down her cheek, signifying a fresh wound on her head. She prodded at the sore with her fingers, wincing, and decided she couldn't tend to it here.

The movement in the dust cloud changed. Difficult to identify much, she thought she saw a man. Staring at him, she lost herself, struggling to make out legs and arms, a face.

Another man burst out of the miasma. "Over there! Two of you! The rest, on me!"

Now there were others, peeling off all around her, some of them stopping for a brief second to look at her. They wore masks, their voices muffled, but she could make out most of what they were saying.

"Base, this is Alpha 5," a woman said into a radio, her mask up, eyes squinted. "Operation Grasshopper is underway." She slipped her mask back down, released the radio on her shoulder, and moved in on the rubble of the nearby buildings.

What was Operation Grasshopper? How'd they even come up with such a silly name?

"Ma'am?" Sheila felt someone tugging at her arm. "Are you okay?"

She only stared at the masked man.

"Do you require assistance?" he asked.

She still didn't answer. And now he was escorting her away. She went with him, too stunned and unable to process all of this.

Then, as realization dawned on her, she yanked her arm away. The man staggered to a stop. He looked frustrated and threw his hands down, cursing her before running to catch up with the others.

There must have been two dozen men and women, all of them scouring the ruins of the city, ducking into destroyed buildings and back out moments later. She did not know what they were looking for. Perhaps they sought the terrorists who'd destroyed this town.

Walking down the road, she happened upon a few of those soldiers. They were setting up camp, starting to patrol the area. An odd thought came to her, as she didn't know where she'd parked or even if her car was still intact. What vehicles she saw lay mostly on their sides, windows smashed, dented heaps of metal. Those that weren't overturned were burning. And she heard something familiar, an engine.

A Humvee sped out of the dust, its tires spinning in the dirt. They had no interest in her or helping her get to safety. As they passed, one soldier, a man, leaned out of the window and wolf whistled. The sound of it froze her, most inappropriate given the circumstances. She watched the vehicle round a corner, hearing laughter burst through the open window.

All she could think right then was *boys and their weapons, big or small. It's always one or the other.*

The troops started to clear out as they spread around the impacted area. Suddenly she found herself alone, with only the occasional cry for help, and little else.

She had greater concerns, too. If she couldn't find a working vehicle, how was she going to get to the train station? She supposed she could call her dad if she could find a working phone, but he'd have to come all the way from St. Louis. That was close to a three-hour drive. She had doubts any of the payphones worked; lines were down all around her. Even the electric was out, a few downed cables sparking in puddles of spilled liquid.

There were other issues, too. As her eyes began to refocus and the tearing eased, she spotted other people. Bodies lay all around her, among debris and fallen stone. Their faces looked bruised, mouths unmoving, eyes still open.

Surely one of them has a working cellphone. Could she even bring herself to check?

She approached one, a woman she thought, seeing the streaks of blood in her hair. Her body lay twisted at an impossible angle, one arm separated from the shoulder, still in its sleeve but thrown behind her. The woman's purse lay next to her; at least Sheila thought it was the woman's. That face haunted Sheila as she forced herself to kneel beside the woman. She closed her eyes and dug through the purse, felt credit cards, some papers, lipstick, and finally a cellphone.

Withdrawing the phone, she opened her eyes and looked at

it. The screen was cracked badly, but it appeared to be working. She dialed her parent's number and waited, listening closely.

All that came was an odd busy-like sound, only different. That probably meant the tower was down, and she wondered how long she'd have to wait for service to return. For now, she turned the phone off and stuffed it in her back pocket, before proceeding down the street.

Someone out in the haze was moaning. She could hear that much, but also voices moving toward that moan, talking back and forth. She went about her way, trying to ignore the sound, until she couldn't.

A gun shot, and the moaning stopped. Had the soldiers killed this person? What would bring them to that? She didn't want to find out and moved with purpose.

As she progressed, she saw fewer and fewer corpses, but of those she happened across, they all appeared to have been shot in the head. The wounds looked fresh, too, evidence that whoever had committed these atrocities, friend or foe, they'd done so recently. She couldn't be sure of the culprit, as she'd seen no one perform these acts of violence, but hoped they wouldn't be coming back this way.

Had some plague broken out in Southern Illinois? Why on Earth would any terrorist attack a nowhere place like this? More importantly, if it came at the hands of those troops, why had they let her live? Did they let others live, too? Was it only the wounded they were killing? Was that only temporary?

Trudging through the debris, she stopped to look at the sign, which informed her she'd arrived at the Gadeson Hotel. From the brief description beneath the plaque, she read how the building had stood for four decades. A large section of wall remained, its pale-yellow paint covered with sprays of blood. The colors shimmered in contrast, making the edges appear orange. In front of the wall, three bodies lay crossed over one another, twisted in positions that would be impossible to manage while alive. Sheila identified a large gold wedding band on the finger of the elderly gentlemen on top, staring at it thoughtfully, wondering only now why she'd never married.

To her left, a large wooden front desk remained in perfect

condition. It was a stark contrast to the destruction surrounding it. A young man sat in the chair behind the desk, a hole through his forehead, his feet still propped up on the desk. She read the nametag aloud, "Jay Colsten." The customary ledger sat atop the desk, a pen lying next to it. The book was still open, too, as if the Gadeson's last customer had written it in moments earlier before everything went bad.

Sheila shifted around the desk, tripping over Jay's legs by accident. This knocked them off the desk, causing Jay's chair to spin. He lolled to one side, rolling outward, and spilled off the chair, his legs knocked into Sheila's, throwing her off balance.

She regained her footing and pushed her way past Jay's stiff legs to get to the desk. Standing there, she perused the ledger and saw a red X first, then a note scribbled on the same page.

Chapter 2

The day of the devastation, Marty left the family farm. He almost wished he hadn't, certain he would have died if he'd stayed. That would have been easier. But life was never easy.

Fate had taken both his wife and daughter and now, he'd lost his brother, too. He'd found some hope in the form of travelling companions, but even as he got to know them better he couldn't stop worrying about losing them. This world seemed to have it in for him, so he didn't trust his surroundings, always mindful of every sound. Nowhere felt safe, and a large part of him had died back at that house. Still, there was this underlying need to survive despite it all, and, that if nothing else, pushed him on.

He brushed his hair back with both hands, sensing a greasy feeling on his fingers. In need of a wash, he reminisced about the sting of a hot shower. Steam always calmed him, both mentally and physically, washing away the tension as if it were dirt. There was no time for such luxuries now, though. They had to stay ahead of the soldiers.

Arms falling to either side of the ledger, he read the names on the left-hand page. He didn't recognize any of them, as he'd lived out in the country prior to the bombing. He wondered if either of his companions knew any of these names, but he didn't ask. Being the only hotel in town, there'd been many people here. A handful of those people had survived, all of them standing in the lobby. He'd tried to convince them to come along, stressing the importance of leaving and even pointing out what they'd seen on the way through town. But the desk attendant just kept on assuring them otherwise.

In Marty's experience, having once been a teacher, teenagers thought they knew it all. Jay hadn't seen what Marty had, so he had no way of knowing these soldiers weren't here to protect them. Something must have gone wrong because the soldiers were exterminating the innocent. That meant they didn't know who was infected by whatever disease they were trying to prevent from spreading and who wasn't. That had to be the reason they'd taken to killing off anyone the slightest bit suspicious.

Still, no matter how much Marty pleaded, the most he got from the stubborn boy was permission to use the half of a ledger page to leave a note in case others wanted to join them.

The boy sat there, feet propped up on the desk, tapping a steady beat on the counter with his outstretched foot. Every rap unnerved Marty, bringing him to the point of wanting to smack the kid upside his head. But he knew doing something drastic like that wouldn't further anyone's cause. Likely, it would sever any chance of convincing the others to join them and dismiss any hope of the kid letting him leave a note behind.

Turning his attention to the ledger, he was at a sudden loss for words. One would think a man who once taught English literature would have words spinning around in his head at all times, but over the years he'd lost touch with that man, distancing himself by focusing on his work at the farm. He still read from time to time, but he didn't enjoy it like he once had. And it took him ungodly lengths of time to get through a single book. Thinking of it all now, he didn't want to dwell on the past. Doing so could debilitate him.

Pressing the pen to the ledger, he noted the dimple it left on the page. Such a slight touch of the tip and already he'd done the damage. Seeing this urged him on, though. So, with little hesitation, he started rewriting a familiar letter that had transformed over the past few hours.

February 4th

If you're reading this note, you already know about the bombing. Maybe you aren't aware of how bad things have gotten. I don't have time to explain all of what I've seen or know, but I'll do my best.

The soldiers are heading east. Do not mistake their purpose. They are not here to help you. I have witnessed their crimes first-hand. I'm hoping they won't be so thorough to notice my notes. They appear to have their hands full with more pressing matters.

Be careful. They're afraid. They'll shoot without hesitation at this point. I know this because they've shot at us twice so far. I'm not clear on all the details, but I've overheard a few of them talking. They've mentioned the worry of government officials, how they'll do anything to keep this from spreading any farther than it already has. It's clear they either haven't found a cure or aren't interested in one.

What has them so worried are monsters. I know that sounds silly, but they very much exist. I've witnessed my brother go through this transformation, and all I can say is, I understand why they've taken such drastic measures to eradicate these creatures. Whatever started this hasn't moved on, and I can't help but worry the real hell is still yet to come. When they finish this business, they won't care who you are or what you might offer them.

We're heading for the Indiana border, hoping to sneak out of state if we can. You're welcome to join us. We stop frequently, trying to help others, and occasionally, I leave behind a letter or note. If you spot a red X, you'll know you're on the right path.

My sincerest wishes for your survival,
Marty

He sat down the pen and perused his work. There was something satisfying about leaving these notes. About helping others. It made him feel somewhat normal again. He retrieved the can of red paint and shook it.

Jay went rigid, but he didn't get up. "Hey man, what are you—"

Marty sprayed a small X below what he'd written.

"Jesus," Jay said. "You could have warned me."

Stepping away from the desk, Marty nodded at Jay, then the others. "Are you certain I can't convince any of you to come with us?"

An old man puffed away on a cigar. A blonde woman looked nervous. None of them seemed interested.

"I told you," Jay said. "We're good. We'll be okay here."

Marty didn't argue. He just turned to leave, waiting a second longer in case any of them reconsidered. When they said nothing, he joined his companions outside and went on his way.

Chapter 3

Sheila dwelled on Marty's salutation, considering what she'd meant. She didn't like the fact his note confirmed her suspicion that it had been their own forces attacking these people and not some terrorist cell. But it was the other details he'd conveyed that intrigued her most. What had he meant by... transformation? And monsters? Was this the all-famous zombie apocalypse finally come to fruition after a multitude of movies and TV shows on that very subject?

A smile found her face. Even thinking it sounded farfetched. Perhaps this was all a joke. Maybe Marty had lost his marbles. Would tracking him down lead to something worse? Surely *everyone* in his group wasn't crazy, though. Was that even possible?

She didn't know, but she felt inclined to find out at this point. Part of her wished she had the energy to catch up to Marty and his friends this very night, so she could ease her concerns once and for all. Besides, she couldn't help but feel a little lonely. But she did not know how far ahead of her they were.

By herself, she was vulnerable. And she was still right smack dab in the middle of town. At some point, those soldiers might come back. Maybe they'd remember seeing her, start looking for her. She didn't like being hunted.

Peering into the night through a hole in the far wall of the hotel, little moonlight lit the world outside. Somewhere nearby a downed power line sparked, though it provided no extra light. She didn't think she could sleep through that noise, and if she wanted to catch up with Marty's group tomorrow, she'd need a good night's sleep. And she couldn't sleep here where there were so many corpses. And it would take too much effort to move them, and even if she could, she worried the smell would worsen before daylight. At least one of them looked awful heavy.

Sheila exited the hotel in search of a better place to hunker down. A quick glance to her left, then her right, revealed a dumpy corner drug store down the road. It looked like it had taken little damage compared to the adjoining shops. Hopefully, there'd been a lot less foot traffic in the store, too.

Making her way down the street, she remained cautious of her surroundings. Alert of every sound, she kept an eye out for any soldiers. And oddly enough, she scanned for monsters, too.

"Great," she whispered. "Now you're losing it, too."

Still, being exposed in the open like this made her to feel like a mouse making its way across a long field where hawks and even owls swerved in the sky above, and cats and dogs and all the other creatures roamed the surrounding ground. She wasn't so sure that analogy was far from the truth, either. And she wasn't sure she could outrun anyone, let alone a trained soldier.

At least Marty had given her a good idea. Maybe she could escape to Indiana. But even this concerned her, because she did not know how far this devastation reached? If nothing else, Marty and his friends wanted what she wanted more than anything right now—to get out of harm's way. That was enough to warrant her tracking them down. She'd be safer in a group.

When she reached the front door of the drugstore, her paranoia dissolved. The thought of getting off these streets relieved her. But the door stuck when she pulled, as if it had somehow swelled shut in the doorframe. A sudden flash of panic washed over her, and she tried to look through the spider-webbed glass but couldn't see anything. But, in leaning against the door, it opened slightly.

"Really?" she said to herself. "Duh."

She couldn't help but laugh at herself. But her nerves didn't ease any because something kept the door from opening all the way. She leaned to one side and peeked in, instantly seeing why.

An older woman's legs wobbled when Sheila pushed the door. The woman's ancient blue dress suggested her age, despite not being able to see her face. She could see the wrinkled skin on one hand, and the varicose veins on her calves. And judging by her ankles, she was a rather large woman, which likely was the reason Sheila was having so much trouble opening the door.

Sheila leaned back and thrust her shoulder against the door handle, pushing hard. The woman's feet bounced, then slid slowly along the floor a yard. Sheila kept on pushing, putting her back into it. All at once, the woman's round body rolled to one side.

Sliding into the building, she braced the door open with a bucket she found on the floor. The first thing Sheila did was look for others. The warm glow of a battery-operated lantern that sat on the counter filled the room, probably placed there by the owner or left behind by the soldiers after they completed their business. It was bright enough to see the woman was alone here, which was far better than the situation at the hotel. The place was a mess, nearly all the supplies on the floor beneath their respective shelves. She decided a nice place to bed down for the night would be behind the counter.

A flicker of electricity caught her attention, originating from somewhere at the back of the store, what she believed led to the back storage area. This concerned her some, wondering if the electrical failure could catch fire in the middle of the night. The last thing she needed was to wake to a wall of flames. But she was also too tired to care. She considered leaving the front door open for a quick escape, but decided against it, and yanked the bucket free. She left it cracked, though, and rolled the body back over to block anyone else from entering.

Making her way over to the counter, Sheila cast a concerned eye back at the owner. In the dimming glow of the lantern, she could see the dark red stain on her forehead. She couldn't imagine sleeping around a dead person. What if Marty was right, and she somehow came back to life in the middle of the night? Maybe Sheila could drag the woman outside, but she'd have to risk being seen. And it would be no easy task. She supposed she could roll the woman—

Do you realize how crazy this sounds? You're being ridiculous.

Dragging her feet through the clutter, she went behind the counter and stepped over a pile of condom boxes. The floor was littered with nicotine gum packs, batteries, candies, and an assortment of other impulse items. Using the edge of her foot, Sheila slid the mess away enough to clear a large enough area to lie down. She lined the spot with an "I Love Illinois" sweatshirt she found hanging in a storeroom closet and kneeled upon the garment, closing her eyes. She folded her hands the way she had when she was young, trying to focus on something positive, the thought of her parents. For a moment, she stayed in this position, dwelling on everything that had happened so far, and how fast it had occurred.

"Deliver us from evil," she said, the only words she could manage.

The floor was cool against her cheek, seeping through the cheap fabric of the sweatshirt. It was hard, but she was too tired to notice. She was sure she would feel it in the morning, but with a flicker of electricity from the back hall, she drifted off.

Chapter 4

Among the sound of the chirping crickets and throng of locusts, Sheila woke, staring into total darkness. Somewhere outside, she heard a downed power line crackle. The light in the back hallway flickered, a sound she'd grown accustomed to over these last few hours of restless sleep. But what really woke her had been something else, an unfamiliar noise.

She didn't dare move for fear of being discovered by some intruder. So she kept her head tilted up, her ear tuning in the noise. And sure enough, there it was again. She heard something rustling among the debris right outside and something else, too. At first she couldn't make the second noise out, then she realized it was her heart rapping against the floor. At least whoever made that first sound was still outside, which she was safe for...

The drug store door banged, the corpse of the woman keeping it from opening. She heard a whomp-whomp-whomp as if something were batting against the door, pushing to get inside. And she heard the woman's body give. One of the woman's arms slapped against the floor as the door forced her to roll to one side. Whoever was outside pushed harder, the door ramming against the woman's weight, sliding her a little more out of the way. Sheila heard it all, the corpse knocking into several small boxes scattered across the floor. Then, they pushed in through the opening, scattering several boxes of medicine across the tile floor. She heard their feet moving through them for a split second, as they seemed to stop and take in the store.

A second later, there was nothing but dead calm, similar to the moment that no doubt came right before a rattlesnake struck. She considered her options, thinking it might be best to thrust herself up, whip out an Uzi and blow her intruder away. The problem with that was Sheila didn't have a gun, and she wasn't even sure she'd know how to use one if she did. She considered throwing some boxes of condoms at her intruder, maybe she'd get lucky and poke an eye out. Perhaps that would give her enough time to run away.

Who are you kidding?

She'd never been the violent sort, let alone athletic. She was fit and had a decent body, but she rarely even used the hardcore vocabulary that went along with any of this action hero stuff. If this ended up being one of those soldiers, and they were looking for her, she'd be better off using charm over fisticuffs. And she didn't like trying to charm anyone given what they'd done to some of the citizens. So instead of being reactionary, she kept her face plastered to the floor hoping whoever or whatever had come inside wouldn't discover her.

The gleeful chirp of crickets returned, growing louder and louder as they regained their confidence. She heard a hum, too, which could be the electric wires outside. Or it could be a truck idling somewhere, ready to speed her off to some destination upon her capture. Then another noise followed, closer, what sounded like a rat scurrying across the floor.

It surprised her when she looked down and discovered her leg was twitching. She grasped the leg with both hands, trying to calm her nerves. Even then it kept twitching, each time making more noise. Worse yet, that other noise returned, louder and more obnoxious, whomp-whomp-whomp-whomp repeatedly. She thought it her heartbeat and checked, but although it beat wildly, the sound she heard came from elsewhere in the store.

It felt like several minutes of her lying there, waiting for her intruder to leave. But they didn't, and her patience grew thinner. She wondered how far away the back entrance was, whether it was locked. Eventually she would have to make a run for it.

That humming sound intensified. She turned her head, trying to single out that sound and what it could be. And she heard other strange noises, a steady click and a grinding crunch, then a wet sound, too, one that sounded like an animal lapping up water.

The electric short flashed, which made her jump with surprise. Although she tried not to, her leg flinched enough to cause the sole of her shoe to screech against the tile floor.

She shrunk into a ball, aware all the noises on the other side of this counter had silenced, even the crickets. Whoever was in the store with her had shifted their focus, no doubt staring her way, watching intently.

The silence lasted long enough for Sheila to count to two hundred and fifteen. Counting eased her nerves. One by one, all those sounds returned. The grinding, the crunch, the lapping, the whomp-whomp-whomp, all of it, and it was driving her mad.

That was when she considered something daring. And even as she began to crawl up to her knees, she was cursing herself for doing so. What was she thinking, being so brave? She wouldn't stand a chance if it were one of those soldiers or something worse.

With a growing urgency, Sheila got to her knees, staying beneath the top of the counter. She waited, taking slow breaths to settle herself. Convinced she was as calm as she ever would be, she lifted her head over the top of the counter and stared out into the darkness.

At first, she saw nothing. The light flickered and what she saw took her breath away at first, as the shadow it cast on the far wall was frightening. A split second later she identified her intruder.

The poodle stopped licking long enough to acknowledge Sheila's presence. It didn't appear startled by her or even scared. It went back to licking the woman's bloodied face. This wasn't a wild dog; it had tags, which jingled lightly as it licked. And it had recently endured a haircut, some areas with bushy fur and others not. Its tail wagged, striking the door with a steady whomp-whomp-whomp.

Sheila watched in amusement at first, her terror subsiding. But she felt gagged at the realization that this dog might do worse than just lick the woman's face.

Another sound, one familiar, made her ears feel like someone had stuffed cotton in them. The gunshot startled her, as she'd been looking at the dog and saw it go down. A fraction of a second later, she ducked behind the counter again, getting lower and lower, praying no one would find her.

Chapter 5

"Marty?" Bernard stood in the doorway, his dark lumbering form swaying. For a black guy, he had a way about him that was humble, more country than city.

"Hey, how are you doing?"

"Fine. Sorry, didn't mean to interrupt."

Truth told Marty was thankful for the disturbance. Leaving a paper trail of letters bothered him. Not only did he think it a waste of time, as it was likely no one would take the time to read a random letter, but he worried the wrong people might find them. That could lead to them being caught long before they even reached the Indiana border. Besides, there was no way of knowing how many survivors were out there, let alone how many thought to trail them. He'd seen the aftermath and how people had scattered off in all directions. Even those he'd encountered had their own plans, most looking for a place to hide out until this was over.

"No. Nope. That's all right." He returned his attention to the ratty piece of newsprint sitting on the table he'd dug up from a pile of rubbish in the room's corner. "Give me just one second."

Marty jotted the last few sentences down while Bernard came closer. Right as Marty wrote the last few words, he did so in Bernard's shadow. The big guy waited patiently for Marty to finish, as he'd been the catalyst for Marty writing these notes at each stop. Marty sat down the pencil and looked up.

"You finished?" Bernard's eyebrows rounded.

"Yes, sir. I'm done."

Bernard eyed him with suspicion, as if he didn't fully believe Marty was telling the entire truth. "You sure?"

Marty nodded, but they remained in a stalemate for a

moment until Marty conceded. Finding a spot in the middle of the page with his finger, Marty jotted down one last comment in the margin before setting the pencil down. "Happy?"

"Quite." Bernard smiled. He grabbed the spray paint off the table and made an X across the surface. Then he leaned over and patted Marty on the shoulder. "Now, was that so hard?"

Marty laughed. "Not at all, my friend."

Something about Bernard always reminded him of his brother, Jake, which made Marty feel like a young boy again, being teased by his older brother. How the two of them used play war. Jake always got to be the countries that won World War 1 and 2. Only when they pretended they were in Vietnam did Marty get to play the U.S., and he'd gotten good at playing dead because of it. He'd hated losing as much as Jake had, but those playful days seemed so far behind him now. Bernard had that same flare for winning.

As much as the big lug gave Marty a hard time about these letters, he considered Bernard to be a brother. Besides, the letters had proven to be therapeutic for Marty, and for Nancy, who liked to read them before they left. Though his suggestion, Bernard never read a single letter, which made Marty wonder if he could read at all. The guy was as big as a house, a gentle giant. He wouldn't hurt anyone unless he absolutely had no other choice.

"I spotted something out on the horizon." Bernard pointed at a small hill through a hole the size of a limousine in the back wall.

Marty got up and walked over to Nancy.

"Other side of that hill there."

"One second." Marty glanced back, then handed the note to Nancy.

Though a little rough around the edges, he thought Bernard had grown fond of her. And perhaps Nancy had grown fond of him, too. They'd make a good pair, Bernard tall and thick, chest like a whisky barrel. And Nancy was a medium build woman with short dark hair. She had a beauty on the inside Marty couldn't deny. The way she looked at the guy, Marty couldn't understand why Bernard hadn't asked her out sooner. He seemed oblivious to her hints, even when Marty reacted to them, egging on Bernard.

Turning his attention back outside, Marty stood beside Bernard and found the spot in question with ease, as there weren't many large hills in Illinois.

A frown creased Bernard's round face. "I don't think that's gonna bode well for us."

Marty wasn't sure what to think about it. "So," Marty spun to Nancy, "what's the word?"

Bernard followed his gaze to the woman. She smiled then nodded.

With a sideways glance, Marty swore he saw love brewing in the big lug's eyes. Then, as if a hiccup of emotion occurred, the want in his eyes transformed to one of endearing appreciation and innocence. Marty knew then just how much Bernard loved this woman. They'd known each other for a long time. But Marty began to doubt Bernard would ever relay his longing to Nancy. And he couldn't get a solid read on her, either so who knew whether she would reciprocate those feelings.

"Okay. So, not good in what way?" Marty asked Bernard, pressing his lips together.

Something about this role he'd taken on bothered him. It reminded him of all those childhood days playing games with his brother. How his entire youth seemed to encompass leaders and followers. He'd tried to stray from any resemblance to those childhood games, as he had no desire to be a leader of any sort. But those games returned with ease, as did the role that best suited him.

"Well, I can't be too sure, but something just seems off," Bernard said, returning his eyes to the hill and scratching his balding head. "I think these armed forces we've been seeing around have been here all along, maybe even before the bombs fell. Maybe we just never saw them."

This notion played on Marty's concerns. "Well, you would know better than I, as you lived right outside of town. What do you remember?"

"I wasn't paying too much attention, but I'd swear I saw military appear right out of the gate. Even out by where Nancy and I lived. They seemed to come out of nowhere."

Marty sighed. "Well, that would be something, wouldn't it?"

"Yep. But that's not all. I'm not so sure anyone bombed us from a distance. I think those were charges, maybe planted days earlier." Bernard wasn't a big thinker, but he knew things. He'd served a short stint made shorter by an injury. He knew something of the weaponry and war, having read many books on the subject along with his training. "And despite that, I don't think they were trying to kill innocents...not at first. Which means, of course, that came as an afterthought, even if it was one they'd planned for up front."

Marty scanned the horizon and saw the crowd. He should have known they'd set up posts on the borders. It would be even worse if they got there and found out these were reserves guarding the points of entry. Reserves were expendable, which would make them so, too. At a glance, the men and women guarding the border appeared to be local militia.

"That is disappointing." Marty tugged at the gray hairs on his chin, caught in deep thought. "Are you certain of this?"

"No." Bernard looked lost for a moment, as if trying to run these thoughts back through some mental checker to see if he could confirm any of this. "I'm not sure of anything." Bernard's eyes lit up. "What the hell was that?"

Marty hadn't been looking. He scanned Bernard for the answer.

Bernard's eyes widened. "I think I just saw a tank."

"That most definitely is not good." Marty watched, trying to see it himself. "If they've moved on to heavy machinery, we could be walking right to our own graves."

Did that mean things had progressed? Had the troops let up on the killing as they got farther from the epicenter or were things only getting worse? Either way, with a tank, they could roll in any time they wanted, take their time and clean up any mess they'd missed on their first wave. Marty wasn't sure, as leaders could be so unpredictable with matters like this, where some strange contamination had broken out. They'd do anything to contain it.

Bernard squinted at Nancy as she returned the letter to the table. It appeared his large friend had grown overtired. Maybe Bernard was just seeing things, as Marty still hadn't seen the tank. After a moment of indecision, he decided the ex-gas attendant's eyesight was fine. Marty trusted his gut. "Well, we better go check it out to be sure."

"Why not just head south?" Bernard asked.

"If they're setup like this in the east, they'll be set up around the entire perimeter. We can't be sure of their intention yet. It reminds me too much of a pigeon shoot."

Bernard glanced back at Nancy with a boyish look in his face, such a caring man trapped within that large frame. Love like that seemed impossible for Marty after what he'd been through, so he had no business meddling in Bernard's love life.

"Do you think we'll die, Marty?"

Bernard's question was so to the point, it startled Marty. He wanted to say yes, as that was the obvious outcome of this all. But he was no more a leader right now than he was a schoolteacher anymore, or even a farmer. Those parts of him had perished. Now he wasn't sure what words classified him other than the truth, that he was alone. History had proven his greatest enemy, as he'd lost everyone he'd ever cared about. Knowing that made him worry about these new companions.

It's too late. You have an obligation to these people.

"No," Marty said in an outright lie. "We won't die. Not today."

He put on his game face, which he'd learned as a kid playing baseball. Having been a small child, skinny, arms like twigs, he'd been afraid of getting hit by the baseball. Jake had taught him to put on his game face, and Marty had tried. The very next at bat, he made a face at the pitcher, to which the kid had just smiled. The ball came in and Marty swung, but he struck out, again and again. Yet none of that failure mattered had mattered so much back then, even with his game face on. If nothing else, he'd shown that he could stand at that plate and not back out. That pitcher, who'd once thought Marty an easy out, had to face him. That meant he'd earned some level of respect. So he'd won some small portion of that war, even if he got hit by the ball. And he had, too, though it came a full year later.

Something similar was happening now with Bernard. He looked sold on Marty's thoughts. And eventually, he moved on without another word. Marty watched until he could no longer see Bernard, letting out a deep sigh. He hadn't even realized what he was doing, and he regretted it instantly, hoping Bernard hadn't heard.

He retrieved the pencil and turned it in his fingers, stared down at the newsprint, and crossed out the rest of this last paragraph. Hoping to think of something to say in its place, maybe where they would head next. Nothing came to mind. Instead, he drew a large question mark in the margin and hoped this alone would suffice.

Thinking it wouldn't, he hesitated, wanting to add a little more. But he didn't have it in him. He'd worn down mentally, so he had finished the letter as far as it concerned him.

Chapter 6

Sheila had witnessed the bullet pierce the dog's skull, how the impact caused the canine's body to jolt and shudder across the floor. It landed with a loud thump, debris scattering beneath it, medicines and boxes rattling across the floor. For the brief fraction of a second it took for all this to happen, Sheila froze. Then, hearing the men laughing and joking about the kill, she shrank behind the counter.

"What the fuck man?" a man said, his voice shrill. "You scared the crap out of me." His shadow stood in the doorway.

A second man's shadow stretched across the back wall as he pushed by the first man. He didn't respond.

"What was it anyway, a dog?"

"Yep." This man had a deep voice and spoke with a certain pride, as if he'd just killed a grizzly.

"Okay, so why?" The shrill-voiced man's shadow put his hands on his hips. "Noise like that will only scare them off."

"Are you kidding me?" For a long moment, he said nothing. Neither did the shrill-voiced man. Their shadows stood unmoving on the wall, and she worried they might have seen her.

"I guess you're right," the shrill-voiced man finally said. "Can't have anything running around here making trouble."

The other man only grunted.

Now the shrill-voiced man entered, crossed the room and bent. "You kill her, too? Two for one shot?"

Perspiration beaded on Sheila's upper lip. The feeling behind her eyes made her woozy, her heart beating so fast she could barely contain herself.

The deep-voiced man said, "Nah, someone else tagged her."

"Does she look familiar?"

"Nah. But do any of them at this point?"

"I wouldn't mind seeing that one gal again." She imagined him wearing a big grin. "Where ya reckon she's run off to?"

Were they referring to her?

"No idea." The shrilly voiced man chuckled. "But I hope we find out soon enough."

At this, they both giggled.

"Wonder how far she got." The deep-voiced man said.

"Can't be that far. She's just a girl. Ain't nothing like Edwards, either. This one was thin as a rail." He walked across the room, the sound of his shoes on the linoleum getting closer.

The deep-voiced man followed.

What was happening? Were they teasing her?

"What?" said the deep-voiced man.

"Nothing. Probably just nerves."

The short in the electric flashed, and one of the men jumped. The other raised his rifle instinctively. Slowly, they both moved toward the back area. But the worst part was that this brought them ever closer to discovering her.

One of them started, then stopped. "It's a short," the shrill-voiced man said. "The blasts must have shaken something loose."

There, the two shadows remained for a long moment, staring off in the spark's direction. She held her breath, feeling she had been breathing too heavily. The longer she held it, the more it wanted to come out. Afraid she might make some odd noise, she kept her hand pressed against her lips. Even the thumping in her chest sounded too loud, but she couldn't think of any way to quiet that down, not under these circumstances.

"That what you saw?"

"Nah, wasn't that." The shrill-voiced man said. "And I heard it first. Maybe right when we came in. A slight shuffle. Then a quick visual, maybe eyes."

"Eyes? Whose eyes? The dog's?"

Sheila cursed herself for not being more attentive.

"If I knew that I'd say." His shadow on the back wall indicated he was moving toward the counter. With each inch that shadow stretched across the wall, she scrunched up more, closer to the counter. She wished she could somehow melt right into it once she'd run out of floor.

His shadow froze.

"What?" said the shrill-voiced man.

She considered running, was close to it because her nerves were getting the best of her. She felt a slight warm sensation trickle down her thigh.

The shrill-voiced man sniffed. "I smell something."

"You think it's one of those *things*?"

His face came into full view, hovering over the end of the counter. She couldn't move. Even if she could, she'd have to run right through him.

The shrill-voiced man moved in, and now she could see both of them. But they still hadn't discovered her. The deep-voiced man's eyes widened on her. His upper lip glistened with sweat, and he smiled in a way that made her skin crawl. Sheila told herself to hop over the counter, to get away, but her legs felt rubbery and useless.

"Well, will you look at that?" the deep-voiced man's grin grew.

"Huh?"

The deep-voiced man nudged the other soldier. Now he saw her, too, and they were both smiling toothy grins. They were a wall of meat and guns, blocking her exit. She did not know what to do, so she just pulled her legs up and scrunched into the smallest ball she could, all the while looking at them, terrified by what they might do to her. She couldn't stop shaking, especially when a much larger shadow spread across the wall behind the soldiers, drawing their attention.

She saw little of what happened next, but she heard it all. The first sounds were the obvious ones—flesh pounding flesh, a helmet cracking, bodies being slammed against the walls and on the ground—flailing arms slapping anything and everything, their shadows being lifted into the air. At least a dozen bullets ricocheted off the floor or punctured the walls and drop ceiling. Several shattered the glass of nearby counters, missing her by inches. Puffs of plaster and ceiling tile debris rained down on her, getting in her eyes and making it difficult to see. Then, there were the screams, those of grown men being tortured, which only heightened her terror.

There were sounds Sheila hadn't heard before, too, and those were the ones that shocked her most. She'd never heard meat being torn. Their screams sounded almost inhuman as they experienced pain off the scale of what most mortals would ever experience. Hearing these things made her want to scream, but she couldn't. She could only tremble, her throat feeling swollen and scratchy, the panic consuming her and forcing her body to tremble. Only then did she notice the spittle dripping from her gaping mouth to her lap.

Then, something unimaginable happened. A few small bits of viscera showered the walls next to her, striking the shelves and counter like tiny cuts of prime beef. Some stuck to the wall momentarily, before sagging to the floor, leaving a trail of red that slowly ran down the walls. Some landed on shelves, the blood pooling there, spilling over the edge like a fresh coat of crimson of paint and trickling to the floor beside her. Something growled, a guttural sound from deep inside whatever this thing was, and as the sounds of battle faded, whatever being remained moved about the store freely. A horrifying thought encompassed her, wondering if the soldiers were being eaten. It sounded as though they were, and now more than ever, all she wanted was to peek over the edge and see for herself. But doing so would reveal her, so she did nothing, listening as this new intruder dug through the debris and clutter and even the glass of the counter she hid behind.

A brisk rush of air worked its way into and over the counter, making her cold. She shivered, her eyes focused on the large shadow on the back wall. It was just standing there at the counter, for what seemed like a very long time. Then, finally, its form faded from the wall, and only then did she chance a look. The two soldiers weren't there, not really. Very little viscera remained, as if they'd been bugs smacked with a newspaper, their guts smeared across the floor and their bodies carried away by the follow through of the swipe. The woman had gone missing, too.

The shortage in back flickered, lighting the room enough so she could see all the blood. It looked as though someone had painted the room by casting the paint out wherever it landed. Her guts twisted. She couldn't hold it back any longer.

Her stomach purged.

For the rest of the night, she didn't leave her makeshift bedding. She also didn't get a single wink of sleep. Instead, she remained curled up, eyes wide, watching the blood dry. Every once in a while, she heard a sound, the buzz of a fly or a mosquito. Then the short would flash, bringing light to the darkness. The sounds and visions of what she'd seen continued to haunt her.

Chapter 7

Marty could see now Bernard had been correct in his assessment of the soldiers. At least forty troops took positions in the distance, but they didn't seem to notice Marty's group, so he wasn't so concerned yet. They had their hands full with a mob of at least fifty people that had swarmed their gates, wanting only one thing—to pass. A few men and women sat perched atop Humvees and a tank. All of them appeared calm despite the raucous crowd, likely confident in their artillery should matters get out of control. Marty wondered why they weren't just killing them, whether someone had rescinded their green light. Perhaps they were only killing those at the epicenter of what had happened. But how would they react if things got out of control?

The troops on the ground were not so relaxed. They worked hard to maintain a human wall, and each time a member of the mob made a break to pass, they were quick to bring that person down. Thankfully, they'd only used the butts of their rifles so far. But Marty didn't think the kindness would last.

Somewhere among the crowd, Marty identified a soldier he couldn't quite make out barking orders at the soldiers. This was obviously their leader. The man's deep voice stood out, though Marty couldn't make out what he was saying at first. As Marty crept a little closer, he could see the man was using a bullhorn, and his words became clearer. The man directed his comments both at his soldiers and the crowd, ensuring everyone would be dealt with accordingly, that they should remain calm, stay patient. He also gave the soldiers instructions to maintain order.

A thick-bodied man came into view, strutting back and forth with a bullhorn pressed to his lips. "Hold that wall, soldier!"

With his free hand, the man indicated where the problem was, but the soldier never even hesitated, as if he'd identified the issue for himself.

The soldier closed in on a woman in her mid-thirties and lifted his rifle, bringing the butt end down on her head. Marty cringed at the blow. Her children followed as she scrambled back into the crowd, her hands pressed to her head.

"You'll all get your turn," the man with the bullhorn said. "But not a one of you until I get some order. Do you hear me?" He shook his fist at the crowd, what Marty believed might have been more symbolic than anyone in the crowd thought. "Now get back or so *help* me..."

No one budged an inch despite what force they'd already exhibited. These people seemed oblivious to Marty's greatest concern, that although they weren't killing these people, they still would not help anyone. But at least they had killed no one... yet. That intrigued Marty, because one shot from a big gun would leave a heap of fifty dead bodies just like that.

Marty heard an engine. In the background he identified several large trucks weaving back and forth across the landscape. They dragged tanks behind them, the men and women stationed there dressed in special yellow Hazmat suits. The horde of trucks crisscrossed each other's paths, spraying some chemical into the air that left a thick mist that hung like a dense fog.

"What do you think they're up to?" Bernard asked.

Marty didn't know. He could only surmise this had something to do with what happened to his brother. "I'm not sure."

A handful of others dressed in white, doctors or scientists, approached the throng of people waiting to cross over. A few soldiers helped them with their equipment, setting up on a table where several supplies already sat. Though they wore no protective clothing, Marty surmised they could be infectious disease doctors.

"Here's how this will work," the man with the bullhorn said. "I want you all to form a single line. One by one, these fine men and women will inspect you." He sounded calmer now, perhaps trying to exude this feeling among the crowd. "If you test negative, you'll go through after a brief consultation. If you test positive, we will evacuate you to a safe zone for further evaluation. Is this understood?"

For a moment, no one said anything. Maybe they were too afraid, but for whatever reason, as the soldiers made their way through the crowd, the people settled, forming a long, wavy line.

After several minutes, the first person stepped forward, and the doctors examined her. It was hard to see through the binoculars, but Marty felt certain he'd seen them draw blood. Another doctor took the sample and appeared to prepare a slide that she then examined under a microscope while the others performed a relatively routine checkup. Marty suspected this latter part was more to kill time than determining one's wellbeing. They shined their penlight into the woman's eyes, her ears and throat, and poked and prodded her lymph nodes. One woman shoved a stethoscope up the back of the woman's shirt and listened for a moment. A full minute later, the doctor who reviewed the blood gave a thumbs up, and the led the woman through the makeshift gate where she waited for her son to undergo the same procedures.

Marty frowned when it became clear her teenage son didn't fare so well.

"My son!" The woman flailed her fist in the air, but one soldier kept her from going anywhere. "Give me my son!

The boy hung his head like a criminal as two other soldiers escorted him away.

"You bastards," the woman said. "Bring my son back!" Her voice sounded stricken with panic. "Charlie? Come back Charlie!"

The soldier dealing with the woman withdrew his baton, using it to persuade her to stay put. Upon seeing that, the woman collapsed, crying as she watched her son disappear, perhaps forever. Whatever she said amid sobs, Marty couldn't make out, but she looked traumatized.

"I can't believe this is happening," Nancy said, coming up behind them.

"Believe it." Marty said. At least a dozen of those who'd been standing in line tried to leave, heading in their direction. "Wait." Marty turned to them. "Stay down."

"Don't let them leave," The man with the bullhorn barked out, confirming what Marty had long feared, that none of those people were safe.

A handful of soldiers raised their guns and flanked those who fled in a wide semi-circle. These people ran, zigzagging through the high grass best they could, trying to avoid being captured. But the futility of that became clear when one soldier shot a man in the back twice. The others slowed upon seeing this and trudged back to the checkpoint reluctantly, the butts of the soldier's rifles herding them back in place.

Once accounted for, two soldiers patrolled the end of the line until everyone had passed through the checkpoint. About a third of the people failed, which Marty guessed would lead to their immediate disposal.

"We best keep our distance," Bernard said.

Marty scratched his chin hair. "I agree."

For whatever reasons, Marty continued to observe the fog in the background, how the people who had passed these scientists' tests were being forced to walk through that smog. Were they safe? Unaffected by whatever virus has taken to the area? Where were they being taken? What would be their fate?

In the distance, several shots reported, evidence of what happened to those who hadn't passed. Although expected, it was a grave revelation.

"What now, Marty?" Bernard asked.

They kept looking to him for answers. He didn't have any good suggestions, and he busied himself by focusing on the troops as they reformed their wall, waiting to snag any others who came their way. Whoever came would endure the testing, then lead away one direction or the other.

He wondered what means they'd used to identify this affliction, whether it was effective. There was also the matter of that fog, the place where they took all the others. What was it and what did it do? But what bothered Marty most was the simple fact that no matter how big anyone built the wall, no matter how strong or reinforced it was, someone would always find a way through. History had proven as much.

As the thought crossed his mind, he watched a little girl dash from bush to bush, too small for anyone to notice. The girl bounded through the tall grass, barely detectable due to her being so young. She reached the barbed wire fence and carefully crawled through at the widest opening. A minute later the girl disappeared into the vast blanket of smog beyond.

Chapter 8

Exhausted by her lack of sleep, Sheila had trouble reading the next letter she found on a table beside a red X. The pain seemed to radiate behind her eyes, forcing her to blink, and the words almost looked like little bugs squirming across the page.

Woozy, near passing out, she shook her head. She brushed the hair out of her face, holding it there with one hand, and she used the other to shield her eyes from the morning's light that stole in through a large hole in far wall. This helped her focus enough to read the words written in heavy lettering across the front of the folded paper, "Please read."

February 5th

If you're reading this note, you already know much of what is going on. You may have even read one of my previous letters and are hot on our trail. What you might not know, though, is how bad things have gotten. I can tell you some of what I know, but I'm certain I haven't seen everything yet myself. I'll do my best.

My name is Marty, and I am not traveling alone. Everything started yesterday as far as you're likely concerned, but I assure you the true issue dates dates back even farther than that. I watched my brother transform into one of the creatures you might have heard people talking about. What they are, I can't say, or even whether they are dangerous. I will say that my brother's calm demeanor quickly eroded into an unexplainable rage, and he tried to harm me. To what level of danger I was in, I'm uncertain, only that I felt it best to leave.

Sheila wondered what it must be like to watch a family member go through this transformation. And now she could confirm Marty spoke the truth, that these creatures were dangerous. The creature that interrupted her sleep had torn two men to pieces. Worse yet, it appeared the creature had perhaps taken their remains, which likely meant they were carnivores.

You're best to avoid any soldiers if you can. They may seem like they're here to help, but if you've encountered any of the deceased, you've probably seen the bullet hole in their head, and you can guess where those are coming from. They appear desperate which could signify they've been unsuccessful at containing whatever has affected this area.

I should also mention that these creatures have a weak spot at the sides of their abdomen, where the skin is visually thin. To my knowledge, these appear to work as a lung of sorts. Careful aim with the right weapon can bring these creatures down and possibly kill them. Do not bother with the skull, as it's far too thick.

We hope to sneak through to Indiana tonight. You're welcome to join us if you can catch up. I suspect this area will be on strict lockdown soon.

My sincerest wishes for your survival,
Marty

Someone had crossed out the last paragraph before the closing and scrawled a doubtful question mark in the margin. That troubled Sheila, as she wondered if the plan had changed. And, if so, where had they gone instead? What could make a man like Marty change his mind so fast?

She let her hair fall back in her face. After refolding the note, she replaced it on the table where she'd found it. Standing in the large opening in the wall, she heard the crackle of gunfire. Hearing that made her uneasy.

Was that what perplexed Marty? Were they in danger? She had so many questions.

Chapter 9

A strange white haze hung in the distance, which Sheila believed was no ordinary fog. She concluded this because of the unseen truck engines she heard revving up within that smog as they moved from side to side. But she had bigger concerns, too.

Had Marty and his friends made their way into Indiana? Or had they gone elsewhere? If so, where? Also, she couldn't be sure if what she was seeing now, this haze, had come of mankind's doing or whatever creatures Marty had spoken of. She hoped the former, as that could mean she'd be safe getting through to Indiana.

In the distance, a large group of about twenty people approached a line of armed forces on the fringe of a vast cornfield. Men in white uniforms rushed into place at the middle of the formation. Two soldiers carried a table behind them. Some loud and boisterous man belted out orders in a bullhorn, shouting things she could make out from here.

"Your patience is appreciated. Everyone will get through, but you will need to wait in line." He cleared his throat, a sign that he'd gone through this drill than a few times. "If you refuse to wait in line, we will not allow you through."

His words fell on people who dragged their feet, tired of walking, their patience gnawed and spat out like a tough piece of gristle. Somehow, despite the way they looked, many of them mustered up what strength they had and attempted to take what they wanted—freedom. And that should have been okay, at least within the walls of the United States, as it was the right of every citizen. But, for whatever reason, the soldiers fought them off.

Gunfire, sounding much like thunder, echoed across the field and startled Sheila. She was certain it had been many rounds fired all at once. And they kept on firing, the end of each rifle flashing like fireflies in the distance. Half the people fell dead right away. A few kept up the good fight, but the soldiers soon subdued them, either by a hard blow to the head via a soldier's rifle or a baton. No matter how passionate these people might be in their plight to cross over to Indiana, bare fists did little to help their cause, and soon all was calm again.

Sheila thought she'd be better off staying away from the border, at least for a while. Then again, a few people who'd undergone a brief physical were being let through. Armed guards escorted the rest away. A crackle of gunfire from that nearby destination signaled to Sheila at least some, if not all those people, had met their demise at the hands of those soldiers.

She wondered if she could sneak past this checkpoint. But what if they caught her? Could she survive on her looks alone, as she might have at least once before? She doubted it. Any advantage looks gave her ran out long ago. And she dared not risk being one of those folks led off by the guards to be shot.

Blurry eyed, she squinted, feeling the weight of eyelids because of the lack of sleep. She struggled to keep them open, watching the men in white walk away, their table carried off behind them. They cleared the landscape, leaving behind a few soldiers to stay their ground. She watched as these soldiers talked and laughed, perhaps exchanging stories of their bravery in this latest brawl with frightened men, women, and even children. They were everything that was ever wrong with men in her eyes.

Boys and their toys.

Now that their numbers had dwindled, she wondered if she could make it past them after all, perhaps through the nearby cornfield. Focusing on this, she stepped forward when a rustle of leaves crunched behind her. Hearing this alerted her, and she was wide-awake and scanning the area behind her with paranoid eyes.

She saw no one. Then, a second after she'd come to that conclusion, she felt a large hand press over her mouth. She tried to scream and failed. Tried to run but felt herself being pulled back against a broad chest. Somewhere inside of her, a steady drumming began, rapping loud and out of control. She felt lightheaded and worried but kept fighting. Though she kicked and bit, her efforts amounted to nothing. But she refused to stop trying, praying she'd free herself somehow.

A man, maybe in his early forties, came into view. But she ignored him, refusing to give up her struggle with the large man behind her. What did they want with her? They weren't even soldiers.

And she worried she already knew the answer to her question, that these were bad men with worse thoughts.

She spotted several soldiers in the distance and thought if she couldn't get away, maybe she could alert them to their position. Maybe they'd help her. So she screamed, louder and louder, muffled by the large hand, doing whatever she could to draw the attention of those soldiers. They might be her only hope. And she prayed there was yet some chivalrous act left in this lawless society.

"Quiet," said the pepper-haired man. A look of genuine concern crossed his face. "If you keep this up, you'll attract those men over there. And they aren't looking to help anyone."

She made the big man behind her work to keep his hand over her mouth, swinging her head back and forth to shake him. "Listen to him, lady. He knows what he's talking about."

Sure, he does. Of course, he does.

Sheila kicked her foot back, finally making contact with the large man's shin. To her surprise, the man lost his footing. He staggered back, her still in his arms, stumbling left and right as he clumsily tried to regain his footing. When he couldn't prevent the fall, he loosened his hold on her, and she fell to a squatting position.

She didn't scream. Instead, she darted forward to avoid the big man's failed attempts to regain hold of her. But in her effort to escape the large man, still dizzied from shaking her head, she ran face first into the pepper-haired man's chest. They both fell, her on top of him, and him struggling to fall on his side. She had no breath to scream now, so she fought to keep him on his back, to lessen the blow to herself so she'd be able to escape moments later.

But the large man was already on his feet and coming for her. The man looked to his side, and Sheila saw a woman. "Nancy," the big man said. "Get her."

With that everything seemed to freeze. Sheila felt her heart beating, more so a result of the fight to escape than anything, but now it had intensified. She realized whom these people were she was fighting, and an instant wave of guilt washed over her despite their offensive approach.

She threw herself sideways, and they hit the ground in unison. Nancy was on her right away, but Sheila didn't put up a fight. Instead, she asked the one question that came to mind above all else. "Marty?"

He stared at her for a moment, wincing, breathing heavy. His eyes softened on her, perhaps realizing this had all been some bad mistake. He waved Nancy off and with some effort, pushed himself up to a sitting position. An abrupt laugh escaped him.

Sheila couldn't help but laugh, too. It was funny in a twisted way. "I…I read your notes. Well, two of them. Sheila. My name is Sheila."

"Well then," Marty said, "it appears Bernard's brainchild succeeded. I'm sorry for all that. There were better ways for us to approach you, but we worried you might alert those soldiers. You don't want to get caught up in that mess over yonder."

Sheila shook her head and sat up. "It doesn't look promising, does it?"

"It's an instant death for anyone they deem as being ill. I guarantee that much."

Marty stood and brushed himself off before offering her his hand. He hefted her up to her feet and dusted off her shoulder, offering a kind smile. That was when Sheila first noticed it, the charming quality about the way he carried himself. He was a humble man. A good man. Only then did she realize she'd been smiling, too. She tried to gather herself, brushing the hair back from her face. But her heart was still racing a mile a minute.

"You're welcome to join us. We have a few others for you to meet if you so choose. But we also won't stop you if you want to try to get through to Indiana. We only wanted to make sure you knew the consequences."

She studied them all with curious eyes. Every one of them, including herself, had all been through a lot. But the most alluring fact about going with them was that she'd finally be able to get some decent sleep.

Marty led the way to a nearby farmhouse. And she followed, eager for some rest.

Chapter 10

Marty moved to the scraggly-looking man he'd learned just yesterday was only slightly older than he was. The guy looked far older, perhaps the result of whatever life he'd lived before this.

Marty turned back to Sheila. "This is Ike."

Ike extended his hand, without even a hint of a smile crossing his face. He shook Sheila's hand briskly, much harder than Marty cared for.

Marty had introduced Ike first because he the one person he least trusted. He never minded his own business. And he complained about everything, to no end.

Funny thing was, less than a week ago, there wouldn't have been any reason to think anyone suspicious. But now, after seeing what these soldiers had done on repeated occasions, he found it difficult to trust anyone who didn't ooze kindness. He'd even had his doubts about Bernard and Nancy at the beginning, which made him feel guilty even now. He knew it all was just foolish paranoia, but the lack of sleep had driven him all too often to unsubstantiated conclusions.

Another part of him, though, the part that was still a teacher, had learned to identify the bad apples early on. Ike fit the profile well enough, and just seeing him set off many bells and whistles in Marty's head. Call it a teacher's intuition. Marty would stake his life on it; Ike was one messed up guy. And guys like that attracted trouble like bees to honey.

Without knowing he'd been doing so, he evaluated Ike for a long moment. The slender man dressed nice enough. But he was always squinting, as if he had trouble seeing and had lost his glasses. Beady eyes like those could only hint at what one could expect of Ike. And the way he always wore a scowl did nothing to smooth over Marty's opinion, either. The fact Ike was so bitter all the time only added to Marty's distrust of the man. Still, the group wasn't all about trust at this point. Not yet. But that would all change soon enough if matters kept up this way.

Ike let go of Sheila's hand, and Marty moved to the newest addition to their group before Sheila. "This is Sandy."

She was a youthful Hispanic woman. While shaking Sheila's hand, Sandy offered a warm smile. Then she pulled Sheila in close and gave her a big hug. This was a brilliant woman, far beyond her years, with a kindness unmatched in these difficult times. Her only flaw was her clear interest in Ike. Perhaps this was the only reason Marty continued to allow the angry sod to tag along.

"Last, but not least, we have Andy." He patted the young man's back.

Andy looked as though he'd stepped right out of high school. He was the sort of kid who wanted to do something about everything wrong in his world, and it always needed seen to right away, before things got any worse. Marty valued his passion, but also recognized it as the naivety of being young and full of rebellion.

Andy nodded the way cool kids did. Sheila returned the gesture, giggling as she did.

Andy broke any formality in their introduction, changing the subject. "I think we should break through that line and get into Indiana right—"

"Andy," Marty said, interrupting him before he got too far ahead of himself. "Please. Sheila has only just joined us and judging from her eyes, she's pretty well worn out. She'll need some rest before we decide on anything…as a group."

They all looked at Sheila. Marty had identified the dark red circles under her eyes. Having been alone, she looked far worse off than any of them did. Then, as if responding to this, her body hunched over, struggling to stay afoot.

Marty couldn't help but wonder if she had the infection. But reason prevailed, the knowledge that any of them could have contracted the infection and might not know it. He considered how the contagion could even be the catalyst behind Ike's bitterness. That at least made sense. Jake had shown a similar aggression toward Marty.

No. Marty figured that was too easy of an explanation. Ike had likely always been hard on all sides, with no smooth edges. He couldn't understand what Sandy saw in him.

"I can stay awake." Sheila's eyes drooped, revealing a much different story.

"Not now, Sheila." Marty grabbed her arm, leading her away. "Rest some first. Then we can go over everything."

She fought him at first, doing her best to stay in the moment. The others had already moved on, a few of them discussing a much more vital discussion whether TV was still being broadcast. They relied on Marty to make these sorts of decisions, and Marty somehow always slid right into the role.

His arm dragged. Marty looked to Sheila, not surprised to see she'd fallen asleep and could barely even walk. He lifted her into his arms and carried her to some bedding he'd placed in one corner of the room for himself. A fraction of a second later, she was fully asleep and dreaming, even before her head reached the ground.

Poor thing.

He laid a sweater he'd found over her, staying there to watch her for a bit, unable to take his eyes off her, creepy as that made him feel. And just the thought he'd looked at her in that way made him feel guilty.

Someone moved behind him. He spun to find Bernard, who was studying him. Marty's red-hot face gave him away. Still, he put on an awkward act which didn't appear to fool Bernard.

Funny. The guy can't even figure out his own love life but *can so easily decipher my interests.*

Marty motioned for him to come over. Bernard did as requested, standing over him, smiling now. Marty stood and led Bernard to the next room, where they could speak in private. He wanted to discuss matters with none of the others chiming in. This was important to Marty, because if there was one person he could depend upon for solid ideas, it was Bernard. The guy had a knack for these sorts of things, much as he had with the concept behind the whole paper trail.

Bernard had served in the Marines, a detail one could glean just by observing the way he carried himself. That, and the way he always stood at attention, how well he took orders, the guy was a regular old grunt. But he'd spent the last ten years working as a gas station attendant. War had a way of changing a person, of forcing them to get creative when they were in the down and dirty. But working at a gas station offered plenty of time to think, and Marty thought Bernard had done more thinking than anything. He wasn't a brilliant man, just a good thinking one, and now Marty needed a trusted opinion.

"What do you think?" Marty pulled at the hairs on his chin.

"I think you like her," Bernard said, still smiling.

"What? No. Not that."

Still, Marty glanced over at her, saw her lying in the corner of the next room. She was beautiful, but it was nonsense to even consider such a thing at a time like this. Besides, Marty had only brought grief to those he loved. He wasn't about to go through it all again. Didn't have it in him.

"What then? You asking 'bout Ike?"

"No," Marty said. "What do you think we should do?"

"Oh, hmm."

Bernard rubbed his thumb and forefinger together as if he were holding a lucky rabbit's foot. Marty had seen this before. The guy always did it whenever he was deep in thought, though Marty doubted Bernard knew he was doing it.

"Well, I think trying to cross is one idea," Bernard finally said. "Maybe we could even walk right through that cornfield out there."

"I've considered it. I'm not sure that's our best option, though."

"Yep, I agree. When I was in the Marines, I learned a hard and fast rule, the objective comes before all else. I can tell you without a doubt it comes before any sense of humanity. If you're infected by whatever this is, you're dead. Plain and simple."

"That's what I thought. And who knows if any of us are or not?"

"Well, I have seen nothing to indicate otherwise. Course,

we could always hunker down right here and hide, try to fight things out if we need to."

"Fight it out?"

"Well, I'm not sure how things are going to play out yet, but I'd reckon eventually they're gonna sweep the entire area. They might find us. The fact they set up a checkpoint implies it's in or out at this point."

"Their checkpoint has flaws," Marty said.

"Flaws? How so?"

"I saw a child sneak through earlier today."

"Well, we could try that ourselves. That's what Andy wants."

Marty thought about it for a moment, trying to play out the pros and cons of such a risk. There were a lot of cons—much more than he expected. Seven people made for a greater chance of being caught. Going one at a time might better those odds for each individual, but it didn't guarantee everyone's safety. The safety of the entire group was his main concern, whether he fully trusted every one of them or not.

Marty released his chin hairs. "It might be too risky."

"That's my feeling, exactly." Bernard looked as though he wanted to add something but didn't.

"What?"

"Nothing, it's a bad idea."

"What is it?"

"Well, I think if they've set up this perimeter out here, it means two things for sure."

"Okay. What then?"

"Well, for one, they still think they can contain this problem."

"And we already know they've failed at that," Marty added.

"Yep. Another thing, they likely have evacuated ground zero. If they think they've contained this, they'll eventually move to minimize the containment zone."

"I see. So being out here on the edge isn't in our best interest?"

"I don't think so. Course, this only applies if we think any of us have been diseased. Eventually that door will close to us, I think."

"Maybe it already has." Marty's throat felt dry getting the words out.

"Could be. I've heard more gunshots this last hour or two." Bernard rolled his eyes back in his head for this next part. "We'd have to deal with whatever it is they couldn't contain."

Marty winced at this. "Not the best of situations, either. Trust me."

"Nope," said Bernard. "I doubt it is. But there would be plenty of places to bunker up and defend. Plenty of people had weapons, which would've all been left behind. We might be able to secure a place until all this is over...if it ever is."

Marty didn't respond to this. He didn't want to give the man any notion they wouldn't make it through even the hardest of times. And he was certain that time was quickly coming.

"So, what do you think?" Bernard said.

"I'm not sure yet. I think I need a good night's rest to think on it still."

"Could be. You would think–" Bernard stopped short and leaned back, looking out of the room. "Ike?"

The miserable man lurched forward from the side of the doorway.

"Can we help you, Ike?" Marty worried they might have already done just that.

Ike didn't answer. He only stared at Marty with an accusing gaze. Or maybe that was what Marty thought he saw. He couldn't be sure.

"What is it, Ike?" Bernard asked.

Marty cursed himself silently. They should have taken their business elsewhere, far enough away they didn't have to worry about this happening. But it was too late now. And he doubted even taking that care would have kept Ike from listening in. The guy was sneaky about stuff like that.

"Just wondering what you guys thought is all," Ike said after a long moment.

Marty didn't trust the guy's scowl, an expression that suggested he'd heard details that bothered him. Then Sandy was behind Ike, her hand on his shoulder, almost as if protecting him. This conversation was over whether or not Marty wanted to continue.

Marty shooed all of them out of the room. "Okay, let me

finish this letter. We can talk more in the morning and decide what to do then. Get some sleep. I'll take first watch."

While Marty might be their de facto leader, he very much believed in the Democratic way. He wasn't about to turn this into a dictatorship, not that he could accomplish that if he wanted to. These were strong people, every one of them, and their biggest strength was in their numbers. He didn't want to diminish this advantage.

He lifted the pen, readying to write his note when he realized he didn't know what to say. He couldn't convey what they would do or even what they might do. Where were they going next? And so he sat there alone, the light of the room eventually creeping in, illuminating him. There, he sat most of the night until Bernard relieved him.

Chapter 11

"Hey, Marty?" said a familiar voice.

Marty rolled to his other side, expecting to see this person. But no one was there, so he assumed he'd imagined it.

Just hearing that voice again made him shiver. Even dreaming Jake might still be out there somewhere concerned him. And knowing that made him wish he could somehow discern which Jake it had been calling his name, the man or the monster. He couldn't be sure, though the monster had a certain intellect to his voice Jake never had. Either way, it had been a bitter end.

The worst part of it all, though, was that Marty still wasn't sure whether it had been him or his brother who crossed the line first. They'd stopped communicating, mostly because what happened terrified Marty. And they'd both done things no brother should. Even before all this happened. Before the monster. It all boiled down to these simple trespasses, the simplest disagreements between brothers. That's what severed their relationship. That's why Marty had to do what he did before he left the farm.

"Marty?" said the voice again.

And he knew it this time. That was his brother all right, but not the human Jake. Not the one he wanted to see again, the man he longed to hold in his arms, to make everything okay between them again. He missed Jake very much. But this was the Jake who came after, the one who talked without stumbling over his words. The one who no longer walked with a limp. This voice came from the perfect Jake, the new Jake, flawless in every way. This was the monster.

But there was no way Jake—or rather what Jake had turned

into—could be here. So this couldn't be real.

Unable to ease his mind, Marty rolled over. Again, there was nothing. He let his eyes explore the room, delving into its many shadows. They had avoided starting a fire, as it might alert any nearby troops to their presence, so there were plenty of shadows. Only the moon offered any light, making difficult to see much of anything. What he could see was that Andy wasn't where he'd gone to sleep anymore, which meant he'd probably gone outside.

Marty's eyes sank deep into the corner, almost trying to create Jake, standing there, his silhouette not human but that of the creature. It was almost as if he were trying to summon the monster from the very depths of darkness. But the form didn't come from there.

"Marty?" said the voice again.

This time he didn't roll over and instead turned his head to look over his shoulder. Sure enough, there he stood, a blistered wound puckered up and healed over his side.

Marty trembled, unable to say anything. He couldn't do anything, frozen in place on the floor. His throat felt scratchy, like it was swelling.

The other side of the creature's abdomen inhaled and exhaled with a wheeze. That single cycloptic eye gone now, yet somehow he was sure this Jake, the monster, still saw him very well.

"No. It can't be," Marty said, managing a whisper. Warm tears stung his eyes.

The monster towered over him. "It's me, brother. I've come for you."

"No. You aren't real." Marty expected the others to wake, but not one of them stirred. His throat had to force the words out. "I killed you."

"Oh, you tried. But you can't kill me. And now, we have a score to settle. A score among brothers, yes?"

"No," Marty said. He turned away in defiance of the vision. "You aren't real."

"Look at me."

Marty refused, shaking his head.

"*Look* at me."

Marty twisted his head back to the monster only to see him lunge at him, jaws wide, arms flailing, claws like daggers.

Marty scooted away as fast as he could like a worm wriggling on a rainy night. His back struck the wall, and there, still seeing the vision of his brother, he curled up his legs and held them with his arms. And even when he realized the monster wasn't really there, that he would survive this, that the others were safe, he felt dead inside. His tears came faster now, sprinkling his cheeks, and the sadness overwhelmed him.

"I'm coming for you, Marty. Count on it." His brother's voice echoed in his thoughts, so maddening in its insistence.

Dripping with sweat, his head swooning, Marty woke to find himself drowning in darkness. He couldn't move, didn't want to look, but did so anyway. When he saw nothing, he shuffled across the floor on his hands and knees until he reached the window they'd blocked up before resting for the night. With gnarled fingers, he pried the large plywood board away and let the moonlight spill in. The room glowed a dim blue, but it was enough to see something had gone wrong.

Andy really was missing. And that made him question the rest. A quick scan outside didn't reveal Andy, either. It appeared he'd abandoned them. Marty feared why.

Chapter 12

Andy made his way across the field, feeling what he likened to some magnetic-pull tugging at his back. There, he'd find comfort, maybe even safety in their makeshift hideout. But for how long?

Hiding from this was pointless. All these old people ever wanted to do was hide. They had to take turns keeping watch, stay here for the night, there the next. It was tiring, and most of all, boring. They wouldn't risk making a break for the border, so that meant Andy had to take it upon himself to make the first move, the right move, if he wanted to survive.

When he saw the patrol, he ducked behind a large forsythia bush, the aroma of its yellow flowers teasing at his nose. Being allergic to most everything, he felt very close to sneezing. So he pinched his nose harder than usual, and the tender flesh inside his nostrils burned with irritation. At least he didn't sneeze, though.

He had to admit it felt good being accountable for himself and only himself. The others had just been holding him back. So, if nothing else, he was his own man now, a free man. That was all that mattered.

The patrol headed back toward the outpost, so he kept low, moving across the field to a tree. He threw his back against the large trunk with a girth wide enough to hide him, which wasn't too difficult a task given how thin he was. That was his biggest advantage.

After a quick glance around the tree to ensure the soldiers were heading away from his position, he lowered himself back against the tree. For a moment, he stared at the hideout in the distance, noticing only now someone had removed the plywood from the window. Soon, they'd know he'd abandoned them if they didn't already. Even if they knew, he doubted they would come for him. Confirmation of this notion came when six individuals exited through the ragged doorway. They stood watching him, or at least he imagined they did. He couldn't say for sure, but no one was flagging him down or waving for him to come back.

Andy shook his head. "Whatever."

He got to his feet and studied the five guards on duty, the patrol had returned to the others and now all of them were too engrossed in conversation to notice him. This was the chance he'd been waiting for.

Keeping low, he scampered across to another bush where he kneeled. There, he spotted two more soldiers, and altered his course to stray from their post. He didn't want to go too far, though. Certainly not to the place he'd heard the gunfire yesterday. Not only would there be dead bodies, but there might be more soldiers he hadn't yet identified as that area had been closed off with a large fence with only one visual access—the front gate. And if he ventured too far, he'd likely just encounter a whole other post, anyway.

Turning around the bush, he squatted, watching closely. Seeing no problems, he crossed the vast open area in a squat-run. This was the last tree before the cornfield which he breezed through the entire length of the field undetected despite the stalks he pushed aside. When he came to the end of the cornfield, he stared out at patrols. If he wanted to make it across the border, he'd have to risk being seen.

He slid himself flat against the ground. The soldiers had stopped talking, and two of them headed away from Andy on another patrol toward a large military RV. Everyone else, though, must have taken to the barracks which were likely within the tall containment fence. He believed they'd rest for the night, entrusting a handful of men to watch over them, to make sure no one crossed undetected.

He noticed something else, too. They'd stacked a bunch of sacks not too far from his position. He couldn't make out what they were, but the stack was almost eight feet tall, looking like sandbags from what he could tell.

"Why sandbags?" He hadn't meant for the words to come out so loud. Biting down on his tongue, he monitored the remaining guards. Not a single soldier stirred, which meant he was still safe.

He refocused on the stack of what looked like sandbags and identified another object—a hand. Just seeing it surprised him. But he held back any reaction, knowing that would get him captured. Besides, he didn't think it was really a hand. How could it be?

One of the other two guards turned, said a few words and then retreated to the same trailer as other two. He waited, watching as all three gathered outside for several minutes before finally entering. After what felt like a long time, the sole light inside the trailer dimmed.

Andy couldn't help but let a wicked, boyish grin grow upon his cheeks. Now there were only two guards posted here and two further down. This increased his odds.

He crawled parallel to the barbed wire fence, heading for a place between the two posts. Stopping to check on both posts often, the guards at each remained in conversation. He couldn't believe how patient he was being given the situation. But it appeared his tolerance had proved worthwhile. It felt liberating. He'd never felt so free in his entire life. If the others wished to spend their remaining days wilting away in hiding, avoiding creatures and some illness and the armed guards, then so be it. That was their choice. His destiny lay elsewhere.

In a few minutes he would be home free, leaving behind the devastation of one state, the worry of imprisonment. He'd be safe in Indiana.

They should've listened to me when they had the chance.

He grew anxious. Every nerve ending came alive, and before he knew what he was doing, he'd sprung into a sprinters position and took off running. He ducked behind every bush, the skinniest of trees here and a growth of heavy weeds there. Crisscrossing his path, he paused at each post long enough to make sure none of the remaining soldiers saw him. His heart hammered out a steady beat in his chest. That excited him. Made it more thrilling. His forehead beaded with sweat, his muscles loose and strong, he pushed himself, while maintaining as quiet an escape as he could manage.

I'll make it. Just a little further.

He neared the line.

You can do it.

He would have, too, if not for the sudden appearance of the small glowing orb. Out of his peripheral vision, the orb wavered to intersect his path. He tried to duck it, but the orb followed. He leaped back and tried to make out what this orb was and saw the camouflaged soldier holding a short spear-like staff. The end of the staff was not sharp but glowed with a silver ball of electricity.

The soldier thrust the staff at Andy and connected with his chest, knocking all the air out of him at once. More so, it felt like a truck had run him over and had parked on the middle of his chest. To his surprise, Andy was flying, too, reeling back and spinning out of control. Unable to move his arms or legs, his body convulsed, the spasms giving temporary life to his limbs. He tried to use that to break his fall but still crashed hard to the ground.

There, he tried to speak, to say anything to stop the attack, but managed only a groan. Spit drooled from his mouth, down his cheek. He still couldn't feel his arms, which lay outstretched to his sides. His right cheek felt cold against the grassy earth, and the dirt tasted like clay and the bitterness of grass. Only then did he notice his rear had ended propped up, his legs kneeling beneath him, holding him up. He toppled, landing with a hard thump, and that was when he felt the fresh raspberry on his nose and face, burning, the feeling slowly coming back to him.

The soldier stood over him. "Just where do you think you're off to, Cinderella?"

Andy didn't respond, couldn't.

"Little late for the ball, ain't ya?" The soldier kicked Andy in his stomach, forcing him to roll onto his back.

Thick foam frothed at his mouth, dripping slowly down his chin. He tried to bring focus to the soldier, but the image shimmied back and forth, never allowing a clear view of the man's face. The resulting effect, though, horrified Andy, and a trickle of urine warmed his crotch. But he held it back.

"What?" the soldier said, the contempt thick in his words. "Did you think we were just standing there telling war stories, and not a one of us saw you coming through that cornfield? People like you make me sick. You ruin everything."

Another kick landed square in Andy's side, driving the air straight out of him. His eyes swam in a sea, and right then the urine released, wetting his entire left thigh.

"What the—" The soldier folded over in a fit of laughter. "You done pissed yourself."

A tear streamed out of Andy's eye and down his cheek, followed by another. Slowly the soldier's face became clearer, less shaky, looking angrier. And behind the soldier, high in the air, he saw something else. That, too, became clearer. The sky was no longer the purple Andy remembered. It had flooded crimson red, and it moved and swayed as if it were alive, as if it were the sea.

Then the sky came crashing down, and the soldier screamed. Andy flopped to one side and despite his failing limbs, tried to crawl away. He wept, he drooled, but he made little progress.

A flurry of activity surrounded him. A shower of wet fell over him. An object slid across his back and rolled off to his hand. He barely touched it, and he couldn't make out what it was, only knew it was wet and bloody, that it was meat. Then, realizing he could meet his own demise, he tried to scream. A strange gurgle escaped his throat.

More sounds filled the night. Other soldiers appeared, men and women alike, possibly five of them. Guns crackled. At least two of those staffs whirled in the air. All the while Andy tried to escape.

The feeling was just coming back to him, enough he might escape when two muscular arms wrapped around him like a hawk seized its prey. He felt himself being lifted high into the air, that sudden sinking feeling in his stomach, losing all that grounded him to reality. Something batted against his face as they climbed, a webby thing, flapping steadily. Wings, he thought.

Marty never said anything about wings.

The creature's arms cinched tighter around Andy's midsection, pulling him in closer. Gunshots reported below, what looked like fireworks on the ground some hundred yards below. A few of those shots whizzed by, but they just climbed higher and higher, the sensation of being weightless overwhelming Andy. His legs and arms dangled, still somewhat numb by the shock of that staff. And his head swam, the disorienting feeling of flying adding to his confusion.

At one point he saw a small group of people near a shack that had seen some heavy damage. They were blurry, but he glimpsed them all the same. They watched him be carried away. More gunfire followed and soldiers shouting at each other.

"It killed Jackson!" a woman screamed in the distance. "Find it! Kill it! Hurry..."

All of that sounded so far away now. Andy felt close to the brink of death, slipping, the world now some surreal Dali painting, melting all around him. At some point he just stopped caring. The cool breeze teased his hair, soothing and relaxing, like cold river water on his face. And Andy found himself able to do something he hadn't done for two whole days. He slept.

Chapter 13

"What the fuck was that, Marty?" Ike said.

Marty loathed the way the guy always seemed to throw an expletive into everything he said. And that made him question Ike's intelligence, thinking maybe he didn't have the vocabulary to speak like a sophisticated human. More so, though, it was that he didn't like Ike's question. Not because he wasn't thinking the same thing but because Ike clearly expected Marty to explain this, as if he were responsible.

"You never said they had wings," Nancy said under her breath, and though she wasn't directing this comment at Marty, it sure came off that way.

Marty hadn't realized he was looking at Nancy, somewhat hurt by her accusing tone and feeling the frown on his face. He tried to get rid of the scowl but failed. How was he supposed to provide any reasoning to what they'd just witnessed?

"Marty?" Bernard sounded anxious. "Hey, yo. You still in there?"

He was still too shocked by it all to answer, but his eyes fell on the big man. Even worse, there was an underlying consideration eating away at Marty's thoughts, one that wasn't allowing him to hear everything the others said. Had that creature been Jake? Was Jake—no, not Jake but the monster—still alive?

It can't be. Jake was dead. Then again, last time he checked, he'd fallen behind on his study of alien life forms. Not that he had much basis for an understanding of alien life to begin with. Jake had undergone a huge transformation, actually more than one, but he couldn't know if his brother was dead or alive because he left. Maybe this was just another in a series of alternate forms for his brother, a flying one.

"Marty, you gonna wake up and answer us, son, or have you lost your mind?"

Marty's hazy vision faded, his eyesight clearing.

Bernard grinned, suggesting he was teasing. "Did you even hear a single word of what we just said?"

"Huh?" Marty felt his fingers pulling at his chin hairs. "Sorry, it's just that... Well... I'm not even sure what we saw there."

"You gotta be frigging kidding me," Ike said.

Marty sighed, annoyed by Ike's comment. Still, he knew one truth above all else. "It's possible it mutated."

"Mutated?" Bernard started rubbing his invisible rabbit's foot.

"He's saying the genes mutated," Sandy said. "That they changed somehow."

Bernard shrugged. "And that makes wings?"

Not wanting the discussion to degrade any further, Marty held up a hand. They both stopped. "It means what it means is all. And as a group we still know very little." He nodded toward the soldiers in the distance tending to what Marty thought was at least one dead soldier. With them so preoccupied, Marty gave some thought to making a run for the border. But would that see all of them safe? Probably not, so he kept the thought to himself. "And as long as they're watching the border, we have no choice but to go elsewhere. What Andy did should prove that much."

"That frigging thing just took Andy," Ike said. "Took him right up in the damn sky, and then what? Why would it want Andy? To eat?"

He was looking right at Marty. "We don't know that." He hated to admit it, but Ike had struck upon Marty's worst fear at the moment. "But it's something we need to take into consideration. It might not be any safer at ground zero, or even anywhere close to it." Marty pointed at the distracted guards this time. "But I don't think Indiana is a way out for us any longer. Not after this."

"So where do we go then?" Bernard said.

Marty shrugged. He looked up at the sky. The morning sun had already tinged the horizon a deep, vibrant orange. Soon it would be full daylight, and they'd be out in the open. If those soldiers checked the perimeter, they'd find them before long. They had to leave, and right away.

"How about the old bomb shelter in Redsdale?" Sandy asked.

That sounded promising to Marty, but he looked each of them in the eye with a raised brow to measure their reluctance. They needed to all agree on this, so there wouldn't be any naysayers after they got on their way.

"Blasted! I knew it!" Ike had a surging intensity growing in his words. "I sure as hell knew you'd want to go back."

Only Ike wasn't looking at Sandy when he said that. He believed Marty had planted the seed, and Sandy merely took the bait. And maybe he was right to a degree, but how had he missed the fact that Redsdale had been Sandy's idea?

"Relax, Ike." Bernard had a calm tone. "My man Marty is just trying to figure out what's best for us all."

"Fuck you, Bernie. You know what he's saying, where he wants us to go. He's leading us right back into that hellfire." Ike kicked at the ground and spun around in anger. "We'll die there."

Sandy's hand found Ike's shoulder, working up to his neck where she massaged. It didn't calm him down much, but at least it quieted him up. The guy was a short fuse, and once ignited, he was a difficult one to extinguish.

"Well, we might run into hard times there, for sure." Marty approached Ike and spoke directly to him, perhaps trying to form some bond where none existed, or maybe to offer some sense of reassurance. But Ike took a step back. "And I won't lie to you, we may meet our end. But I think our chances are better *there* than here. And we might just find Andy. We owe him this much, don't we?"

"Marty's right," Sheila said. "I know I'm new here, and you might not care for my opinion just yet, but he's right."

Bernard stopped rubbing his imaginary good luck charm. "Plus, an old shelter like that might have a good food stash. That alone could last long enough to see us through the worst of this. The walls are relatively impenetrable, assuming we can even get inside, but it would be an easy place to hunker down and defend. I've heard they built it strong enough to withstand twisters, but I'm not sure anyone has used it. I reckon this is just as good a reason as any."

Marty felt a twinge in his chest at the mention of a tornado.

"Won't it be locked?" Nancy's face was full of doubt. "Maybe we'd be better off if we turned ourselves in."

"And get shot?" Ike stepped forward, and Sandy grabbed for his hand. But he pulled away and walked a good twenty feet away from the group, perhaps trying to make everyone think he was leaving. But Marty suspected they all knew he wouldn't, even if some wished he would.

The sun shone through the trees on the horizon. Just seeing it refreshed Marty. It wasn't too hot or too cold. "It might be locked. But it might not be. Other people might be there, too, maybe some who can help us."

"Strength in numbers," Bernard said, echoing this notion.

"That's right," Marty said, and went half the distance to Ike. "Listen, I can't make anyone go with me even if I wanted to. I'm not much of a physical threat. Heck, I'm not even a good leader. All the same, I am going. And you're welcome to join me if you wish."

Bernard cleared his throat. "I'm—"

"We're in." Nancy interrupted.

She put her arm around his waist, and they moved together, taking a position next to Marty. Sheila said nothing but stood beside Marty. She gave him a jesting punch to his shoulder and flashed a grin. He couldn't help but smile back.

"Christ!" Ike threw his fists up in semi-protest. Then he took a place alongside Marty, too. Sandy, of all people, was the last to join them, and she'd been the one to suggest it.

"It's settled then," Marty said. "Let's pack and leave before those guards come looking our way."

It took ten minutes to pack up. By the time they headed out, they could hear the troops behind them. Judging by their path, Marty thought it obvious they'd made the right choice.

For the first few hours, conversation was infrequent. When they talked, it was quiet, between two and three people only.

As they neared the end of the day, to everyone's surprise, Ike broke the silence. "What the fuck is that thing?" They all followed his gaze. "Is that? Oh, Christ—"

Marty couldn't believe what he was looking at.

Chapter 14

Andy's head started clearing, but he did not know where he was. Some strange orange glow loomed all around him, and his heart struck a steady beat. But it wasn't just that this orange background illuminated him, it was moving, too. This was a living, breathing substance of which he still couldn't make any sense.

He tried to turn, surprised to find the space smaller than he originally thought. As he touched it with his hands, he felt the satin texture of the walls surrounding him. It was everywhere, too, all around him, a gelatin-like substance enclosing his now naked body. This made his heart race faster, the thought of being smothered to death within these walls. His mind obsessed over it, worrying him to the point—

That was when he noticed one side of this pod remained open. Relief fell over him, his thoughts easing as he leaned his head out of the pod and checked his surroundings. A corridor stemmed off from his position, running either direction. Remnants of clothing, a few books, a tube of lip balm, some other odd objects lay scattered along the ground. Both passageways darkened as they twisted around a bend. But to the right, he identified something odd and didn't like the look of it.

Even with his blurry vision, he saw the demon-like form emerging from the darkness. Seeing that terrified him, and he swallowed hard. Hoping it wouldn't see him, he shrank back into his pod, pressing himself against the back wall, keeping still, holding his breath.

The creature moved at a steady pace, growing closer and closer, and if Andy hadn't pissed himself earlier, his bladder might have released itself again. For now, though, the creature stopped some fifteen feet away, where it appeared to service another pod. Andy couldn't see who was in that pod, but with this creature distracted, he considered trying to escape before it was too late. Yet, when he tried, something held him in place, an unnatural force he couldn't identify. Then, as he inspected the walls, he realized that satin texture was also tacky, like some giant fly strip. The more he struggled against it, like a bug trapped in a spider's web, his situation only worsened, as the walls tightened around his body, encircling his arms and legs, around his waist. This brought back the panic, the feeling of being strangulated, of losing his breath, of being buried alive, and he couldn't stop breathing heavily, his heart hammering away against his eardrums.

The demon finished what it was doing and stepped closer. Andy didn't want to look but couldn't help himself. Just the thought he would have to face this monster made him tremble. And not only did he see the creature when it came into view, he also saw some cart toting behind it, pulling it with one of its many arms. The cart, large and metallic, floated behind the creature, carrying a huge vat filled with some strange bubbling goop.

With luck, the creature stopped at the pod next to Andy's, and although Andy couldn't see if a man or woman or some other race lay inside, he identified the silhouette inside the pod. He was sure it was a human, though he couldn't be sure. The monster reached one of its clawed hands into the bubbling vat, withdrawing a huge wad of some gelatinous orange jelly-like substance. It then spread the substance with its hand over the open wall of this neighboring pod, and although Andy couldn't see it happening, he knew exactly what was going on, that the monster had sealed in whatever being rested in that pod.

The creature finished and towed the cart to Andy's pod, where Andy got his first look at the inhuman creature close-up. He stared into its lone weepy eye, its unnatural upside-down face, that large mouth with all those teeth, drool dripping from both corners of its horrible frown, which Andy knew right away was more of a smile. Right then Andy understood more than anything, this wasn't just any old pod—it was a coffin.

"Please," Andy said. "No. Please don't—"

But the creature reached into its vat, returning with a palm full of that gelatinous material and started sealing up his pod.

Andy didn't know why the others hadn't screamed, but he did now, constant and without end, the air leaving his lungs so fast. When he'd expelled every breath, he gasped to refill his lungs as fast as he could and screamed again.

Still the creature sealed off his pod.

"No!" Andy said. "Stop! Just stop!"

Andy knew one thing in that moment; he would not go down without a fight. He kicked and thrashed, thrusting his body out in all directions, doing everything within his power to damage his pod. Trying to pull himself free of its imperceptible grasp. But his hands and feet only sank deeper into the spongy walls, as it swallowed him up. And the creature continued sealing up his only escape.

He screamed louder this time. So loud it hurt his throat. None of it, nothing he did or said even fazed this creature. The monster dipped its hands into the vat again, retrieving more of the gelatin, and in one swoop spread it across the remaining open wall to his pod like a bricklayer might use a trowel to spread mortar.

Andy screamed, and he fought so hard that at one point, he ended up twisted in the pod. Somehow, in his terrifying plight to free himself, he face-planted into a nearby wall. All at once he felt the goop in his mouth, in his eyes and nose, almost sucking at his skin. He tried to pull away, but all that did was pull him in deeper, farther into the mass. His only concern fast became whether he'd soon stop breathing altogether.

Sucking in what little air he had left, he held his breath. His eyes felt as though they would soon pop right out of their sockets. His cheeks burned, his eyes aching. He started convulsing, knowing that eventually, he'd have no choice but to give in to death. And when he neared that point, he fought not to scream, not to waste one second worth of air. But scream he did as the walls swelled, fully enclosing his body. The madness of it was too much to bear, as he expelled all his remaining air at once. He felt his throat straining, unable to produce anything.

His lungs felt hot, warm, as if they would burst.

Then, a little at a time, the ability to breathe came back to him. At first it felt like he was breathing through a straw, then a water hose, and soon a small window. Bit by bit he grew calmer, no longer wanting to scream because all that mattered was the breathing. As a flush of pinkish fluid flooded his pod, the realization came over him that this was more of a uterus than anything.

He felt the cool liquid cover his body, smothering his face, and he breathed it in. At first, he struggled against it, the natural reaction when sucking in fluid. His body convulsed, fighting the unnatural act of inhaling liquid. It ran into his mouth, down his throat, up his nose, into his stomach and lungs. He felt very close to blacking out but fought it off long enough to comprehend his condition.

He wasn't dying. In some strange way, they were using him. But he was no longer human, not fully. There was something growing inside of him, a tiny voice he couldn't yet fully hear. But it was more than that, the feeling he was part of something bigger, an entire network of pods, human bricks that were all connected, a single thread through them all.

With this knowledge, he found peace. His body went limp, and the white-hot sensation lessened, slowly at first and then altogether. Andy drifted off, asleep in the fluid-filled pod.

Chapter 15

Sheila saw what everyone else saw and didn't have the words to describe it. The structure wasn't like anything she'd ever seen before, and yet she had.

"What the fuck is that thing?" Ike said. "Is it? Oh, Christ—"

It seemed no one else had the immediate words to describe this, either. It was both horrifying and unthinkable and most of all, it told the truth of just how much the armed forces had controlled matters.

"It's a heart," Nancy finally said.

A dreadful silence followed until Marty said, "It isn't a heart."

Sheila liked Marty's deep-set, kind eyes. How had a man like that stayed single for so long?

Already, an unspoken friendship had grown between them. She was aware she'd been flirting with him, too. And though she believed he knew it, he hadn't reciprocated.

Bernard grunted, pulling her out of her thoughts.

"Well," Bernard said, "it's gotta be some type of heart."

Sandy pointed to the top. "There aren't any ventricles or anything of that nature. I don't think it's—"

Marty interrupted. "It isn't a heart."

"Well then, what is it?" Bernard was rubbing his fingers together.

"It's a hive," Marty said after a long moment.

They all gasped quietly, Sheila included, seeing this horrid object in a new light for the first time. Noting the distance between them and this hive, it had to be at least ten miles away, maybe more. But from their position it still looked very much like a heart. She was certain, though, upon closer inspection, they would find it was precisely what Marty described it as being, and that was a dreadful thought.

Judging the size of the structure from here, it must have been three and a half or even four football fields tall and as wide as two. Oddly, it pulsed on the horizon, as if beating ever so slightly, but enough that she could see it doing so. And there was a rhythm to its beat, as if in fact it were breathing. All of this only made it harder to deny the organ it so much resembled.

"Ah fuck!" Ike, he had a way with words. "So you're sayin' there's some queen-like monster stuffed up the ass of that hive."

Marty studied the structure for a moment, likely considering Ike's words. Sheila followed his gaze, wondering just how much room there was inside. Were there other hives, too? Did each have its own unique queen, like a beehive? Or was one queen controlling them all?

Squinting now, Sheila believed Marty was trying to figure out just how the thing worked. Or maybe he already had some ideas and just hadn't worked out how best to convey his findings. He was a calculated man, one who thought things out, made sure he wasn't causing a panic, and that alone was likely the reason they all treated him like a leader, including herself. But she wished he would say something now, anything.

"Maybe not a queen," Marty said, shaking her out of the thought. It looked like he was still dwelling on the matter. "I mean, we can't say whether it's male or a female, can we? Or maybe there's more than one. They could even reproduce by asexual means." He pondered it all a moment longer. "Of course, they didn't used to have wings. Who knows what all has changed regarding their anatomy?"

"I'll say, shit has changed," Ike said. "It's right fucked up."

Sheila didn't trust Ike. And because of her gut feeling, she'd taken to monitoring him. At least Sandy kept him somewhat under control.

"So, what?" Bernard asked. "What should we do, Marty?"

Sheila felt warmth on her fingertips and looked down. Her hand had grazed Marty's. He didn't seem to notice, too lost in his thoughts. She took his hand briefly and squeezed, encouraging him.

He smiled weakly, then shook his head to let her know he had it under control. But did he? Did anyone really have anything sorted at times like these?

"Well," Marty said, "if we hole up in the shelter, we might last two months, maybe more. Sweating it out in there is definitely our safest option."

They all nodded in agreement.

"But if we do, by the time we resurface, there might be nothing to come back to. If we don't, someone might hunt us down. Maybe they already are." Marty shook his head.

"Marty's right," Bernard said. "I don't think they see us as being any different from our flying monster friends out there, not anymore." He waved at the hive.

"True," Marty said, confirming the notion and tugging at his chin hairs again.

Sheila liked that he did this when deep in thought. It was kind of cute.

"We might be digging our own graves if we do nothing," Marty said.

"Fuck that," Ike said.

"I agree," Marty said. "Fuck that, indeed."

Sheila laughed. She hadn't heard Marty curse yet, and it didn't sound right coming from a man like him. When she looked around, she saw the others choking back laughs.

Marty turned and looked each of them deep in the eyes. "If we choose not to fight, we give in to one side or the other."

His cold words disheartened Sheila, his stern gaze falling upon each of them again. They really had no choice but to fight. And she hadn't realized her eyes had welled up with tears just thinking about it.

Seeing this, Marty put his arm around her shoulder and pulled her in close. "Let's not discuss this any further just yet," he said, as if sensing the growing tension. "Let's think about it on the way to the shelter, where we can get some rest. We can decide later once we've all let it soak in. Besides, we still have a while before we get there."

They all agreed. And Sheila wiped her tears away on her sleeve. Marty's hand found hers, and he walked with her for a short while, speaking of better things, trying to calm her down. But from the corner of her eye, she saw that hive, and couldn't stop dwelling on it. At some point they'd each need to make a very difficult decision, and that time wasn't far away.

Chapter 16

Ike's world had gone off kilter. The train had derailed. But, having made acquaintances with these people under the presumption they would leave this state as soon as possible, Ike trailed behind the group on his way right back to nearly the same damn place he'd left only a few days ago. And what about that frigging thing out there, that giant heart Marty thought was a hive? Now they were planning to do something about it?

He did not know what went on inside a hive like that, but he also didn't want to know. Who fucking cared? He didn't care if there was a queen or not because, either way, whatever was on the inside was frigging awful. It had to be something otherworldly, something related to these goddamn creatures, and that alone meant it wasn't safe. He liked to gamble, but no matter what they said, no matter how hard they pushed, he wasn't going anywhere near that thing.

Besides, had there ever been a hive that didn't have a queen? He didn't think so. And what did a queen do? Why they produced larvae, always hatching new brood to do their bidding. He knew this would not be any different. Asexual or not, there was some creature inside that thing squeezing out new monsters left and right. And who knew what those bastards would look like? Wings? Sure. But how much worse could it get? Ike had a good imagination, and he could think up all sorts of bad stuff. He could sense it like he could the ace of spades being the very next card drawn from the deck.

He also didn't like hashing things out later. If he'd had his way, they'd be across the border to Indiana by now, wolfing down some chicken and waffles. Screw those soldiers, too. If they caught him trying to cross, he'd put up a fight to the bitter end. And he'd make sure to fare better than that ninny Andy, too.

What bothered Ike the most, though, was this Marty guy. Who died and crowned him Lord Almighty King Shit, anyway? People like him always had a way of keeping Ike down over the years. They were the reason he'd been forced to work in the sanitation business these last fifteen years, barely making enough to survive let alone place a solid bet. After everything he'd accomplished, he should have been a shoo-in for a desk job. But *no*! Only uptight asshats like Marty got those jobs.

And guys like Bernard weren't any better. Those sorts of people always ended up being supervisors, each of them following around their bosses like lost sheep. God help guys like Ike when those supervisors turned their beady eyes on them, too. Because of those dolts, Ike often found himself knee-deep in the shit...literally.

Ike didn't trust those two arm-candy gals who walked around clinging to Marty and Bernard like ticks to a dog, either. In fact, he might trust these monsters more than he trusted any of those four. They had a way about them that made him feel small and insignificant. And he didn't like that feeling of being lesser than anyone. It made him sick, and once he got it in his head, he just couldn't stop thinking about it. That was the worst part, too, constantly dwelling on how they made him feel. He hadn't had that issue with Sandy.

The way she walked made Ike stiff as a tent pole. She showed interest in everything he did, how he thought. When she spoke, she looked at him, not through him, and she was the only one here who made him feel important—or better than a sanitation worker. Not only this, but he believed if they made it through all this bull crap, he might have a real shot with her. Even if he didn't, maybe she'd give him the time of day for the high and hard pickle tickle. That was, of course, as long as all those four cock blockers didn't get in his way.

For a long while they all remained speechless. Ike supposed there wasn't as much to say as there was to see. For two days the dust had been ungodly, but it was settling some. Even then, it left behind a strange fog-like appearance hovering across the landscape. He couldn't even see that far, which made the hive more ominous as they passed. They took a wide berth to avoid being seen, but even then they were walking straight down the middle of a road to avoid any debris that might hinder their travels.

Ike stopped to examine the hive. Something was flying around the top, circling the hive. He squinted, trying to bring one of these things into clarity, but realized what they were a second later. It was three or four of those blasted winged creatures guarding the hive.

"It's a few more miles to the shelter," Marty said, startling Ike.

Ike hated the righteousness in Marty's voice. He didn't believe for one second the guy had been a farmer, not with the way he spoke all proper and all. And the guy walked like someone had shoved a frigging broomstick right up his ass, too. Most of all, Marty exhibited a certain intelligence well beyond that of the everyday seed sowing sap. That likely meant he'd gone to college, and Ike resented such privileged assclowns.

Bernard stopped some few feet down the road. "It's larger than I thought." Everyone else stopped, too. "I'm not sure I like going anywhere near that thing."

"Well, we might have to, my friend," Marty said. "We might not have a choice. But that's not a choice we need to—"

"We're going to that hive, like it or not," Sandy said, the first words she'd spoken in hours.

Ike couldn't believe his ears. Why would she come out like that and spew such bullshit? They'd discussed this, and he recalled her being in favor of heading to the shelter. The fact this road passed so close to the hive hadn't even crossed his mind. And hadn't she been the one to lead the way down this road?

Marty faced Sandy. The others gathered behind him, even Ike. "Sandy? Care to explain what's going on?"

Ike loathed the way he said things. Why not just say what they were all thinking? "Are you fucking nuts?" But he held his tongue and waited for her response to Marty's...question. Besides, opening his trap now would only sour his chances of getting laid later. The fact she might be bat shit crazy did nothing to lessen the fact he still wanted to boink her. But he'd be damned to hell if he would walk right up the ass of that hive.

"I think that's a real bad idea, Sandy," Nancy said.

"I agree," Sheila said.

All five of them waited for Sandy's response, but Ike noticed something different about Sandy's demeanor just then. Suddenly, she didn't look so soft, and he didn't think she was that easy-going sensitive girl he'd once thought she was. The way she carried herself, she stood tall, straight as an arrow, like she was carrying around every ounce of pride. Her face appeared rigid and tense, like someone was about to do something—

"I'm not crazy," Sandy said, barking out the words, bold as a dog in its own backyard. "And that wasn't a request."

Marty started pulling at the hairs on his chin, another act that always got on Ike's nerves. He couldn't care less what the guy did so long as they started moving again and got the hell out of here. Marty said, "Sandy, listen—"

She withdrew a handgun from behind her. She must've had it tucked in her waistline, underneath her shirt, because Ike had been staring at her ass all day and hadn't noticed a gun. And Ike wasn't one to go around missing such details, either. Sandy aimed the gun right at Marty's face, then bobbed it to the others, one by one, tracing the frowns forming on their faces. She finished with Ike.

"What the fuck, Sandy? This here's no time for a frigging stickup." Screw getting laid. Ike had bigger concerns now.

Her face twisted with disgust. "Shut your foul mouth! You've tested my nerves enough already, so you best keep quiet, or I'll shut your mouth for you." She pumped the gun his way, and he did as she asked, though he continued to grumble under his breath.

"Why, Sandy?" Sheila asked.

"That's Private Masterson to you, and I expect you all to call me by my name. And here's what's up. We're gonna go into that hive over there and figure out how to take it down, plain and simple. We'll either do it together, or you'll provide enough of a distraction so I can do it myself."

"San—" Marty said, then corrected himself. "I mean Private

Masterson, please, contact your people. Let me reason with them."

"Fuck that, too," Ike said, unable to hold his tongue. "I'll be damned if I'm going to—"

Sandy's gun found him again. "What did I tell you, loud mouth?" She used her free hand to brush a few strands of hair out of her face. Her eyes gleamed with ferocity. "Listen, none of you are gonna make it out of this alive, anyway. This is the end of the road. You've even discussed as much. The second you stayed on this side of the blockade, you sealed your fate. So why not go out with a fight? Isn't that better than just dying?"

"No!" Sheila took a defiant stance.

"You've got to be kidding me." Private Masterson's face flushed red. "Don't you get—"

"This isn't the way things have to shake out." Even as Marty spoke Ike saw Bernard readying to assault Private Masterson. "We can—"

Sandy turned and fired. Ike felt himself jump. The gunfire echoed across the landscape.

For a fraction of a second, Ike patted himself down, feeling for blood. He found none. Then he saw Bernard, the large man's hands pressed to his stomach, the blood seeping out through his fingers already soaking his shirt.

Fuck.

Ike stared at Sandy, at the smoke drifting from the end of her gun. She looked so ugly now.

Bernard stumbled back, collapsing to his knees. "I'm... I..."

He dropped back on his rear, sitting there in the dirt-ridden street. A dazed expression washed across Bernard's face, what Ike recognized as confusion.

Ike knew something else, too. He'd seen it before, perhaps a few times even. Bernard would die.

Only a few seconds had passed, and in that time they'd all frozen, perhaps equally unsure of who the private had shot. Nancy ran to Bernard and knelt beside him, doing what she could to slow the bleeding, pressing her hands against the wound. But Ike knew it was a futile effort.

Bernard's eyes rolled back in their sockets as pain clearly

overwhelmed him. He never made a sound, not a single grunt or cry of pain. All the while Nancy poked and prodded at the wound, trying to save him. But when Bernard rolled back on his side, and Ike saw the exit wound, that only confirmed his initial suspicions. She was only making things worse for Bernard, worse for her, worse for all of them.

Unable to contain himself any longer, Bernard wailed out a long, horrific cry. He sounded like a demented wolf-like creature howling at the moon.

"Let's go!" Private Masterson said, but no one moved. "Now!" She waved the gun to enforce a sense of urgency.

"Marty," Bernard managed. "Get them out of here." He coughed, and a spray of blood splattered the road beside him, some dribbling down his chin. "Go. Go."

Just getting that out must have hurt bad, because Bernard writhed on the ground, clenching his stomach himself now. In that moment it became obvious Nancy no longer knew what to do. Her hands moved but touched nothing. Tears streaked her face.

"I'm not going anywhere!" Nancy said.

Bernard waved her off, but his hand fell weakly back to the ground. "Please, Marty." A pool of blood had formed on the road beneath him.

Marty stepped forward and took Nancy's arm. He pulled her up despite her fighting against it.

"I'm not going!" She pulled away from him, trying to escape his grip, but he held her tight.

"Go," Bernard said again, his voice fading.

"Why?" Nancy said. "I want to stay, Bernard. Please let me stay."

"We have to go, Nancy." Marty pulled her arm, which got her moving somehow. Her eyes stayed glued to Bernard.

"Walk," Private Masterson said and buried the end of her gun in Nancy's ribs.

"Fuck you!" Nancy said. "Fuck you, you asshole!" She spat in Masterson's face.

Lucky for her, Masterson only stabbed the gun forward, causing Nancy to wince.

Ike's contempt for Bernard faded as he watched the large man suck in a deep breath. The guy convulsed in the road, trying to keep breathing. Bernard's lips quivered as he tried over and over to force out his last words, "I love you." Then he froze, the air coming out in a long quiet hiss. Bernard was dead.

Nancy fell to her knees, crying hard and loud. Marty tried to support her, but she'd given up.

Private Masterson kicked her, but Nancy didn't move, didn't even seem to feel it. But just seeing that enraged Ike. He stared at Sandy with contempt. "Leave her be!"

The private eyed up Ike, but he didn't even flinch. Not even when she aimed her gun at him again. Why? Because fuck her, that's why.

After a long moment, she lowered the gun and waited, her impatience obvious.

Marty helped Nancy back to her feet, and they kept walking. Sheila moved to Nancy's other side, doing her best to assist and comfort the woman. Nancy kept looking back every few steps, as if she still couldn't believe her eyes. Even when Bernard was far behind them, the poor woman continued to glance back. Nothing shook her out of this grief, and rightly so. Not even the impending threat of entering the hive.

Ike couldn't stop thinking about what he'd seen. How he'd trusted Sandy. It was more than a shit thing she'd done. And that had him reassessing his entire life, everything he'd believed, including how he viewed these people.

Chapter 17

It bothered Marty that he hadn't seen it coming. And thinking back to his days as a teacher, hadn't it always been the quiet ones who made the poorest decisions? Had he not learned anything from those days? He'd seen it time and time again, a good kid gone bad. It made sense to him, too, that they would send one of their own to penetrate these groups, to be friendly before taking control, and force ordinary people to attack. Who better for this next wave of ground assaults than the most expendable of all soldiers, the civilians?

He wished Bernard were here to confirm these thoughts. And now, thanks to Marty being too slow to see it for himself, Bernard would never come back. Judging from the way Nancy looked she might not come back, either. What did that say about Marty as a leader? That he was inadequate? Why did he ever let it get to this point?

There were implications in government leaders choosing to use citizens this way. It meant they believed they'd lost control of the situation. Perhaps, they'd depleted their forces, however far this now stretched. And there was no better recruiter than a gun to the head. But how many others were being forced to do just that, to charge in blindly with no forethought, in the hopes they might somehow defeat this unknown force?

What it also meant was that there was no control within the containment zone. So it seemed probable that as this spread beyond their reach, they might soon use bigger bombs. At some point, likely when they felt they'd started grasping at straws in bunches instead of one at a time, they'd look to end this the only way they truly knew how. But then why hadn't they done so already? Hadn't it already gotten to that point?

Marty believed that could mean the enemy had somehow neutralized those weapons. If that were true then so help them, because that clearly gave their foes the upper hand. Even worse, it meant he and his small group were walking right into the fire. He knew that would lead to their extermination and many others. So, worse than Marty's role in this, was theirs.

He looked at their faces one by one. Each of them looked tired, too worn to go on, and yet they did. He felt guilty for causing them this grief, for not being able to think of a way out of this. And considering that, the memories of his old self washed into his thoughts like a vicious tidal wave. He missed his wife, his daughter, and more than ever he missed his brother. They were all gone now. He was alone.

So it was on the path to the mammoth heart-shaped hive, gun pointed at his back, he started crying. And once he started, he couldn't stop, as visions of his estranged brother and what they'd gone just a handful of days ago swirled in his mind.

Chapter 18

When Jake slapped one of his beefy hands against his chest, Marty thought the worst. A hurt, twisted look wrinkled across Jake's face, and that was when he suspected his brother might suffer a heart attack. Images of what he'd lost shot through his mind like flashes from an old camera, seeing his wife and daughter sucked up into a tornado, even though he hadn't been there to witness any of it, and his thoughts became infected with the worry of losing his brother, too. He couldn't let that happen.

He took three cautionary steps toward Jake. When Jake's knees buckled, Marty took four more, not wanting to hold back any longer. But Jake waved him off, the independent sort who wanted no one else's help. Though Jake had always been bigger and stronger, able to stand on his own two feet, Marty felt rather overprotective of his older brother. And so he maintained his position on the front lawn for a few seconds, still some thirty yards away, before creeping forward.

"Are you okay?" Marty said.

Jake nodded, his hand working its way over his shoulder to the nape of his neck, where he rubbed. This put Marty at ease, as much as he could be after such a shock to his system. But he didn't like Jake trying to do all this work on his own. That had been part of the reason he'd come here after losing Fiona and Gina, to help with the farm, a task that had grown more difficult for his brother because of his bad hip. Truth told, he owed this service to Jake, as he'd been there to pick up the pieces when Marty couldn't do it on his own. Now, with their roles reversed, he stood a short distance from the front porch, watching his brother steady himself, still unsure whether he should help.

Jake never worried about much of anything. He'd left school early after their father had a stroke. He'd tended to the fields so that Marty could finish school. And Marty had finished, becoming an English teacher at Lakewood Falls Middle School. But lack of knowledge had never concerned Jake. He'd always known what he wanted to do with his life, and that had always been enough for the large man. Jake had enjoyed standing in the fields, watching the blazoned sun fade on the horizon since he was a young man.

When Marty lost his family, Jake hadn't had time to worry about himself. Marty had been a mess, to the point he couldn't recall much of those days. Jake did what he always had, what seemed to come naturally to his brother. He took Marty by the arm and dragged him back to the farm and gave him something to do. Something to keep his mind off everything. And Marty had done so ever since.

Marty had depended on Jake. Yet he never felt that need in his brother, even now, when Jake's situation almost begged for help. Marty had also come to depend on the farm, a place where Jake had given him a life to fill the void of everything he'd lost. This farm gave Marty a renewed sense of being, a second wind so to say. But he also knew the truth—that this farm, his brother, were only distractions to keep him busy, so he didn't have time to think about the horrible incidents that ruined his life.

Whenever the workday ended, Marty found himself with an abundance of time on his hands. While Jake slept, his snoring loud enough to wake the chickens, Marty sat watching TV, ruminating on the past. He often wished Jake would stay up with him, to keep him from thinking about it all. But being ten years older, Jake was all about routine, one he'd adhered to ever since quitting school. And even now, Jake stuck to his plan, waving Marty off, despite him being within twenty yards of his brother.

Marty stared at Jake's face, noticing the way he winced. Something about his eyes looked different just then, as though they'd glazed over, like a man struck by a profound thought but could not hold on to it as his thoughts drifted back to reality.

Jake wobbled as he straightened himself, his hand on his

knee, supporting his weight. "Gosh darn skeeter got me."

"A mosquito?" All the worst feelings ran through Marty's thoughts: the Zika virus, the bird flu.

"Up and bit me," Jake said, still rubbing his neck.

"All that drama for a mosquito bite?" Marty laughed. "You ·
had me worried."

"Well, it hurt like hell."

But Marty's thoughts were already wandering, laughing that he'd let himself get so worked up over nothing. He had an awful tendency of doing just that, worrying too much. He thought back to something his father always told him, "99% of what you worry about never comes to fruition." Which made it all the more concerning he'd gotten to this point, where he worried about everything, all the time. It was all so debilitating. And even more troubling, he knew now, long before he even thought about going to sleep, that he'd have trouble dozing off. That and spending all day out in the fields half asleep wouldn't make things any better. Once he missed a few hours' sleep, he never got them back. And there were no sick days for lack of sleep here on a farm. He'd pull his weight no matter what the ailment.

Marty wished Jake didn't do so much around the farm. Not only did he have an aging ticker, but he'd had his second hip replacement three years prior. That first one had looked like it had gone through an oversized garbage disposal when they took it out, evidence Jake did far more than he should. And the doctor had warned him, too, informed both of them if Jake kept it up he'd be in a wheelchair before he turned sixty. So Marty helped where he could, trying not to let Jake notice and doing his best to keep his brother from doing any of the heavy work. This meant more than ever Marty couldn't miss a day of work.

Thankfully, over the years, Jake had taken to more of the household duties such as the cooking and cleaning. This afforded Marty time to do those things he needed to, even though he'd always suspected Jake had done so because deep down, he knew himself, that he couldn't do the work he used to. Though Jake would never admit to such a weakness, Marty had caught his brother watching soap operas on several occasions, a guilty pleasure he'd tried to keep hidden from Marty.

Withdrawing out of his thoughts, Marty observed the way Jake kept rubbing his neck. By the time he finally stopped, Jake held his hand to his face and stared at the palm awestruck.

"What? What do you see?" Marty figured he might have splatted the mosquito, gotten blood and bug guts all over his hand. A smile crept over Marty's face, replaced by alarm when Jake didn't do the same. He saw no look of satisfaction in his brother's eyes, evidence he'd mushed the mosquito. All he saw was disgust. "Are you going to let me in on this or what?"

His face twisted in confusion. Jake didn't look up. "It's just blood. A whole hell of a lot, too."

"Well," Marty said, "I guess you squashed a juicy one." Marty laughed when Jake only glanced up long enough to shoot him a mental middle finger.

"I told you," Jake said. "It bit me real hard. This blood ain't from killin' it, either." Jake held up his hand for him to see, and Marty gasped. This wasn't just a little blood. It covered his whole hand. And it was dripping from Jake's fingers like a leaky faucet, too.

Jake's eyes flickered. Marty felt his doing the same. But while Marty stood there, still considering everything that had happened, Jake went to do what he'd come out here to do. He bent over with some trouble and retrieved the metal bucket and rested it over the nozzle of the well's hand pump. He gave a handful of good solid pumps and the water burst into the bucket—much landing in, but more splashing out.

After filling the bucket, he took it in the hand absent of blood and headed toward Marty. All Marty could think was how he wished he'd gotten the kitchen sink fixed so that Jake wouldn't track blood all across the carpet. The carpet was old enough as it was, and they couldn't afford to replace it. Heck, they couldn't even afford a cellphone, and everyone had one of those these days. He wasn't even sure if they had coverage out this far, anyway.

Jake's body shot out in all directions, like a bolt of lightning had struck him and run right through his spine, throwing his arms and legs out as though in the middle of doing a jumping jack. Only there wasn't any lightning. And though he'd somehow held on to the bucket, the water in it sloshed about. Even from here Marty could see half of it had emptied before Jake's grip finally gave. The bucket struck the ground, rattling as it rolled back down the slight hill, spilling the remaining water. Jake's body convulsed like he was having a seizure, his mouth spread wide as he tried to speak. "Mar-ty?" he said in a shaky voice.

Frozen by what he was seeing, Marty stumbled forward on numb legs. "Jake? I'm coming, Jakey."

It registered for just a moment, a split second where Marty had somehow regressed to his childhood self, back when two boys tried to find common ground in playing war despite their age difference. Those precious few moments, though quite frustrating, welled up inside of him and already tears sprinkled his cheeks, feeling warm, his eyes blurring.

Jake dropped to his knees, even then his legs appearing too weak to support him. All the while, his arms and torso still shook like some horrible ghost was trying to tear him limb from limb. "Ho-ly cr-a-p." Jake's eyes were as wide as they could be, nothing but the whites of sunny side up eggs. But the tremors lessened some, his eyes calming again, and Marty slowed, watching his brother return to the man he'd known his entire life.

"Thank God," Marty said, folding over to his knees and breathing heavy. A long sigh escaped him. Thank God for small miracles. It appeared whatever came over Jake had passed.

After catching his breath, Marty made his way toward Jake anyway, deciding he'd help even if Jake refused. Once inside, he'd check Jake out, convince him to let Marty drive him down to see Doctor Showalter to find out what had caused this mess. Marty would need to pick up some extra hours around the farm, but he'd do whatever must done, and he'd take care of Jake until he got better. He couldn't risk—

Jake's stomach shot forward, his shoulders rounding back. Both of Jake's arms shot out again as if some surge of energy was passing through him, unable to find a way out. Jake's Adam's apple vibrated, pulsing like Jake's heart had somehow become dislodged and wound up in his jugular. His head jerked back, lips parted and drawn back from his teeth in an awful sneer. Jake howled into the bruising sky as Marty hurried to him. "Ahhhhhhhhrrrrrrr gggggggggddddd!"

Reaching his brother's side, Marty didn't know what to do. He braced each arm to either side of Jake, preparing to catch him if need be. But Jake only kept trembling, his body swaying back and forth, the whites of his eyes staring up at Marty. He couldn't bear seeing it anymore. Crying, terrified he would lose Jake, too, Marty fell to his knees and embraced his brother. "Please, Jakey. Stop. Please."

And there it was again, little Marty pleading with his brother to make it stop, as he had many times when they were younger, and Jake got too rough. One time, Jake had even tickled him until Marty pissed his pants. But that was what big brothers did, they tormented their younger brothers, especially when their parents only ever spoke of said younger brother's achievements. When the younger brother got all the attention.

Marty shook away the thought. "Jakey, please..."

Then, as suddenly as it came, it left. And Marty pulled back, staring at his brother, who kneeled in a lethargic state, appearing devoid of all strength.

"Come on," Marty said, getting to his feet and pulling at Jake's arm. "Let's get you inside fast."

But Jake didn't move. He kept kneeling there, barely moving with each gentle tug Marty gave. It felt like pulling a fifty-pound sack of potatoes, sluggish at first but then easier once you got started. Only Marty hadn't gotten him started yet.

He pulled a little harder. "We'll get you in and call Doc—"

Jake stood all at once, and without even the slightest misstep or falter. Dumbfounded by the unexpected vigor, Marty felt his jaw slacken. He considered letting go of Jake's arm but couldn't. Not until Jake pulled it away himself, and even then, Marty kept his hands out in front of him, slightly lifted, and stared at his brother.

Realizing this, Marty withdrew his hands, and brushed his lengthy hair out of his face, his focus still on Jake. "You okay?"

"What in Sam Hill was that?" Jake said, his eyes blinking with each word, as if trying to emphasize them. He brushed himself off.

Marty supposed the way Jake spoke came of whatever surge of energy had passed through him. It had probably lit up his nervous system like a Christmas tree. Perhaps some of that energy was still in there, too, bouncing off each nerve ending like ping pong balls. He wondered what it must feel like, all that energy still inside of him, and likened it to drinking one too many cups of coffee. And that's exactly what Jake looked like, too, like a guy coming down from some caffeine high who still hadn't shaken the aftershock. Marty couldn't shake the worry the invisible-looking burst of electricity might return, and even several minutes later when they started back to the house, he kept one arm out behind his brother, ready to jump in should Jake experience it again.

"Come on," Marty said, looking at Jake's blood-smeared neck. "Let's get you inside and look at that bite. Maybe get some Monkey Blood on there if it's that deep, before it gets infected."

Deep down, Marty still hoped he could convince Jake to visit the doctor. That was, in fact, his sole task, one he hadn't fully worked out the details for yet.

Everything they needed, they had delivered to them. The companies who bought their crops sent trucks. Vendors of farm equipment came to their farm, providing much of what they needed, or they could always ask if something particular struck them. Their food came directly from their hard work, right from the farm onto their plates. And they never went on vacations. So they didn't own a car. Any greater needs they had beyond this, they obtained by use of a bus or cab, and if an emergency arose a well-placed phone call. They owned a bike and a mule, though. They also had the tractor which they'd used more than once to get into town. But that wouldn't work now, when he felt like this was more of an emergency. So he considered calling 9-1-1 once they got inside.

What seemed like a whole other lifetime ago, Marty had a car. He used it to get to and from school. That felt like a different time now, but, like riding a bicycle, he was certain he'd be able to pick it up right away. And that's what got him thinking about calling the Joneses, who lived six or seven miles down the road. If he convinced Jake to go to the doctor, maybe they'd let him borrow their old pickup. That would be quicker than waiting for a cab, but it was still quite the hike to their place by foot, so they'd need to take the tractor.

Jake reached the front stoop and hesitated, which was why Marty eased his arm around his brother's waist. Only then did he realize just how much Jake's health had declined over the last few years of doing less and less around the farm. His skin felt softer, having lost much of that leathery feel one accrues after years of hard labor. And his skin had paled, too, evidence he'd been spending more and more time inside the house. At least he still had a few calluses on his hands, but Marty believed they were a byproduct of light household chores, the duties Jake took to while watching his soaps.

"Did you see that, Marty?" His eyes blinked over and over, as if being irritated. And his voice sounded thicker and a little less hick-like. He looked like a child standing at an ice cream truck. "I think I got struck by lightning. Gosh darn, did you see a bolt of lightning?" Jake's face twitched, and so did his body, almost to the point Marty thought he might start dancing. He swore if Jake pirouetted he wouldn't be able to hold back his hilarity. Why was he so excited about this?

Offering Jake a steady hand under his left arm to get up the stoop, Jake shook him off. Marty didn't see any resentment in his face, but Jake never liked needing anyone's help to do anything. Jake offered a sideways glance and his face wrinkled as they got to the door, all the while Marty clinging to his arm. Funny enough, it almost felt like Jake was pulling Marty along instead of vice versa.

Marty, still considering what Jake had said, mumbled, "There wasn't any lightning."

Jake stopped and looked Marty straight in the eyes. There was a hint of resentment behind that gaze, and Marty couldn't fathom any reason for such bitterness. "Then what the hell was it?" he said in a cold tone.

"I'm not sure." It had looked like a stroke, or perhaps a heart attack. It could have been either one, given Jake's previous condition. Both were more probable than an invisible bolt of lightning striking some hick farmer from southern Illinois. He could almost see the headlines now in all the tabloids. No, that hadn't been it at all. That's why he still worried and wanted to convince Jake to visit the doctor.

Jake pulled away from Marty's hand. Marty couldn't detect that his brother was experiencing any pain in his hip, which would have been a miracle. But he thought the underlying pain of what had happened could have taken away from that normal ache; deep down his brother was just as concerned as he. However, the way Jake had fallen down, it was a wonder he hadn't broken his other hip. If nothing else, Jake should be complaining of a much greater pain from that tumble he'd taken.

The screen door clattered shut behind them, and Jake took an immediate chair at the kitchen table. Easing up behind him, Marty examined the mosquito bite. A blood smear covered most of Jake's neck, so Marty found a washcloth and wet it. He dabbed at Jake's neck, wiping the blood away to reveal what they were dealing with.

"What the—" Marty said, staring at the sore.

"What is it? Is it bad?"

Marty could hear the angst in Jake's voice. That made him wish he'd been more sensitive about the matter, maybe not so audible about his amazement. But that also seemed like an impossible task as he stared down at Jake's neck.

"Well," Marty said, tapping a finger on his chin. "It looks like the biggest pimple I've ever seen." Marty pinched his fingers close together and held his hand in front of Jake's face.

Jake's eyes widened on Marty's fingers. "A zit? That's all? You sure?"

The circumference of the wound was as large as a dime. But more concerning, Marty swore it had grown in the few seconds it took him to show Jake how big it was. And the center of the thing had become pasty white, as if the pus had suddenly gathered beneath the sheath of dead flesh, wanting instant release.

"Well, I'm no doctor, so who knows for sure. Maybe we should—"

"Marty, will you just tell me what you see and stop this doctor business?"

His brother's stubbornness often bothered Marty. "Okay, well, maybe it's infected. I think we should call the Doc—"

"No doctors," Jake said, shaking his head back and forth. "You're so set in your ways."

Truth told, Marty wasn't the one set in his ways. But he didn't let his brother's words get to him. He was too concerned for Jake to feel offended. Plus, he understood Jake's issue with doctors, and why he refused to see them.

Doctors had found various ways to make Jake's life difficult. It had taken them years before they diagnosed his thyroid disease properly. Before that, they blamed his constant tiredness on being overweight. And while Jake was a rather large man, he never had been fat. He had a bit of a belly which was enough for them to proclaim him pre-diabetic. But even once they diagnosed his issues, it took months to zero in on the proper medications and dosages. Marty remembered those days well; how tough they'd been for Jake. His brother hadn't slept right for much of that time, often working out in the fields in the wee hours of morning, long before even the roosters woke up. And Jake swore it was those days, where he'd been working the hardest because he couldn't sleep, that he'd wrecked his hip. Then they botched the first surgery, so he'd had to go back a second time just to get it right. All that time away from the fields healing had taken a toll on Jake, and maybe that's why he'd gone back to work so soon, long before doctors advised.

So, whether Jake needed help no longer mattered from his point of view. All his doctors had near taken his livelihood away, and surely Jake still resented them for that if nothing else. Marty tried to put the thought out of his head.

"They'll just come up with some dumb disease," Jake said. "And all that will happen is I'll be doing less and less around here, to the point I'm nothing more than a maid."

Marty tried but couldn't keep the words from reaching his lips. "Maybe that's for the best, Jake."

Eyes like daggers darted up at Marty. And a sneer crossed Jake's lips, evidence he didn't care for talk like that, even if it was the truth. But Marty saw something else, too, a strangeness to his brother's eyes. Maybe they looked browner or had more orange flecks, but something felt off about the way he looked at Marty.

"Okay, okay." Reminding himself that people's eyes didn't just change colors so quickly, Marty pushed the thought away and leaned over to examine the wound a little closer. He didn't like the looks of it. Not only had the whitehead grown in size, but now it wriggled and squirmed as if something were growing inside. "Jesus."

"What?"

Marty stepped back, afraid the whitehead would blow at any moment. Realizing what he'd done, he laughed nervously. "I swear, something's moving around inside of that bite, Jake."

"What do you mean, something's moving around in there? Like what?" he said, his accent drawn out, sounding almost tired.

"I'm not sure, but it doesn't look right. Looks like something's in there and whatever it is, it wants out."

Jake's hands rushed to the back of his neck where they found the wound and probed the circumference of the sore for a moment. Marty couldn't believe his eyes, as now the bite was as big as a nickel. When Jake's hands pulled away, there was a slight wetness gleaming on his fingertips. Jake gazed at them for a moment, then he held the fingers to his nose and sniffed.

"What the?" He raised the fingers for Marty to get a whiff. "They smell like crap."

Marty shook him off. Whatever Jake's fingers smelled like, he had no interest in confirming that for him. Jake withdrew the fingers with reluctance. Sensing his disappointment, Marty moved in to examine the wound again. "It's bigger now. About the size of a quarter."

"Why would it get bigger?" Marty could hear the worry in his voice.

"I think we need to get whatever is in there, out." He considered his words before he spoke them, knowing already what Jake's stance on the matter would be. Still, he tried. "I really think we should get you to a doc—"

Swift as a barn swallow, Jake's hands swooped behind his neck, found the sore and squeezed. "Eeeeyoww!"

"I really think we should—" But Marty was too late. A split second longer and he might have finished his sentence. Instead, he jumped to his left, to avoid contact. A glob of white goo shot through the air, missing Marty by inches.

Jake squeezed harder, and while Marty expected a drip of blood, none came. "Ow!" Jake said. And he kept on squeezing, as if sensing something more was in there.

Thankfully, Marty dodged the second pale wad of pus as it shot through the air. Unfortunately, this second passing had come close enough for Marty to get a whiff of that smell Jake had been talking about.

Relief fell over them both in an instant. After what felt like minutes, Marty tiptoed over to the pool of pus and examined it. "Looks like the cream off a fresh bucket of cow's milk."

It had been a long time since Marty needed to pop any zits. In fact, he thought it had been thirty years on the dot. Though what few he'd experienced had been bad, not one had ever been this bad.

"See anything in there?"

"Nada," Marty said. "So you got that going for you." And he laughed, unable to control his nerves.

"Hush now. That ain't funny."

But it was to a small degree.

"You okay?" Marty looked back over his shoulder and found Jake's eyes. Something about them seemed even more different now. They looked...brighter.

Without knowing he was doing so, Marty investigated the lighting and the windows, trying to decide if something affected Jake's eyes in some weird way.

"Actually, I've never felt better," Jake said.

Marty supposed that would be true. Having gotten some relief from a sore like that must have felt good. Jake wore a dumb grin, as if all concern about the bite had left him in mere seconds.

Marty started questioning what he'd seen. Had it really been that bad? Or had he imagined all of it. He glanced at the pool of pus. "Let me take another look."

Marty approached again, and already he saw that the

wound was no longer throbbing. Whatever needed to get out had done so. A layer of torn skin remained, surrounding a half-dollar sized patch of raw flesh. It looked very tender, like what one might expect when they'd been out in the sun far too long without lotion, and their skin had turned a bright red. Even the edges looked like the fresh peel around such a burn.

"Well," Marty said, "it looks a lot better now. I think we should get that cleaned up and bandage the wound before it gets infected?"

"Huh," Jake said, waving off the offer. "I feel better."

Even Marty could see something was different about Jake, though he couldn't put his finger on it just yet.

Jake stood and faced Marty. Odd, Marty was certain he had to lift his head a little higher than usual to look Jake in the eyes. It was a subtle difference though, and he believed if Jake's hip was in fact feeling better, that could cause his brother to stand a little taller than usual.

Marty stared into Jake's eyes. "You look better."

That was true, too. The wrinkles Marty had grown familiar with all these years he'd spent with his brother had mostly vanished. Years of laugh lines had vanished. Jake's drooping aged eyes now looked bright and more alert, as if he were ready for anything. And while Marty supposed he should find such an unusual restoration alarming, truth was, he almost welcomed it, because a healthy Jake would be around for a long time.

As quickly as he stood, Jake turned away. "Other than feeling dog tired, I feel better than I have in decades." He kept staring off at the stairs that led to his bedroom.

To Marty, it looked like Jake might fall asleep. It was clear he needed to get to bed as soon as possible. That might explain some of this, too. Maybe Jake was just too tired to notice the pain. Could the exhaustion be making him feel better? And aside from Jake being tired, Marty sensed he wanted to be alone. It was such a reclusive feeling his brother emanated. But at least Marty had seen that look before, and he had a way of crowding Jake, especially when he thought his brother hurt.

When Jake took a step for the stairs, Marty headed for the couch. "Go get some rest. I'll catch up on some TV."

They didn't have cable out this way, and they'd opted against satellite. So there wasn't any Internet or much of a selection of channels. What they got came via their old antennae. But Marty only needed some background noise. He always did when he got thinking about his wife and daughter.

He sat on the couch and observed Jake standing at the foot of the stairs. To his surprise, Jake took the stairs a few at a time. Startled, he shot forward, waiting for a cry of pain. When none came, he slowly eased back on the couch, listening to his brother's heavy footfalls on the wooden floor above. There was something about all this Marty didn't like, even with Jake looking so spry. But he reckoned he could call Doc Showalter in the morning. Maybe he could guilt Jake into going. He'd always been more receptive when Marty applied some pressure.

Struggling to keep his thoughts focused on the day's events, Marty's memories flooded back in time as expected. His heart ached for both of them. He longed to hold his daughter again. To feel his wife's skin pressed against his. The soft touch of her lips, the small of her back as he pulled her closer. He missed looking into her eyes, seeing the love, and remembering everything they'd been through together.

With the TV volume low, watching a concert on public television, Marty started drifting. As he slid into sleep, the first thing he saw was a broad desk forming in his mind's eye. Sitting on that desk was a black office phone, its cord twisted and knotted. And it was ringing.

Chapter 19

Sheila saw the look in Marty's eyes and thought it anger at first. She imagined him blowing up on Sandy, perhaps wrestling the private to the ground where she hoped he would defeat her. Then he'd take away her gun, and they'd...

That wasn't Marty's style. She thought him more likely to use his words to diffuse the situation, but she worried that if he tried, he might end up meeting the same fate as Bernard. Yet she knew it wasn't that either. Something else was bothering Marty, and it wasn't the gun at his back.

"What is it?" she finally asked.

Marty dismissed her with a shake of his head.

She took his hand. "Please, Marty? Let me in."

Was that what she wanted? She wasn't sure. But holding his hand in this moment made her stomach flutter. She felt attracted to him, and maybe she wanted more. It made her sad they'd never have the chance to—

"Oh yeah, do tell." The private said, mocking Sheila.

Sheila swung around only to stare down the barrel of the gun. Still, she eyed up the woman almost daring her to pull the trigger. And she would have continued to do if not for Marty, who kept trudging onward, pulling her along with him.

She went but didn't care for the private's tone. So what if she'd been playing them for fools? That didn't mean she had to treat them with disrespect. How appropriate this woman who once held power over Ike, now clearly despised the man, and even reminded Sheila of Ike. Sheila almost wanted to reveal that detail to the private, thinking it might somehow wound the woman's pride. But she kept it to herself, for now.

Still, Sheila had to say something.

"Don't tell that fucking bitch a single goddamned thing, Marty," Ike said. "Just ignore her like one would crotch lice at a whorehouse."

That earned Ike a good pistol whipping. He reeled away from the private, rubbing his shoulder. But his grin grew a mile wide.

Before settling back into his silence, Ike grumbled something under his breath none of them could make out. But Sheila had some good ideas what he might have said. And just hearing what he'd said made her feel somewhat better about the man. Still, it was mildly ironic the private now held a different power over him.

"It's—" Marty turned to Sheila, his eyes straining to hold back what she now saw were tears. "It's my wife."

Sandy stabbed the gun into his chest, and while it annoyed Sheila, Marty ignored the gun. Sandy urged them onward and if not for Sheila, he might have gotten going again.

It felt like she had to pull him along. "Oh. Marty. I'm so sorry."

She knew nothing about him, and now the pieces seemed to fall into place. Had Sheila crossed some boundary? Made him feel uncomfortable? Was this her fault?

"Thanks." Now he was full out crying. "It's just been so long. I miss her."

Sheila felt a little better about her flirting, knowing she wasn't to blame for his hurt feelings.

"My daughter, too," he said, and that made her heart ache.

"Was it—" Sheila looked around. "This?"

Marty didn't look capable of answering. "No. It was something else."

Whatever happened, Marty hadn't gotten over it. She wondered if he ever would. How long had he suffered like this, kept everything bottled up inside? What had even brought this on? All of it made her eager to reveal her growing feelings for him, but she was certain that would only complicate matters. Plus, that wouldn't be fair to him, not now, maybe never so long as he had such deep regrets.

Suddenly, Marty stopped. And most everyone else did, too.

Sheila could see he didn't have much left in him. He needed to get this out.

"All right, lover boy," Sandy said, shoving the gun in his back.

Marty didn't budge, and Sheila shot the private a glance that might have knocked her out if it had been a punch. Still, she thought it served as warning enough to back off for a second. The private didn't receive the look well, but at least she didn't press them to move.

Ike tugged at Nancy's arm to stop her. She kept shambling on until the private rounded her up. When she did, Nancy sighed, perhaps in relief, but likely more out of grief. What Sheila knew about a woman like that, one that was so inconsolable, was that they could be unpredictable when it came down to it. Sheila worried Nancy might try something stupid at some point and get them all killed. But for now, Nancy remained so dazed Sheila didn't think she could do much of anything, let alone walk.

"Listen, Sandy," Sheila said.

"That's Private Masterson, bitch." The look on her face was almost too much.

"Okay, okay. It's almost night," Sheila said. "We need to find shelter. At least for a little while."

"That's fucking brilliant," Ike said. "My dogs have been barking all damn day."

Sheila looked at Nancy, her concern for the woman growing, and then turned to the private with hopeful eyes.

Masterson surveyed the land a moment. She pointed out a small barn on the horizon. "There."

Marty remained distant, as though trapped in some other world. The pain of what he'd endured showed on his face. But she could do nothing for him now but offer comfort and her condolences. She gave him this with all her heart, holding his hand, walking with him, hoping he'd open up to her once they stopped.

Chapter 20

When the phone rang, it derailed Marty's thinking. It also disrupted the young minds he was trying to make an impression upon. As it continued to ring, the children began to giggle, quietly at first and then louder, until they rivaled the phone.

He held up his free hand, signaling for them to continue reading. Seeing the students hadn't done as directed, he rested the phone against his shoulder and pointed to the book in his hand, *Romeo and Juliet*, making sure they got the message. He depressed the line button. "This is Marty Sanderson."

"Marty!" Fiona was crying. Her voice sounded full of panic, her tone rushed. His heart skipped as he heard a roar like that of a lion in the background.

"Fiona? What is that?"

"Gina ran upstairs!" The way she said this made the hairs at the back of his neck prickle. It felt like a spider crawling across the nape of his neck.

"Wait. What? What's going on?"

"It's a—"

He couldn't make out everything she said. The noise was too loud. "Hon, I can't hea—"

The phone crackled. "...a tornado!"

He dropped the book. The phone slipped from his shoulder, rattling against the floor. Several students jumped, but he barely noticed them.

Somehow, he still hadn't fully processed what she'd said. It was like some vortex in his head spun the words around and around, jumbling them up. But then he understood everything and dropped into his chair, where he bent to retrieve the phone.

She'd said it was a tornado. The word twirled around in his head a moment longer until his mind broke free of the hold. He stared out the window, seeing how dark it was, how the storm raged. But they lived a good half hour away from the school, and he saw nothing of the danger she spoke of. His fingers curled around the receiver, and he held it tight.

"Both of you get to the basement," he said. "Under the stairs. Hurry! I'll get there as soon as I can."

As he waited for her response, the sounds froze him. Fiona must have sat the phone down. It clanged against the floor, then slid across the linoleum. The roar was louder now, much louder than the animal he first likened it to. Dishes clanged against one another, some shattering. Wood snapped. Then he heard a nightmarish scream. But he couldn't tell if that scream belonged to his wife or his daughter. Why'd Gina have to stay home sick today of all days, with Fiona calling off work to stay home with her?

Marty stood, wanting to run to them, but realized he'd never get to them in time. He pressed the phone harder against his ear and barked out orders. "The basement! Get to the basement!"

The entire class was looking at him. Their grave faces reflected concern over his breakdown. He didn't care, and he didn't bother telling them to get back to work, either. That was no longer important to him.

He brushed his hair back feverishly, but strands kept falling back into his face. An urge to rip his hair out overwhelmed him. "Get to the basement!" No response. "Please!"

Right then he sounded like that little boy again, the one whose older brother always had to win. It made him feel equally weak and useless.

Fiona started yelling, which was good. It meant she was still alive. He tried to make out what she was saying.

"Leave the dog, Gina!" She said something else he couldn't make out, her voice struggling against the roar. Then she said, "Get to the basement!"

Marty felt a bit of hope. "Thank God," he said aloud.

Only she didn't stop calling out for Gina, and that worried him. The roar just intensified, sounding closer now, perhaps right on top of them. That was when Marty noticed he'd started trembling. Terror flooded his eyes. But he kept standing there, the phone pressed against his face, waiting for a sign…anything.

Things got worse fast. Fiona's cries grew impatient. The louder that roar got, the less he heard. But he thought Gina was yelling now, too. No, not yelling but crying. He heard Gina calling for the dog, which meant she hadn't given up on saving the dog.

All Marty could do was listen, a prisoner to the atrocity holding his family's future within its daunting winds. Fiona's cellphone clacked against the floor again, as the wind slid it from room to room. He heard bangs, rattles, and cracks. How much more could this phone withstand?

The wind whistled through the phone now, making it difficult to hear anything else. Marty squinted, as if trying to bring something into focus, but only wanting to clarify what was going on amidst the noise on the other end. Then, it became clear Fiona's impatience reached its end.

"Stay there!" she yelled. "I'll come get you!"

He didn't know what to think. This was bad. He couldn't hear her running upstairs, but he could picture it in his thoughts, all the bad things that could happen. He could see her there, hunching over their daughter, the dog frantic between them. Tears streamed down his cheeks, and he waited to hear something, anything other than wind.

When the roar lessened in ferocity briefly, he heard two distinct screams—and those screams were fading fast.

His legs became rubbery, as if he had been out to sea for a long time and only just stepped back ashore. The world around him began to spin and twist, a cascade of colors and featureless young faces, haunting faces. Some students whispered, which sounded like a swarm of locusts to him. Only these bugs were hungry for flesh. They wanted to eat him, to swallow him whole and right then, he very much wanted to die.

Both knees turned in on each other. His arms felt heavy, and the receiver clanged to the floor again. He couldn't even use his hands to break his fall. His body spiraled down, and as he face-planted onto the tiled floor, a loud *Thwap* froze him in the air, mid-fall.

What's this?

He had a fuzzy awareness of a sting on his head. Wanting to rub it away, he hesitated, thinking maybe the bugs were consuming him.

So be it. Let them feed.

Thwap! This time it hurt worse, his arms just hanging there, unresponsive to any suggestion of movement. But there was something else, too, as though this world struggled to exist.

Thwap! It felt like he was drifting into nothingness, being erased from this *now*. And that made him happy, as it would be an end to all the pain.

"Dang it, Marty, wake the heck already," Jake said.

Thwap! Still in the half-numb state of sleep, he saw his brother withdraw the newspaper.

His body wasn't frozen in time somewhere above the floor. And he was rubbing his head. He hadn't been eaten by bugs or faded out of existence. He was just lying on the living room sofa in front of the TV. He'd fallen asleep, and it was morning already.

"All right. All right," Marty said, fending off another attack with his other arm. "I'm up already."

Jake towered over him, waving the newspaper back and forth, sporting a most devilish grin. He reached back with the newspaper, readying to let loose on Marty again. But now Marty had both hands out in front. In the past, throughout their childhood, it had proven a weak but effective defense. He stood up.

"I said I'm up, Jakey." His eyes softened on his brother. "And yes, I know I need to get out—"

"No," Jake said, pulling his collar aside. "I wanted to see if you'll check my neck again."

Marty was foggy with sleep. He needed at least one cup of coffee before he could make much sense of anything. What was Jake talking about?

And then he remembered the wound.

"My neck. The mosquito bite. Remember?"

Marty nodded, doing his best to shake the life back into his head. In some weird way, he wondered if this might be another dream. Maybe some Sci-Fi B movie had been on and somehow he'd applied the details of the movie to real life. If so, he hadn't watched his brother look like he was being electrocuted, there hadn't been a bite, and there had been no pus shooting across the room, missing Marty by only inches. He very much wanted to believe that was exactly what it had been, a dream.

Jake sat and hiked an anxious thumb over his shoulder. Marty obliged, standing behind the chair and—

"What the—" Marty said.

One thing was for sure; this was all too real.

"What?" Jake said.

Marty hadn't meant for that to come out loud. But, in this half-asleep state, once it was on his tongue, it just came out.

"Has it gotten worse?" Jake sounded anxious. "I thought about checking it out in the bathroom mirror but couldn't bring myself to look."

Right then, Marty figured out something he should have noticed the second Jake said anything at all. Somehow, Jake's speech had lost some of that southern Illinois slur. It no longer sounded like he had a bag full of marbles stuffed in his mouth, like Jake's tongue was three sizes too big. He'd been a dropout, of course, so he'd never been a great speaker to begin with. But now his words came out both slick and concise, and always to the point.

Had this mosquito bite somehow given Jake a *real* education? Marty didn't know. It didn't sound so realistic. He remained suspect of any knowledge that came from any means other than school or perhaps a good old-fashioned set of encyclopedias. Did they even have those anymore?

He doubted it, with all the kids having access to the Internet anywhere they went these days. But there was too much teacher left in him to think any different. Whatever this was, it wasn't natural.

"Marty? Are you going to let me in on this or what?"

"Yes. Sorry. Was just lost in my thoughts. I haven't had my coffee yet, you know?"

"Cry me a river. Now what's going on with my neck?"

"Well, looks like the wound cleared up mostly," Marty said.

"That's good, isn't it? Wait. What do you mean by mostly?"

Marty didn't really want to get into this anymore than he already had. He worried what might happen when discussing the reality of this situation. Jake might have a heart attack if he heard his skin had changed color. What Marty was interested in, though, was hearing from someone with authority to give his or her opinion. If not the doctor, maybe someone at the University. He needed to convince—

"Marty!" Jake was glancing at him over his shoulder. "Will you stop that? Please. Now what's going on back there?"

Something inside prevented him from answering, though. There was something peculiar about Jake now, the way he acted, that Marty hadn't yet fully grasped. Until he figured out what that was, he thought it best to keep any speculation to himself.

"It's healed up is all." Marty shifted his head left and put on his best fake smile for Jake's benefit. The gesture wasn't believable judging from Jake's continued impatience.

Jake thumbed at his neck again. "And? Is it ...well...is it normal?"

"That's just it, no. I really think you should see a doctor." There, he had gotten it out. "Doc—"

"I'm not seeing any doctor, so let it go, man." Jake shook an angry fist, much like he had many times throughout their childhood, threatening to pummel his brother, albeit playfully, even at this age. "Now tell me what it looks like."

Marty noticed his brother's anger. If it didn't arise out of fear or frustration, then what made him so irritable? He knew his brother well enough to know all his quirks. Jake was holding back, which meant he was chock full of resentment. But why was he so irritated with Marty, who was only trying to help?

Marty yielded to his brother's demands. "Well, it's red. I'm not talking the freshly healed skin that follows a bad sunburn, either. It's as crimson as the Devil himself."

"The Devil?"

Marty saw the contempt in his brother's expression and ignored it. "Now if that doesn't warrant a visit to the doctor, I don't know what does."

Frustrated, Marty jammed both hands in his overall pockets

and started to walk away, set on making some coffee. Then, he turned back, hoping to see some concern in his brother's face. He didn't.

"So, it's dark red?" Jake wore a bewildered grin.

"It's a dark red," Marty said. "Red, like dried blood."

Marty had some hope Jake might have changed his mind about seeing the doctor. But the moment passed, and Marty saw something else in his brother's face. He saw that Jake almost welcomed this change, no matter how unexpected it might be, no matter how bad it might get. And Marty suspected some of that arose out of his hip feeling so much better, like a drug the absence of pain could be addictive, and now Jake was nothing more than a junky. He even looked younger, and so much stronger than Marty now, so that, too, had a tendency to be addictive. But that crimson flesh, coming from a mosquito bite like that, could mean so many things.

It was possible the flesh looking like this was the start of an infection, perhaps a very serious one. Or perhaps this was more like gangrene, the coloration a result of some pigmentation failure. That was about as scientific as Marty got, and it was only speculation, something to keep his mind occupied, as he couldn't stop obsessing over the matter.

Then he considered another theory, though it sounded more fictitious than anything. Was it possible Jake was turning into a demon? Perhaps that thought only arose from watching one too many late-night horror shows.

Jake laughed suddenly, seemingly for no reason. But Marty didn't see the humor in any of this. Having a patch of red skin was unusual, horrifying even. The fact Jake was laughing, though, made Marty nervous. It got him toying with the notion of his brother might have heard Marty's thoughts. Was that even possible?

Maybe Jake was becoming the devil. It was a silly thought, as Marty was never very religious. Even if it were conceivable that his brother was turning into the devil, Marty reckoned the devil might be a busy man or demon or whatever the hell he was, and if that were the case, Jake wouldn't be around much. Just the notion of this made Marty chuckle under his breath, considering the absurdity of the thought.

Jake closed in on him. "What?"

Sadly, it was more likely this was some rare disease, and that this infection would eventually consume Jake if they did nothing. This concerned Marty, the thought he might have to go on without his brother at some point. That would likely be true eventually no matter what he did, but he didn't like hurrying that along.

"Nothing," Marty said. The way Jake was looking at him made him feel uneasy.

"Sure, Marty. Come on. What's wrong?"

"Just worried is all."

"Well, don't be. All is fine. Believe me, I've never felt so good."

Marty nodded. But miracles didn't just pop up out of nowhere. Marty was certain of that much. If they did, Fiona and Gina would be here right now. And that just would not happen.

No, he was sure of it, something had gone wrong inside of Jake.

As if sensing Marty's doubt, Jake said, "Listen. Will it make you feel better if I promise to go to the doctor on Thursday? If it gets any worse, I mean. That's a mere two days out. If it worsens by then, we can go get it checked out. Okay?"

Marty smiled weakly. "Sure."

He wondered if his brother could tell he wasn't so confident about Jake's promise. Two days might not sound like much to Jake, but Marty knew just how much could transpire in that amount of time. It had only taken a few minutes to lose the two people he loved most. There was time enough in two days to lose one more for sure.

"Tell you what," Jake said. "You can even get a hold of old Alberta Jones, make sure we can use her truck. It will be quicker than the tractor and likely faster than a cab or the bus."

That offered some reassurance but not much. And Marty had a strange thought then, how much Jake sounded like the devil, tempting Marty with dubious promises. He was sure if he gave in willingly, it would spell his demise.

One thing was certain, though. Keeping on this way would

only lead to him revealing how much he was against all of this. And he didn't want to seem complacent with anything. Jake went to say something else, and Marty faked a cough, twirling his fingers to hurry Jake along. Secretly, he hoped they could just move past this and leave the conversation open-ended.

"Okay," Jake said, content with some level of compromise. Maybe not what he wanted, but he didn't seem to mind that. "So, about my neck?"

Marty circled Jake, not taking his eyes off his brother. Jake's irises slid to the corner of his eyes, watching him closely. Marty had the strangest feeling right then that Jake could see everything he did regardless of where he stood.

"Jesus!" Marty said. "It's bigger."

"Bigger?"

Marty was sure Jake's voice sounded younger, as if the damage years of chewing tobacco had done to his vocal cords suddenly healed some.

"Yes," Marty said. "When we started talking, it was about the size of a quarter." Marty pinched two fingers about as big as a half dollar and held them in front of Jake, so he could see. "I think it's spreading."

And there it was, things had gotten worse in a matter of minutes. The urge to revisit going to the doctor overwhelmed Marty, and he struggled to hold back. Instead, he waited to see if Jake showed any signs of concern. But Jake didn't look the slightest bit worried.

If anything would get done regarding this issue, it would come of Marty's doing, with or without Jake's consent. Likely without. Maybe he could get the doctor to come to them. Jake would put up a fight, but at least the doctor would be here, and Marty thought Jake might be willing to at least let him look. Sure, he would be mad—plenty mad. But dealing with that afterward would be a small price to pay for looking after his brother. Besides, eventually he'd get over it.

He wondered if it might be a good idea to call a local preacher, too. Although his religious views were rather narrow these days, it wouldn't hurt to cover all bases. Either way, he could handle these calls later, after Jake was asleep.

"Interesting," Jake said, rubbing his thumb and forefinger at the sides of his chin where a few days of scruff sprouted. This was something their father had done, and even Marty had a tendency to do so when deep in thought.

"What?"

Jake was looking at his fingers. He laughed. "My hair's falling out."

He held up his fingers and Marty saw all the whiskers on the tips of his fingers. Both sides of Jake's face had smooth patches where he'd been rubbing his fingers.

"You know you're getting old when your hair falls out." Jake was still laughing, so hard he folded over.

Marty squeaked out an uncomfortable laugh, a poor attempt at easing the tension that had grown between them. But he didn't think this was funny. In fact, it was scary. He was thinking about how radiation made someone's hair fall out and wondered if Jake had been exposed to something toxic. Still, he needed to rebuild some trust with Jake if he meant to get the doctor out here to check on Jake.

But Marty couldn't stop watching Jake, who placed his hands in his thick head of hair and pulled. Having so much hair at Jake's age was a blessing, even if it was caked with the grease most of the time because of a lack of daily showers. Long strands of hair pulled away, clumped between Jake's knuckles.

"Going bald up here, too," Jake said.

Marty realized his mouth was agape. He needed to act more at ease around Jake, but that was becoming increasingly difficult.

"It's amazing," Jake said. His eyes twinkled, and that was when Marty noticed the change. They weren't so brown anymore as they were orange.

"Your eyes are changing color," Marty said, unaware he'd said it out loud.

"I know," Jake said, his voice sounding greedy and anxious. "I can see it happening from the inside. I can see better, too."

Whatever was happening, it had consumed Jake. And Marty was certain that couldn't be good, not one bit. Not only were there changes taking place on the outside but on the inside, too.

Jake was transforming into something else, seemingly a new man. Or was he a man at all anymore? Marty wasn't sure.

Marty stifled his concern. It was clear this was no longer an issue of health. Jake's health was fine, if not better. This was a greater concern, that Jake wasn't shocked by these changes. In fact, Jake seemed elated by every one of these changes, no matter how strange or improbable they seemed.

"Well, at least I won't have to worry about a comb over," Jake said, confirming Marty's reservations. And Jake just kept on laughing, too, endlessly amused by these changes and the witty comments he could come up with. But there was nothing normal about a man losing his hair in this manner. Something was wrong, even if all signs pointed to a stronger, healthier Jake.

"Jakey," Marty said. "About those two days..."

Those horrible eyes probed Marty, almost looking at him with spite. "Tomorrow, Marty. Let's discuss that tomorrow."

"It's just that I was thinking, maybe I should call Mrs. Jones tonight. You know, just in case."

Jake's eyes flickered.

What the hell?

Marty felt uncomfortable under his brother's gaze, and he wanted to go to his room. He thought—no, he knew Jake was reading his thoughts, that Jake knew how Marty felt right at that moment. Jake's eyes searched him like a cat focuses on its prey, ready to pounce. This cemented everything as far as it concerned Marty. He would call someone as soon as possible.

"Why that'd be just fine, Marty," Jake said after a long moment. His grin stretched across his face, almost encouraging Marty to do something. Perhaps even challenging Marty.

Marty didn't like any of this. He needed to do something quick, to change the mood fast. "How about we get some eats before I hit the fields?"

Jake hummed. "I'm not so hungry. Haven't been for a while now."

Had Jake eaten at all since the mosquito bite? He hadn't seen him eat anything.

Marty secured half a ham sandwich he'd put there two days ago. He made his way to the door, sensing Jake's probing eyes as they tracked his progress. It made him feel nervous. "Okay then," Marty said, stammering over his words. "I'm off...I guess."

"Why that'd be fine, Marty." Jake's tone held the same mocking contempt it had before.

What that meant to Marty was, do what you want because it won't matter what you do. The confidence in Jake's voice only further unnerved Marty. It reminded him of when they had been children.

"I'll be here waiting," Jake said.

When Marty turned, he saw those knowing eyes again. Jake didn't seem concerned about any phone call. Perhaps he even welcomed the conflict.

As Marty passed through the screen door, the springs caused it slam shut behind him, as it had many times before. This time, though, Marty jumped right off the porch. Jake snickered, amused by the fact Marty was unraveling.

Marty didn't know whom to call, only that he needed to call someone. This was all wrong.

Chapter 21

Marty let his hand fall from Sheila's. She tried to grab it back, but he shifted out of her reach. This wasn't right, no matter how new it was, how innocent the intention. He still missed Fiona. Still missed Gina. He missed Jake. It hadn't even been that long, and he felt ashamed for even thinking he could move beyond any of it. How could he let go of who he was, who he'd been? To hide any of it did them no justice. And he very much felt like he couldn't live without them, with his whole heart. There wasn't room for anyone new just yet. Maybe there never would be again.

She was looking at him with hurt in her eyes. He looked away and tried not to catch her gaze but couldn't help it. When he did, her eyes softened on him. Her hair whipped in the breeze, across her face. She picked the strands out of her face, and he couldn't help but notice how young she looked. Too young, for him anyway.

As if sensing his struggle, she smiled, slight but there all the same. It made him feel so warm inside, and he couldn't help but smile back.

She's only trying to comfort me.

That was all it was, a friendly gesture. Thinking it could be anything more was his mistake. And that alone made him feel guilty, his cheeks burned with embarrassment. He'd only just stopped crying and already he felt that pressure starting again. If he didn't—

She stepped forward and took his hand, put her other hand over his, and leaned into him. Then she sidestepped and bumped his leg with her hip playfully. "You're thinking too much."

That was true. He always had.

She acted like nothing happened. Perhaps that was what was best about her, that she didn't judge people. She could be so understanding and kind.

There he went, thinking too much again. He tried to get out of his head and watched as Masterson inspected the barn.

The inside was big enough to stable a few horses at most. But that was it; there was no loft. Bales of hay lined the far wall, random sized pieces strewn all over the floor. Three pens on the left, each with its own weathered nameplate on the gate, evidence of animals once kept here. On the right, he saw various horse tack, but nothing of much consequence. People had picked it over, taking that which would help defend them. He doubted there would be much left that would help them, but that didn't mean he wouldn't check to be sure.

Masterson angled the gun out behind her, her gaze paranoid but determined. Inspecting the darkest reaches of the barn, she kept glancing back, mostly at Marty. She leaned in, and Marty considered making a move right then. But he was too old to fight like that, especially against someone with a gun and training in hand-to-hand combat. Those days were far behind him. Doing anything now might lead to someone ending up shot, or even killed. Maybe someone he cared about.

He looked at Sheila.

It wasn't worth the risk.

Masterson reached for something, moving farther into the barn. When she returned, she had a pitchfork. How had he missed that?

"I don't think you'll be needing this," she said. "Okay then, everybody in."

"You don't have to do this, you know?" Marty said.

She ignored him, waving them in.

Marty went first, Sheila close behind. And Ike pulled Nancy behind him. Ike grunted some curse after he got inside. Then, the large doors closed, and Marty heard something slide through the handles, probably the pitchfork. Now they found themselves trapped, with no windows, in complete darkness.

He crossed to the bales of hay and loosened one, using it to create a large pile for bedding.

Ike went off into a corner alone. Marty was sure he'd be stewing there, no doubt bothered by how easy the Private had gotten one over on him. It served Ike right. He had a way of making people feel bad, of making them uncomfortable. If it ever came down to Ike or everyone else, Ike would always choose himself. That alone defined the man.

"Are you all right?" Sheila was tending to Nancy, trying to help her over to the hay bedding. Nancy didn't respond, still likely in shock from Bernard's death. Marty empathized with Nancy. It was how he'd felt about his own family most of the time.

Sheila didn't return to Marty for a long while. She stayed until Nancy fell asleep. Marty was thankful for that. It gave him time to think. He needed to get his head straight. In doing so, his thoughts drifted back, remembering what happened to Jake and praying it wouldn't happen to any of them.

Chapter 22

These fields were always so refreshing to Marty. Had been since his youth, back when his father used to tend these crops. Coming here always afforded him a place to think and nothing but time. Worry had no home here. This was a place where good things grew, so he never came here to mourn the loss of his family. This was his place of worship. Until now.

Despite the glowing rays of sunshine poking down through fluffed clouds like spikes of white heat, his thoughts were still a mess. The beams of light were so defined they almost appeared to be all that kept those clouds afloat, much like cake pops he thought. Radiating warmth spread across his tanned flesh and for a brief second all his worry drifted away.

He considered getting some work done, but instead squandered away the morning. Besides, the corn hid him well. He could walk among the stalks alone and without worry.

Row after row passed. He didn't bother looking around. All that mattered was the calm. Still, he saw the green, then the dirt, and back to green, over and over. This pattern continued, the normalcy of it all like ocean waves finding him. There was nothing random about it, nothing out of the ordinary. The plants always went to soil and then back again. Marty began to forget where he was, his thoughts wandering to better days. It was all so perfect, like nothing bad had ever happened. Then he saw a difference and everything, all at once, collapsed into turmoil.

What was that?

Of all the colors he could have seen, it looked...red. He wished he could take it back, return to that feeling he had experienced mere seconds earlier. But he walked faster now, turning to look down every row. It was as if he were testing himself, daring his eyes to see it again. And he did, just for a split second. Then it vanished.

Marty walked faster, trying to zone in on what he'd seen. It came into view only briefly, making this more disturbing.

Was this all in his mind? That was very possible. He hadn't slept well. Maybe he was just imagin—

He spun to the rustle of stalks behind him, expecting to see his intruder. Instead, he saw a half-dozen stalks of corn swaying to a stop. He scanned the landscape, expecting to see someone when a new noise surfaced. That was when he realized how out of breath he was, how his fear was mounting. His heart pounded out a steady drum line not only from fright but also anger.

Despite being exhausted, Marty ran for the barn. He hoped he could find some privacy there, but doubted he'd find that anywhere now.

Behind him, something zigzagged in and out of sight. It seemed like an attempt to draw his attention, almost like he was trying catch Marty up in some game. And he wasn't in control of this charade, either.

This thought drilled a sense of urgency into him, and he hurdled obstacles, running faster. The muscles of his legs were aching, too. And every so often he spotted that red color within the rows of corn. Each time, before he could focus on the target, it disappeared.

Marty picked up speed, looking over his shoulder and side to side. Out of nowhere, something halted his progress. He crashed into it, his field of view filled with crimson. And he was falling backward, trying to brace his fall, shocked by what he saw. He plopped down on his rear, his legs out in front of him and stared up at his brother.

An almost alien-looking Jake stared down at him. "Where are you off to, Marty?"

The crimson color had run its course, having covered Jake's entire body. Marty tried not to look scared, hoping he wasn't giving this away in his expression, but he knew he was failing at this deception. Truth was, Jake terrified him. His heart wasn't racing just because of that or the running, but because there wasn't a single spot of pink flesh left on what he could see of Jake's body.

Marty's eyes reluctantly went to Jake's face, half-expecting to discover a pair of devilish horns protruding from his brother's skull. Thankfully, there weren't any protrusions. But those two glaring eyes were bright as ever, his pupils now elongated, both fully dilated. They looked so big, and an awful thought occurred to Marty just then, something he'd heard long ago as a child.

"The bigger to see you with."

Both eyes fixed on Marty, on every movement. They even appeared to breathe along with Marty, heavily. Only a few sparse strands of hair remained on Jake's head.

"I had to come show you," Jake said with gleeful acceptance. He held out an arm, pulling up the sleeve, showing off his new color as one might show off their summer tan. "Isn't this great?"

To Marty, he sounded like the same boy when he'd shot his first squirrel with a BB gun. Marty remembered that boy well. He very much missed that boy now.

All Marty could manage was an awkward smile.

Jake frowned. "What?"

Marty's eyes traced the contour of Jake's body, identifying the issue without words. This wasn't natural, nor was it Jake. He was certain his face showed all of this, too. And Marty struggled to understand how Jake could be so tolerant of any such transformation.

"You're just jealous," Jake said.

Marty didn't respond. How could he? He wasn't the slightest bit jealous. And he was no longer sure how to relay his concern honestly so it wouldn't sound resentful.

Jake kept staring at him. "A good brother would help."

This was all Marty had been trying to do from the start. But Jake wouldn't allow it. Did that make Marty a bad brother? Should he be more accepting of what Jake was going through? He wanted to for Jake's sake, but this was no small matter.

Jake spun on his bare heels, his disgust obvious. Marty thought to console his brother, but Jake left in a flurry of arms and legs before he could set his mind to it.

Marty watched his brother maneuver around the stalks of corn with ease. Then, after a good forty yards, Jake stopped dodging them altogether and plowed right through them, arms outstretched, taking out large sections of corn. He left a path of destruction in his wake.

Chapter 23

Sheila hadn't gotten good sleep since this started. She couldn't imagine ever feeling fully rested again, especially given what they'd all endured.

After a few hours, once everyone was awake and rested, Marty cleared the floor and sprinkled hay into a small pile. When he finished, he kneeled beside it, reached into his pocket, and produced something she couldn't make out at first. She heard a slight grinding noise and saw the tiny flame of the lighter. Marty lit the small pile of hay on the cleared the floor to create a fire by which they could see each other. The open slats in the sides of the barn provided plenty of ventilation.

Sheila hadn't realized she'd started smiling. And she tried to compose herself when Marty's eyes found her, then the others one by one.

"I have something to share," he said.

The fire cast a glow on Ike's face when he turned to acknowledge Marty. As if sensing eyes on him, he backed away into the shadows.

"Ike," Marty said, "please. This is important."

For a moment, Ike remained his bitter self. But then he grumbled to himself and slid closer to the fire.

Nancy, who seemed distant since Bernard's death, even perked up some, apparently willing to listen.

"I want to tell you the story of my brother, Jake," Marty said.

"Are you sure you want to?" Sheila asked. "No one's making you do this. None of us expect you to."

Doubt clear in his expression, he nodded.

"A mosquito of all things set this whole thing into motion." Marty sighed. "I'm not sure what infected it before it bit Jake, but whatever the case, it changed Jake for good. It's also important to note that if this could happen to one person, it might have happened to several people over the entire containment zone. In my mind, that's likely what sparked the government to consider bombing this area in the first place, without so much as a warning siren. It all happened so quick."

"What kind of change we talkin' about here, Marty?" Ike asked. It surprised Sheila he'd been able to keep any curses out of this question.

"Well, at first, it was only a pus-filled sore. But that changed fast, spreading until it covered Jake's entire body with crimson flesh. Most of all, it seemed to alter him in ways I still don't fully understand. But I think it was a physical change and a mental one."

"A mental change?" Nancy asked, her voice shaky. It was the first words she had spoken since Sandy killed Bernard.

Marty smiled at her, pleased to see her talking again. "Yes. Plain and simple, Jake's intelligence went through as many changes as his body. His speech went from a rustic southern Illinois twang to a clear and concise voice, what you might see of a student coming out of Cambridge or the like. Jake used to stumble over all his words, not always sure what the right word to use was having dropped out of high school. But his grammar vastly improved over those next few days, to the point it unnerved me just to listen to him speak. But these changes, as dramatic as they already sound, were only the beginning. The worst changes came later, and that's why I had no choice but to kill my brother."

And with that, Marty began to tell the story.

Chapter 24

Jake was so restless that Marty couldn't sleep no matter how tired he felt. So he just lay there in bed, staring at the ceiling. Not that it mattered, as his mind was going a mile a minute. Times like this he almost always thought of Fiona and Gina. And right when those two came to mind, he heard something outside his door.

The shadow of a man caught in an endless troubled state appeared to rock back and forth under his door. Marty didn't like the thought of Jake wandering around the house all night any more than he liked him standing outside his door, but he didn't think it was a good idea to complain about any of it, either. Not after the confrontation in the cornfield where Jake, like Marty, needed some time to work through this on their own.

What bothered Marty most, though, was that Jake no longer seemed like himself anymore. There'd been several physical changes already and some obvious mental ones. Not only did his brother look different but he sounded different, and somehow, he'd gained an advanced intelligence. And his shift in temperament worried Marty most.

The old Jake rarely got angry. He had a testy side like anyone else, but he never lost his cool like he had in the fields early today. He'd been the kind of brother who would slap Marty across the back of the head, teasing Marty, but this was also the same brother who'd helped him through the most difficult time in his life. Marty didn't think this new Jake would be so kind.

In fact, Marty wasn't so sure the Jake he'd known all his life was even still in there. That was Jake's voice all right, and it had been Jake's words that stung Marty with guilt. But when

Jake spoke, Marty hadn't heard that same brotherly love in his words. There were glimpses of that old Jake now and then throughout the day, but fewer and fewer.

Marty had taken the phone out of the kitchen and strung it into his room. Luckily his room was close enough Jake might not notice the line. But seeing Jake outside his room made him paranoid, so he picked up the phone and held it close, planted firm against his chest. His fingers curled around the receiver, ready to call the Joneses...maybe. Or maybe he should call someone more important, the doctor or the local authorities.

The doctor might know what ailed Jake, might cure him. But the police would likely lock him up. Still, even that posed as an option at this point. It might be for the best, until whatever came over Jake got straightened out. Only Marty wasn't sure what to say. He'd imagined the call several times, running through what he'd say but couldn't think of anything that resulted in a positive ending. They'd likely just hang up on him, thinking it all a hoax.

Unfortunately, it was unlikely any doctor from these parts could do much for Jake, let alone remedy such a remarkable change. And no officer in his right mind would lock up a large, crimson-skinned man. It was more probable they'd put him down upon seeing him, perhaps more out of fright than duty. The scientists might be the worst of all. They'd want to dissect Jake, to better understand what had happened. And knowing he'd put his brother through torture like that would destroy Marty. Next thing he knew, every two-bit periodical in the world would plaster his face on their front page with the heading "Farmer Turns in His Alien Brother."

Marty was shaking his head, contemplating the disturbing nature of people like that who were always so desperate to make a quick buck. He definitely didn't want any version of that end. But he couldn't stay here, either, locked up like a prisoner in his own bedroom. He doubted that old rusty deadbolt on his door would hold back Jake, anyway. Marty had never used the deadbolt before but was thankful for it now, as the old-fashioned keyhole lock no longer worked.

The restless shadow paced outside his door, then disappeared.

Marty opted to call the Joneses. If he couldn't help Jake, maybe he could sneak away long enough that Jake could get through this, whatever was going on with him. Perhaps time was all he needed to make this problem go away. He could borrow their car to get to town and pay the town mechanic to drive it back the following day. Then Marty could take a vacation from all of this. And by the time he got back, good old Jake would be back in rare form.

He felt guilty for thinking of abandoning his brother. Jake would never have done that to Marty. But time healed all wounds. Sadly, though, Marty knew that wasn't true. Time hadn't done squat for him. Each day he felt that same pain over the loss of his family. Regardless, he couldn't just sit here waiting. He had to do something.

After pressing the receiver to his ear, he listened for a dial tone. The dreadful silence indicated the line had gone dead. He pressed the talk button several times, hoping that would somehow awaken the line, but that did nothing. Disappointed, he slammed the receiver into the base on his nightstand. Outside his door, the shadow reappeared.

For several minutes, Marty stared at the darkened area beneath his door. Jake remained frozen, perhaps trying to identify what had made that sound. Or maybe he already knew. Either way, Marty wished he hadn't been so careless. He blamed it on lack of sleep. But at least he was safe, because—

Alarm struck him when his eyes fell on the deadbolt. He didn't remember sliding it over. Whether by routine or absent-mindedness or fatigue, he'd forgotten to lock the door. Now all that separated him from Jake was a simple twist of a doorknob.

With care, Marty draped one leg over the edge of the bed and went to get up, then heard the knob turn. Silently cursing himself for having not locked the door, Marty settled back in bed and rolled to his side, facing the wall opposite the door. He heard nothing more at first, thinking Jake had left him be. Then the door swung open, and the eerie creaking noise made Marty's skin crawl. It was all he could do not to scream when a tall shadow appeared on the wall and began to grow, stretching upward and across as Jake neared Marty's bed.

His heart beat fast, and Marty pressed his eyes closed, struggling to keep them shut. Regardless of how tired he was, it felt like his eyelids were quivering. He opened them to thin slits and listened as the floor boards complain from his brother's weight. As Jake closed in on him, Marty was certain his legs were shaking. Now his brother's shadow darkened the entire wall, showing Jake now stood over him.

As if confirming this fear, Marty heard Jake's heavy breath. He half-expected Jake to tickle him, yelling "Gotcha!" when he did. That would be the old Jake, though. So that moment never came.

Jake growled then, and Marty couldn't tell if that had been from Jake's stomach or an actual growl. Either way, it made Marty anxious. He wanted to roll over and confront his brother. Besides, he doubted Jake was buying any of this, especially now that he seemed so much more intelligent.

Marty realized he'd been holding his breath. That meant his chest wasn't rising and falling like it should. Knowing that, Marty flipped over in bed, mouth half-open, ready to spout his anger over this intrusion. But Jake wasn't there. He scanned the room, and saw no sign of Jake, but the door was still open wide. Marty hopped out of bed and hurried to the door, careful not to move too fast, fearful of alerting Jake that he was up. He reached the door, curled his fingers around the edge, and closed the door as slowly as he could manage. But his grip slipped, and the door slammed shut. Frozen in place, he hesitated a moment before sliding the deadbolt across.

He made his way back to bed, trying to calm himself, but he couldn't stop looking at the door, checking to make sure he'd locked it this time. And maybe he would have settled eventually, but Jake's shadow reappeared outside his door. The darkness beneath the door paced back and forth, and a second later, the moment passed.

You're overreacting.

What if Jake had only been observing his brother sleeping? What if it had been Jake's good-natured love shining through? Just considering this saddened Marty.

His sorrow transformed into tears, which sprinkled his

cheeks like hot ashes. Soon enough he was thinking of his wife and daughter as he often had. He missed them dearly. And he missed Jake, too.

Marty rolled over in his bed sobbing, when a knock came to the door. But he wasn't sure if it had been a knock or an attempt to regain entrance to Marty's room. Whatever the case, Jake kept on doing it, causing the door to rattle against the deadbolt. Marty worried the door would soon break right off the trim.

Marty sniffed, his fear diminishing. "Go away, Jake." Marty waited for a response. "And keep it down out there. I'm trying to sleep."

Jake's shadow continued to loom under the door, the tips of his shoes visible now, showing just how close he stood to the door. Surely he heard Marty's sobbing. Had Jake been himself, Marty might have let him in. He might have tried to explain what he was feeling, his fears that his brother was no longer the man he'd idolized his entire life. But how could he now with everything that had transpired?

Marty felt alone in this vast world. Soon enough, his tears dried, and his thoughts dwelled on all he had lost as he stared at the picture of his wife and daughter hanging on the wall. It wasn't long before those thoughts turned to dreams, and he was sometimes happiest in that artificial world. In some of those dreams his world remained intact. There, everything was better.

Chapter 25

Bright light crept through Marty's window, searing his eyelids, causing an orange color to fill them. He fought against waking up but already knew this was a battle he would not win. The morning sun could be so demanding. Much more so than the rooster's crow, which apparently he'd slept through. But he'd gotten used to that over the years, so it didn't much surprise him.

He dragged his hand across his lips. They'd dried up overnight, and his throat felt even drier. He wished he had something to quench his thirst. Getting a drink, though, meant leaving his room, and he hesitated to do that after last night's confrontation. This room was his best hope to avoid Jake. He couldn't hole up in here forever. He needed food and drink, sooner rather than later. Already his stomach was in knots.

He didn't bother changing before bed and didn't bother this morning, either. Already he could smell the dried sweat on his clothes, but he had nothing clean to wear and couldn't shower with Jake wandering around like some kind of lunatic.

Marty kept his room simple, so there wasn't much he could use to fend off his brother should he attack. Not that he wanted to hurt Jake, but he had to defend himself. He looked at his bed. It wasn't big, enough for him and only him. The only other furniture was the small dresser against the wall next to his bed and a nightstand with a quaint lamp sitting on top of it, which provided the only unnatural light for the room. A tattered throw rug kept his feet somewhat warm from the wooden floors in the winter. A fan set in the room's corner, but he wondered how difficult it would be to remove the blade without the use of tools.

Moving to his closet, he slid open the door. It was mostly

empty save for a pair of hip waders, which he'd used a few times over the years. But he also saw the shotgun his dad had given him long ago. He wasn't even sure if it worked anymore, but he felt he needed the gun now more than ever. Wishing he'd kept it cleaned, he realized he hadn't even used the gun in years. Was it loaded? Did he even have shells for it? He abandoned the gun for now, mostly because that would be a last resort.

His latest read, a copy of John Steinbeck's *Of Mice and Men* sat on his nightstand, face down where he'd left it to mark his place. He hadn't touched the book in weeks, maybe longer. Sadly, seeing it now reminded him of his brother, how strained their relationship had become. Halfway through, now he longed for those pages, to find out what became of those two men who almost seemed like brothers.

Marty tiptoed across the floor to the door, mindful of any noise he might make. There, he listened for any sign of his brother. Hearing nothing, he rested his hand on the knob and slid the deadbolt across. When he opened the door, he did so an inch. The noise had been negligible. He stared out through the gap, surprised to find what he could see of the house empty. Then, he noticed the trail of dirt and scattered brush across the floor, which led up the stairs.

What a mess.

Marty couldn't say anything to Jake about it. Not anymore. Even if things somehow returned to normal, he wasn't sure if he could ever bring this up. That thought brought an overwhelming desire to leave, paired with his life-long bond and responsibility to his brother. The two emotions clashed, each fighting for higher ground. What finally won out was curiosity.

With care, Marty opened the door the rest of the way, cringing as the door moaned loud and long. Once opened far enough, he crept across the room and glanced back and forth. This was when he noticed the TV wasn't there. He'd spent a lot of time with that appliance. No one even had a tube TV anymore; they were all flat screens. Jake had gotten good at repairing it, too, had done so more times than he cared to remember. But as long as it kept on working, they'd never planned to replace it. Now he longed for the nights of watching reruns on public television.

A fond memory came to Marty, one where his brother learned the hard way how easily those old tubes could hold a charge. Jake had gotten his screwdriver too close, and the electricity had arced out while he was still deep in its belly. The jolt had knocked Jake back a good seven feet, and Marty had thought him dead at first. Even when he came to and got his wits about him, Jake had still looked rather out of it.

Several pieces of broken wood indicated the TV was not only missing but broken. He ignored it and started up the stairs, each step complaining as he ascended. Deliberate in his footing, Marty did his best to make as little noise as possible. But he was unsuccessful, likely alerting Jake to his approach. Knowing this, Marty changed tactics.

"Jake?"

No response. A dreadful silence came from beyond the closed door at the top of the stairs. Marty hesitated to open it, wanting to call for his brother again. Instead, he tried the knob. It turned with ease.

When he opened the door, it surprised him to find the floor caked with mud. Jake had piled limbs in one corner of the room, whatever furniture he saw there reduced to scraps. Only the smallest bits remained scattered across the floor. What concerned him most, though, was that Jake was nowhere in the room.

Noting the clothing sprawled across the floor, Marty eyed up the closet. It was a rather large walk-in, the result of unused crawlspace. Jake had never needed much room, so he'd never used it, opting to keep his clothes in his dresser instead. That space had been empty for years.

This door opened with no complaints, and there, sitting on the floor under the small window, was a large object Marty couldn't identify right away. Try as he might, he struggled to make sense of it.

He moved in to examine the object, trying to make sense of why it looked so familiar. Then, as if he'd known all along, it came to him.

"A cocoon," he whispered to himself.

But what bothered him most was the huge hole in the

cocoon's top, the silky strands of mucus that indicated whatever had been inside had already emerged. A plastic mass sat inside, covered in mucus, but easily identifiable as Jake's plastic hip.

Marty turned and hurried downstairs. When he got there, he saw the creature that blocked his escape. This wasn't his brother anymore. It was something horrible and as it closed in on him, he was too shocked to move.

He took in every bit of the large crimson creature, seeing its alien arms and legs, the face, thin gastric sacs at each side of its slim abdomen. Where had once been a mouth, a solitary bulbous eye studied him, the elongated pupil changing size, the orange-flecked iris almost predator-like in how it examined Marty. But Marty noticed the creature seemed sensitive to the lighting coming in through a window as it neared, lifting an arm to shield its vision. That was when Marty noticed the strange secondary arm underneath the primary arm, its purpose unknown.

Two nostrils on the creature's chin seemed to do most of its breathing. Flaps of flesh at their edges reminded Marty of fish gills. Further up the cheekbone, a pair of fleshy satellite dishes no bigger than a quarter seemed to serve as ears. They twitched and twirled in response to each movement, no matter how small. Many teeth filled the mouth across its forehead, all of them dull like its human counterpart, caught in a permanent but intimidating frown.

When the creature leaped at him, he saw the stubby tail with a stinger the length of a steak knife. Marty shielded himself, ducking into the corner of the room. The creature landed hard, debris crunching beneath it, which luckily threw it off balance, as it seemed still awkward in its new form. It fell back, and Marty fully expected it to crash to the floor. It would have been a great opportunity to escape, only he didn't know where to go. Thinking fast, he went to the only place that offered him any safety, his bedroom.

Once inside, he turned to shut the door and saw the stubby secondary arms and legs, each hidden behind the primary appendages, how they had worked together to keep the creature from ever crashing against the floor. They pumped all at once and pushed the creature back up to a standing position. Without hesitation, the creature ran for the door.

Marty slammed the door shut, putting all his weight against it.

Bang!

The door nearly opened. Marty fumbled with the knob, trying to keep the creature from turning the knob. Even then, it took all his effort to hold the knob and door shut, while trying to slide the deadbolt across.

Bang!

He pressed himself against the door again, reached up and this time managed the deadbolt. Even then, he stayed there, holding the door shut for fear the deadbolt wouldn't hold.

Bang!

This time it came with less effort. He doubted the creature was tiring so much as it was considering other options. And only after a long while with no more attacks, did Marty finally step away from the door. Even then he remained on edge long into the day.

Chapter 26

The creature scampered back and forth outside Marty's bedroom door, stopping for a moment at each pass. He knew in his heart that Jake was a creature now. Whatever happened overnight, some other transformation had taken place. That thing was no longer his brother. What remained was this alien creature pacing back and forth outside his door in the early hours of morning, bothered by not being able to get at Marty.

Whatever the creature wanted to convey, he seemed incapable of doing so with words. He stopped outside Marty's door occasionally, standing there as if about to say something. Seconds later the shadow continued this pattern, passing back and forth in a steady trek with only those brief pauses. He seemed to cover more ground, too, heading farther outside each time, then heading up to his room before returning. More interesting, Marty thought he was dragging something in from the outside with each passing; large masses with a pungent odor he could smell from this side of the door.

What's he doing?

He identified the thump-thump-thump as these objects were pulled up the stairs to Jake's bedroom. Then came more thumps as these items were maneuvered upstairs, almost directly above Marty's bedroom, until the creature had them right where he wanted.

Then came that clack-clack-clack sound of alien feet as he returned downstairs and crossed to the front door. It sounded like a giant crab moving across the wooden floor, past Marty's bedroom, on his way for another load. Occasionally, the creature bellowed a low, guttural sound, as if warning Marty not to leave his bedroom. Or maybe the sound emanated out of exhaustion, as clearly he was exerting himself with this task.

Marty didn't dare interrupt the creature, even if he ended up speaking and sounding just like Jake at some point. No, he was better off here in his bedroom for now, where he could lock himself in. Eventually an opportunity would present itself and then he'd escape. Until then, this was the safest place for Marty.

He stood on his bed, trying to reach the vent on his wall. Even if he could punch through the register, he doubted he could fit through the ductwork. He'd likely get stuck before he got anywhere.

The window seemed pointless, too, as he could see Jake moving along the horizon each time he left the house. Judging from the scene he'd experienced in the cornfield, he was sure Jake would be quick enough to intercept him even if he made a run for it. That meant he needed a plan.

After getting the front cage off the fan, he couldn't free the fan blade. He twisted and turned the nut, trying to free it with his fingers, but that proved futile. Considering the blade, he wondered if he could wield the fan itself as a weapon, even picked it up to try, but it was just too bulky to be of any use.

Maybe he could sneak out between passes. He thought about peeking through the keyhole in that old door, but his gut feeling was to wait until whatever was going on outside his door settled.

So, after much thought, he retreated to his bed, where he waited for what felt like hours. And with so much racket outside his door, he couldn't sleep. Each bump and thump shook him awake. But eventually, when the sun finally spilled in through his window and the rooster crowed, the commotion came to an abrupt end.

He rested on his elbow, staring at the door. Though he told himself not to, Marty dared himself to look. He even got out of bed and crept to the door where he stood, unsure of what to do next. Time seemed to stop as he stared at the door, imagining that he was brave enough to slide that deadbolt across and open it wide. He didn't think he had the courage.

With curiosity getting the best of him, Marty lowered himself to his knees and leaned forward, pressing his eye to the keyhole. In that moment as he observed complete quiet in the room outside his door, he was thankful for this old house, more so for this keyhole. Though the edges of the keyhole ebbed in and out of view, he saw nothing for a long moment. Then, out of nowhere, a single eye with orange flecks slid into view, its eyelids sliding across so fast, one after the other, that Marty leaped back.

He staggered back and fell in a sitting position. His bones ached as he sat a few feet away from the door, still staring at the keyhole. The creature's shadow wavered beneath the door, breathing heavily, either angered or exhausted. Marty couldn't move, couldn't stop trembling. Even when Jake grunted, Marty just sat there frozen in place.

The grunt came again, as if asking permission to enter. Then, to Marty's surprise, the doorknob turned. Thankful he'd taken the time to lock the deadbolt, he didn't move. The knob rattled as the creature tested it but soon stopped. After a few seconds the shadow beneath the door disappeared altogether, and Marty, who'd been holding his breath, let it out all at once.

Bang!

Marty slid back, the bed stopping him. He sat there as the bang came again and again. Each time his eyes shut instinctively, and he wished he could get further away from that door. His legs felt like jelly, and he didn't think he could stand. Even scooting around the edge of the bed seemed impossible.

Bang!

The picture of Fiona and Gina rattled against the wall where it hung. The creature's weight struck the door again, trying to force it open, and the barrier almost seemed to bulge inward. The picture swung back and forth, threatening to fall. Marty wasn't sure what to do.

He shot up, scanned the room for a weapon to defend himself, and picked up the first thing that came into view. The bang came again, this time with more intensity. The steady thump-thump of Marty's heart sounded so far away to him. His eardrums felt swollen, making it difficult to hear anything at all. His eyes strained, focused on the door and nothing—

Bang!

Marty jumped. It had startled him so much it felt awkward readying to fight with—

What are you doing?

Slipper in hand, his body poised to attack, he couldn't help but shake his head. He threw it to the floor in disgust and sought something more menacing. He found a large book he didn't recognize, but its hardcover binding held promise. Holding it out in front of him, he saw what it was and wondered if he could use it to ward off the creature. As if the Bible would protect him from—

From what? My brother?

No, this thing wasn't his brother. Not anymore.

With that Marty remembered the shotgun and went to fetch it. The attempts to gain entry ended. After a few minutes, the shadow shifted back and forth one last time, Marty holding his breath while he watched. He tried to slow his heartbeat, and finally the creature departed.

That was the end of the commotion for the morning, but Marty sat on his bed all day, the gun by his side, wondering if it still worked. When he began feeling tired because of the loss of sleep the night before, his thoughts wouldn't let him rest. Even once he felt convinced Jake would not return, he sat there plotting what to do and when.

Chapter 27

When Marty slid the deadbolt away and opened the door, it popped as if it had swollen in jamb. Thankfully, it wasn't loud enough to alert anyone, or at least he hoped. All he really cared about now was to follow that initial thought he'd long ignored and leave.

He didn't know where he was going, only that he needed to get out as soon as possible. When he swung the door open, he took care in not making any additional noise, moving it a little at a time. He didn't want that creature to have any idea what he was doing.

Still, he'd felt like he needed to even the odds some in case the creature found out. So after loading the old shotgun, he brought it with him despite not knowing whether or not it still worked. Before he left this place, he needed to make sure he wasn't followed.

His heart beating rapidly in his chest, he pushed through the door and stepped out into the living room. He went to the stairs, gun in hand, and inspected his surroundings. The mess was like what he'd seen last night, dirt and twigs and rocks everywhere. He ventured upstairs.

Each step groaned, as Marty neared the door at the top. Before he got there, his foot landed on a twig. The stick crunched beneath his shoe, snapping. Marty froze, listening for any activity beyond the door.

Why am I even bothering? Out of some sense of obligation to my brother?

He'd resigned himself to that. If he couldn't save his brother, he wasn't about to let this *thing* take him. Marty reached for the knob, remembering everything that happened a few hours earlier. Now he was the invasive one, and he suspected the creature wouldn't take it lightly.

Within four inches of the knob, a flash of electricity shot out and struck his hand. While the flash consumed his vision, it felt like a rhino had gored him. He was aware he was flying back down the stairs, gasping for air, but he couldn't feel anything but that punch to his chest. The brightness still burned on his eyeballs, making it impossible to see anything, anyway.

His body struck the hardwood floor like a large sack of potatoes. The jolt of contact sent a wave of pain through his bones. Lying there, he tried to replay it all in his head. None of it made any sense. He could still see the light etched into his vision, the arc of electricity stretching out to touch his hand. And that was when he realized what had happened to Jake that one time he'd been working on that old TV.

That meant somewhere deep within the creature's head, there was still some small piece of Jake in there. The creature had used this knowledge to wire the door, to protect itself. He didn't like that one bit.

Marty stomped back up the stairs, unable to slow himself down. This time he didn't bother with the knob and instead threw his weight into the door, bracing the gun between his arms. The door shifted but held. He tried again, and again, hearing the creature growl beyond the door. But Marty was so angry now he couldn't see straight.

He lay into the door again, and this time the frame gave some. He leaned the gun against the wall and pressed his palms against the sides of the stairwell and kicked out with both feet. The door crashed open, falling to the side supported by a few half-extracted screws. He grabbed the gun and pushed through the fallen door, hefting it out of the way and scanning the room.

The creature wasn't here. Maybe it had been, but it wasn't now. He did not know how it escaped, only knew it had. But more concerning was this room. Not the growth of weeds, plants, and flowers, but the overall appearance. These natural elements served a purpose, something he couldn't put his finger on just yet, but he'd been circling it since entering.

Then it came to him. *It's a nest.*

The disassembled television, along with scraps of other machinery, was wired to the door like some homemade alarm system. He ran over to it and grabbed the wires in his fist, then yanked them down.

He kicked through the rubble, seeing remnants of clothes and appliances and earthen materials, looking for any sign of what might serve as a nest. His feet stumbled on something solid and bent to pick it up, seeing that it was a small ham radio. He did not know where this came from. Jake had never owned such a radio, let alone used one.

He thought to test it and turned it on. The LED turned a dusky red. Static filled the room momentarily. Then the light faded and with it, the static did, too. The radio was dead.

Marty approached the attic space where Jake had holed up in his cocoon. The door was closed, but he wasn't so sure it was a good idea to bust down that door, given the standoff at Marty's door this morning. Whatever the creature was doing, it was on the other side of this door, calculating its next move. He could almost sense its anger.

Turning his back on the door, Marty let his eyes scan the room, seeing beyond the foliage covering the floor and walls. And that was when he saw them in the far corner of the room— three cocoons much like the first. The creature had tried to hide them beneath branches and shrubs. A milky white thread bound them to the wall like spider silk.

Just seeing them made Marty's heart sink. He knew then he had to do something drastic.

Chapter 28

Before Marty left, he needed to take out of those cocoons. And Jake, too. The half-read book on his nightstand caught his eye as he prepared a makeshift pack. The men in that story weren't real brothers, not by blood. He struggled to make any comparison between his life and that story, even if Jake was no longer of the same blood as Marty. He left the book and hefted the pack over his shoulder, grabbed the gun, and turned his attention to his bedroom door.

Tiptoeing across to the door, he cringed at every creak of the floorboards beneath his feet. Already his pulse sped, his heart rapping in his chest. He had a bad case of the butterflies that made his stomach queasy. With him being so on edge, he wasn't sure he had it in him to do what he needed to.

Marty pressed an ear to the door and listened but heard nothing. He squatted and prepared to look through the keyhole again, then hesitated, fearful of seeing that eye again. Having to force his eye forward, in that instant he very much thought he saw that eye again. That alone made him jump. But upon refocusing his vision, he then realized it had only been his imagination.

Pulling away, he pawed at his tired eyes and tried again. This time he confirmed the creature was nowhere in view. Nothing farther out in the room either, except for the debris. That was good.

Rising, he inhaled deeply and let it out slowly. He mustered up all his nerve and slid the deadbolt across, minimizing any noise. Once it slid the whole way out of the track, he heard a small click as the door freed from its embrace. Marty reached for the knob, eager for freedom from his bedroom, from this house, from his brother. Right then the door collapsed in on him, knocking him back on the floor, and the shotgun fell free of his grasp, sliding out of sight under the bed.

The creature burst through the opening, panting like a dog, its sides expanding and letting out the air as the gill-like opening at the edge of its nostrils flared. The wooden door crunched beneath its clawed feet as the creature took a position five feet away from Marty. With no further hesitation, the creature pounced on Marty, pinning him against the floor, his neck angled against the side of the bed. The creature bellowed a deep growl, spittle flung into Marty's face. Its bony structure and hardened crimson flesh provided an armor of sorts. The muscles were formidable. And while the teeth weren't pointy, he couldn't help but wonder if the creature might want to make a meal out of him regardless of that fact.

Marty brought his knee up into the unnatural stomach, which was enough to shift free of the creature's grasp. Without thinking, Marty left the pack and threw his weight up and over the bed, where he landed on the soft top and quickly rolled to the opposite side. There, he clawed under the bed, trying to find the gun. Even once he discovered the stock, he couldn't get a good grip. His fingers kept slipping off.

From under the bed, he saw the creature's small arms and legs push itself back to its feet. Then the creature sprang at him without fear while Marty continued clawing under the bed. His forefinger found the rifle, tried to retrieve it only to lose it again. Then he had two fingers on the gun. As the creature landed over him and dragged him to his feet, Marty made one last grab for the gun. This time he got hold of it, fighting to clutch the gun as the creature lifted him.

With all the strength he had left, Marty drove the barrel of the gun up. Without aiming, he pulled the trigger. Black ooze splattered the bed, the wall, his face, everywhere. The creature staggered across the bed, thumping as it fell to the floor. Once more those extra arms and legs helped to return the creature to its feet, but still the creature staggered away, crashing into the remains of the door as it tried to escape.

Marty pulled himself up, leaning against the wall, and

raised the shotgun again. The eye oozed black liquid, evidence he'd ruined the creature's vision. The creature pawed helplessly as the door, trying to find the way out. And with that Marty stood, aiming the gun to kill his brother.

Get over it, he pleaded with himself. *Kill him. This isn't Jake.*

The creature seemed to say something, what Marty thought might have been, "Kill me."

It was weak, but had his brother begged for death? What remained of Jake suffered inside this creature, and he'd somehow found the will to ask one last favor of Marty. Even thinking this somehow made the job easier, but what if he'd imagined this? What if this was all some lie he'd created so he would have to feel the guilt?

What if I can bring him back?

No, he didn't think that was possible. Not anymore.

Marty leveled the gun, pointing it at the large eye again. "Jake?" A single tear rolled down Marty's cheek. "I love you. I'm so sorry."

The gun thundered and the creature's eye exploded. As if under great pressure, putrid dark green pus splattered everywhere, striking Marty's face and lips. Bile spilled from the creature's gaping mouth; the rancid smell so offensive it made Marty gag. He wiped the stuff off his face with his sleeve, keeping his lips pressed tight.

You're okay. You didn't swallow any.

Still, he spat out what he could.

Amazingly still afoot, the creature scampered through the living room and ran straight into a wall. There, the creature clawed at the wall, finding its way to the stairs, where it then ventured upward.

Marty only watched. Once it left, he retrieved his pack and made his way to the front door.

On the porch, Marty sat the pack down and rested the shotgun against the siding. He hurried to the shed where he found a can of kerosene they kept for burning trash. He carried it into the kitchen and found some matches. Armed with these two items, he headed up the stairs after the creature.

It surprised him that the creature wasn't waiting for him.

He tore off one of his sleeves and shoved it into the opening of the can. Then he let the fuel moisten the cloth before setting it on the floor. He struck a match and lit the cloth. Retrieving the can, he gave a toss into the far corner. It landed near the cocoons, engulfing them in flames with a loud *whoosh*. A chorus of alien cries and hisses filled the room, as the creatures inside burned alive. This was no doubt a harmonious plea for help from their father, and Marty expected just that. But thankfully the creature still didn't appear.

Let him burn.

The foliage caught fire, smelling of fresh manure and what reminded Marty of a skunk. The high-pitched screeches intensified, but Marty still saw no signs of Jake. The creatures inside the cocoons writhed about as the fire spread to the ceiling. Coughing, Marty pressed his intact sleeve to his face and backed to the stairs. He gave one last look before descending.

Marty made haste for the front door, careful not to trip on any rubbish. Upon reaching the door, a distinct growl drew his attention. It sounded different this time, as if the creature were full of misery. Marty reached outside, grabbed the shotgun, and brought it around expecting to see the creature leaping for him. But the creature only stood there, its eye bleeding a dark greenish-black fluid. That same goo covered the creature's chest and face it. Although blind and in pain, the creature's nostrils flared and ears twitched, making up for this lost sense.

The sides of the creature's torso bellowed in and out, as if hyperventilating. Marty knew better. The creature wasn't frightened but angered that Marty had killed its young. Marty translated what he was seeing, the rise and fall at the creature's sides and thought of his lungs. He listened to his own breathing, matching it to the expanding sides of the creature's torso.

With no warning, the creature charged Marty, throwing itself at Marty, all four appendages off the ground. The creature's speed was almost blinding, but Marty fell to one side. There, he lifted the shotgun, aimed, and pulled the trigger.

Blam!

The creature landed on him but wasn't moving. Seeing the end of his gun, smoke rose from the barrel, Marty pushed out from under the creature and slid away before getting to his knees.

When the creature inhaled, a deep wheeze came from its side. The torn flesh sounded like the air being squeezed out of a hole in the side of an airbag. Marty knew full well what he'd done, that he'd shot his brother, each time intent on killing.

The creature looked up at him, and Marty swore then he could see a tear welling where the creature's eye had once been intact. The creature's breathing slowed, and green fluid poured out of the wound in its torso. Marty leveled the gun to the wound, wanting to make sure, and fired deep into the hole. The creature screamed loud and brief, then lay still, his brother's life dimming.

With that, Marty kicked open the screen door. He looked back only once to grab his pack and left before his brother there to breathe his last breath alone. And Marty walked all day and night, contemplating everything he'd done.

Chapter 29

Upon sharing the last details of his story, Sheila watched Marty break, tears flowing down his face. All Nancy and she could do was cry along with him. Sheila felt a strong urge to hug Marty, so she scooted closer and wrapped her arm around his shoulders. He almost fell into her.

"I'm so sorry," she said.

For a long moment, Ike just sat there staring at Marty. He appeared lost in himself. Then, clenching both fists in his lap, he said, "So that's what that fog out there is for? Why the hell didn't they fog us, too?"

Marty wiped his tears away. "I think they have. We just can't see it because...well... we're right in the thick of it."

Ike nodded, still looking rather lost.

Sheila considered this. It had been hazy since the day of the bombing.

"Thing is," Marty continued, "I don't think the mosquitos are the problem. Not anymore. I mean...they bombed them, sprayed them, sent soldiers in to lay waste to them. All that for a mosquito? Who would go through that much trouble for a bug? What it means is Jake wasn't the only one transformed by this contamination."

"What. The. Literal. Fuck?" Ike rose and started pacing. "I can't believe I didn't think of this before." His long strides carried him from wall to wall. "How did they know about it so quick?"

"Exactly," Marty said, revealing a truth he'd been considering for some time.

Sheila didn't understand. She looked from Ike to Marty, back and forth, searching for a clue, tying to put the pieces of the puzzle together. She even looked at Nancy, who appeared as clueless about this as Sheila.

As if realizing they hadn't grasped what he was dishing out, Ike's face flushed with frustration. "For Christ's sake, they knew about it all along." His laughter sounded almost cynical. He held out his hands, as if he couldn't believe they still weren't getting it. "Because they were the ones who caused this bullshit."

The room fell silent as each of them considered their government's responsibility. It shouldn't have come as a surprise. She'd heard stories from the time she was in grade school. Why it should happen in southern Illinois as opposed to say Roswell, New Mexico bewildered her, but she understood it all the same.

"So what? They injected alien blood into mosquitos?" Nancy asked.

"Well, I highly doubt they could or would do that. Mosquitos aren't like mice or any other small, manageable creature," Marty said. "It's more likely they stumbled upon something...maybe even witnessed this transformation before. Maybe that was just the start."

"You mean they captured one of those fucking bugs?" Ike asked.

"Possibly. Or maybe they had the creatures all along and only noticed how the contamination spread. Once they knew that much, they fogged everything just in case." Marty started tugging at his scruff. His eyes widened with conclusion. "Or... maybe they were the ones providing the source blood to the mosquitoes in the first place—in what they believed was a controlled environment." Marty stared beyond them, as if trying to picture this. "Then, all it would take was one stray mosquito to start this whole thing."

Ike grunted. "Those fuckers. Why Illinois? What the hell is in Illinois?"

"Farms," Nancy said, identifying the obvious answer.

"Some big mosquitoes," Sheila added.

"Why not Wisconsin, then?" Ike asked. "Have you ever seen the size of those fucking mosquitos? They're like birds. Really big fuckers."

"I'm not sure any of those details appealed to them. If I had to venture a guess, I would say the fact this state is a central location to the others was the most probable reason. You know the old saying: location, location, location. I'm not sure any of this matters to us, though."

Ike grunted in agreement.

But Sheila heard something strange. She stood and made her way to the door. She saw Private Masterson through a slat, sitting on the ground with her legs folded, her head in her hands. She rocked back and forth, as if bothered by what they were saying. At first Sheila wasn't sure what to think of this but soon realized what this might mean. Had they forced their soldiers to kill innocent people? Absolutely. They sent their men and women right into the fire of unknown demise. The question was, could there be a side to Sandy they hadn't tapped yet?

"Has anyone else noticed," Marty said out of nowhere, after some consideration, "all the bodies are missing?"

Sheila turned and stared at Marty, searching her memories. It struck her odd having seen so many bodies strewn about town shortly after the bombing. She hadn't seen a one since.

"What the fuck?" Ike mused. "What does it mean?"

"I haven't seen any," Nancy said.

"I'm not sure," Marty said, "but I don't think it's the soldiers cleaning up."

"It isn't us," the private said, her voice barely audible even to Sheila who was still standing by the door. The fact she'd been crying was obvious.

Nancy's expression soured, and she withdrew to a nearby wall.

"Sandy? May I call you Sandy?" Marty asked.

"Yes," she said. She stood and approached the barn door. "I'm sorry," Sandy said. "I...I didn't want to..."

She could not finish. But she didn't have to. They all seemed to understand. Even Nancy, though her contempt for the woman still showed on her face.

"We get it," Marty said, moving to the door.

Sheila could tell he sensed an opportunity, so she stepped aside and let him work. But she thought he understood, too.

If his story had taught her anything, fate had forced his hand more than once.

She heard the pitchfork slide away. Sheila wanted to run, to burst out into the open air, but she refrained. The door opened an inch and hope filled Sheila. Then they heard a blood-curdling scream.

There was a flurry of activity as Marty opened the door a little more. It was clear Sandy was fighting someone hand-to-hand. Sheila saw Sandy's gun on the ground.

Marty stood in the doorway. The moon lit his silhouette and in that moment, Sheila saw the shadows of batting wings on his face. She felt the wind, could almost feel Marty's apprehension.

Sandy screamed, "Help!"

Sheila wanted him to ignore this woman's desperate pleas. She wanted him to stay put and avoid being seen, because maybe then they could survive this. Besides, Sandy had shot Bernard. But she also knew Marty wouldn't just stand by, not at a time like this. Not ever. Not when he could help.

His hair waving in the unnatural breeze, he stepped through the barn doors and took a bold step into the night. Sheila followed, seeing him standing there like some saint. She did not know what he planned to do, only that he would do something.

Marty held up one hand and said only one word. "Stop," he commanded.

Chapter 30

Darkness overwhelmed Bernard, yet he felt an odd weightlessness. Likening himself to an astronaut lost in the deepest realms of space, the dark void engulfed him. At that moment Bernard was sure of only one thing, the end was near.

Light flashed briefly, here and there before it left for good. In this gloom, only one thought came to him—that at least Nancy was safe. Thinking of her now made him happy. And somehow it also gave him strength. He tried to get to his feet but found no ground to stand upon. Instead, his feet dangled helplessly in the air, where he seemed to float.

Strong gushes of wind assaulted his face. Soon enough he no longer felt even that. It was as if his body was dying, all of it, slowly, leaving only his brain and a weakened heartbeat. His thoughts wouldn't sleep just yet—his mind aflutter with activity. Together, those organs proved to be a lifeline that was fading fast.

His limp body shot forward, almost like he was a rag doll being stuffed into a box to throw in the attic. Then, the realization dawned on him, what this really was—a coffin—and he wanted to scream. But the ability to do so had passed. He saw himself screaming in his thoughts, as he pictured dirt being tossed over the coffin, burying him alive.

"I'm still alive!" he tried again, but no words came.

Was this what death was like? Would his attempt to escape prove hopeless, all while his mind was still fully awake, aware of what was transpiring? His body felt compact in a cool space, as if he were being submersed into a pool of water. But none of this mattered anymore because he knew the truth; soon even his heart would succumb to his wounds once and for all.

Each beat within his chest rose and fell, a slowing pattern of subtle thumps. The second beat came shallower than the first, his body slowing, growing ever tired of this world. His thoughts pleaded for him to at least try to stay alive, but his body wouldn't allow it. A weaker thump followed, like a note held on a piano, reverberating. And then another, but the next never came. His brain ran wild, various scenes from his life, both failures and successes, flashing through his thoughts in a fraction of a second. These would be the last images he saw before death.

In the distance, a dazzling light approached ready to take him home. Bernard wondered how much longer his brain could survive after his heart ceased. He would soon find out. The light swallowed him in a flash of bright pulses, looking like fireworks without sound.

To his surprise, he was not dead. This was a sudden realization, as the lights faded, and his heartbeat picked up right where it left off. Slow to start, but once it got going again, he knew just how alive he was.

It's a miracle.

He'd never believed in such whimsical things. Not after the Gulf War. He'd witnessed atrocities he'd never forget, things that led to nightmares. Death knew no boundaries in war, and it took greedily from everyone. Bernard had dealt his fair share of death, too. Still, something had changed. He couldn't move his arms or legs because something was holding them in place. Or perhaps something had weakened them; he wasn't sure.

Then it occurred to him that maybe this was the afterlife. Perhaps he hadn't survived so much as he'd passed through to whatever came next. Whether Heaven or Hell or somewhere between the two, he didn't know.

A distant noise rang in his ears. He struggled to bring clarity to the sound. When he did, he realized these noises weren't human. This concerned him, as thoughts of demons raced through his mind. But in his attempt to locate these noises, he realized his situation.

No one had buried him alive, and he wasn't dead. Well, maybe he had died, but he wasn't deceased anymore. Some alien was closing off the wall to his enclosure. And the rubber-like cell was filling with a thick liquid. As the creature finished with the wall, the liquid swallowed him. He struggled for a moment, then upon needing to breathe, he discovered he wasn't drowning. Somehow, he could breathe this liquid in, filling his lungs with the cold fluid, the sting of it all temporary but no less frightening. And doing so connected his brain to this cell and to others. Not only could he sense it feeding him visuals, but he could sense those of the others, too.

He saw an image of a mother with her children, clicking along like an old 8 mm film, the images changing ever so slightly with each new frame. Then, he saw a young man playing fetch with his dog. A man yelled at his wife, then stormed out of the house and got into his car. More visions came, one after another, and he lived every one of them, feeling what they felt, smelling what they smelled, breathing and speaking through their mouths.

There was something else, too, something beyond all the others, a higher power. Bernard closed his eyes and concentrated on the source, trying to focus. When he found it, he envisioned its alien face, how horrifying it appeared with its singular damaged eye and upside-down face, the flesh around the eye puckered, as if wounded. The creature appeared to smile at Bernard.

He pushed hard, trying to force all of it away. But his naked body shook as a wave of electricity shot through him. The foreign sensation made Bernard cry, reminding him of a time he'd shocked himself while changing a wall outlet at Nancy's house. If not for the limited room, he might have thrashed hard enough to knock himself silly.

Feeling some give now, Bernard thrust his fist into the wall. The gelatinous substance binding him slowed the attack. Every subsequent attempt at penetrating the substrate proved equally futile and the more he struggled, the more twisted and bound he became until he found himself face down in the compartment. For a long moment, he felt as though his struggle had ended.

Then an image came to him, that of something in the orange gelatin. And he saw it now, something at the bottom of the compartment, near the corner. Unsure of what it was, he pushed, forcing his body to the object. He could almost reach it and extended his fingers, straining to touch what he now thought was a button. His fingers pressed against it hard, and the gelatinous liquid flushed out of the cell. The thin outer wall decayed like wax melting, drifting into smoke and disappearing.

Bernard watched for a moment, mesmerized by these events. Then, as the air filled his lungs for the first time what might have been hours, he started choking. His stomach heaved, and he fell out of the cell to the floor where the cool of the ground stung his naked flesh. He heaved again, expelling every bit of the orange liquid from his lungs.

Seconds later, as he regained control of his senses, he discovered something new about himself. He was aware. Mindful that he'd freed himself, that he was still alive, and that the odds were against him. But most of all, he was aware the eyeless one knew he'd freed himself, and that maybe, just maybe, that creature wanted him to escape.

Still, he couldn't risk being caught. If they come for him, it wouldn't take long. With that thought firmly in place, Bernard readied to leave this place.

Chapter 31

"Marty, no," Sheila yelled.

But he didn't listen. His posture straightened, and he kept on walking.

Nancy understood Sheila's concern, but she could do nothing more herself. And truth told, Nancy couldn't help but feel proud of Marty right then. Still, she had an unspoken bond with Marty, so she pushed herself up. She felt unsteady when she did. Still, she worried what would come of Marty's bravery.

She stumbled to the door, and it appeared an intensely quiet moment passed outside in the time it took her to do so. Sheila came up behind her and wrapped an arm around Nancy's waist, helping to support her. Nancy gave a quick glance, thankful for her help, but that was all it took to see the worry in Sheila's eyes. Together they watched Marty march at the creature, as it turned its attention from Sandy to the audacious man.

Marty's face twisted with anger. "I said stop!"

This appeared to confuse the creature. Perhaps that might have been Marty's plan all along, the only reason he wasn't torn to pieces. But there seemed some other reason, something she could almost sense as she watched the creature back away from Marty. It didn't want to fight him. Not for fear of losing but for some greater unknown. Nancy could only worry what that might be.

She saw Sandy on the ground, and Nancy's hatred for the woman grew tenfold. Mistake or not, Nancy wasn't about to forgive that woman for anything. And Nancy knew then she would kill Sandy should she make it through this. For now, though, that would have to wait. Still, this realization excited her, and she felt a smile spread across her face.

Sheila was looking at her. Noticing this, Nancy looked away from the fight, faking worry. In reality, her distaste for Sandy was coming out, and she could think of nothing else. Once more the acknowledgement of her plans thrilled her, and the smile returned. She coughed, her hand moving to her face, where she wiped away the grin. A second later she returned her gaze to Marty, feeling actual concern now. But that was when she saw it.

Sandy's gun lay a mere ten yards away. No one else saw it, so no one else went for it. They were too busy watching Marty confront this demon-like creature.

Marty held up both hands, warding the creature off, and still it continued to back away from him. "Leave us!"

The creature stayed its ground, and it even stopped backing away. In that moment when the creature's horrible face stared at Marty, Nancy saw something else in its bulging eye. This *thing* seemed to recognize Marty. It had some connection with Marty. More so, Marty appeared to know this, and his confidence was growing because of it.

Chapter 32

When Marty went for the door, Ike stayed put at first. Not that it had anything to do with caring whether or not he made out okay. No, that wasn't right. It was more that he didn't want to have to care. Compassion never had been his thing. But after hearing Marty's tale, considering everything, he kind of admired the man... a little.

What the— Are you freaking kiddin' me?

In fact, he felt anxious, which bothered him. But that wasn't why he didn't get any closer or try to help. There were other reasons. Better reasons.

Ike was still considering what Marty had said about his brother, his description of being trapped in his bedroom. That recollection had hit Ike with a literal gut punch, one he was having a difficult time recovering from. He, too, had felt trapped, locked away, unable to do anything but pray he'd live to see another day. And he remembered thinking, if he made it through that, he'd kiss his sweet ass and count himself lucky. But, considering his encounter now, he felt anything but lucky. What he felt was...sick.

But there was another problem, too. How would he break the news to Marty, for as certain as he'd been that he'd killed his brother, Ike knew otherwise? Ike had seen Jake with his own two fucking eyes and barely escaped alive. Just thinking of it now, his thoughts drifted back to that memory as if it had happened only moments earlier.

Chapter 33

Ike hid under the basement stairs in the crawlspace of the abandoned house which was in somewhat good condition given the explosion had near ruined everything else. He did not know what was going on, only that he was certain this all happened because the United States had pissed off one too many Middle Eastern factions.

Though he didn't blame the U.S. for stirring up shit overseas. He rather enjoyed it. One of those bastards had cost him his job, so he couldn't help but feel some resentment toward the entire population of people. Every damn time he saw one of them, all he could think of was Akram and the stupid way he talked. He could almost hear the bastard now, recounting Ike's mistakes to his boss.

"He did not even change out the mop water," Akram had said.

What did that guy know about mop water? He should have kept to his own business, always walking around that place with his laptop and his fancy phone. If not for that guy's intervention, Ike might have kept that job. But no, that goddamned suit must have had a thing for Akram, because he didn't even blink twice before letting Ike go. Fucker offered Ike two weeks' notice, but Ike would be damned if he would work for any guy like that.

Besides, the only person Ike trusted was himself. He should have known better than go anywhere near Akram or even his boss. If only he'd waited until Akram left for the day, he might still have a job.

Let it go already, will ya?

There was no reason he should give two shits now, anyway. Heck, it would serve them right if the lot of them burned up in fires caused by this bombing. Ike had enough smarts to survive, and he rather fancied the possibility of being the sole survivor of a war. However, hiding in his crawlspace, he wasn't so sure this was what he had in mind.

It had occurred to him on several occasions he might get what he wanted, that all his dreams of isolation would soon come true. In fact, thinking about it now, this was the first time he regretted those feelings, sitting here in the dark of a crawlspace. He asked God for forgiveness, hoping the big guy in the sky would absolve him. Heck, he'd even requested a pardon for that rat Akram. But God had other plans. He sent something all right, not forgiveness but a real fuckaroo if Ike ever saw one.

He supposed it shouldn't surprise him. Ike had never been much of a religious man to begin with, so it made sense God should make an example of him. But even this seemed over the top.

Ike pulled the rickety door shut slowly and backed deeper into the crawlspace when the creature entered the basement, certain he was staring at Satan himself. He peered through the gap between the door and wall, able to see its formidable body. The monster seemed to sense Ike's presence. It took a step toward the door, and Ike almost crapped himself.

Then it took another step, and a third. Now close enough to smell him, Ike could see the fresh wound in its eye. Dark black streaks down its face appeared dry. Two little flaps on its chin struggled to breathe, gill-like openings around them inhaling and exhaling deeply. Ike could smell something awful on its warm breath, and it made him want to puke. But he held back for fear of being killed.

The creature took another step toward the small door, and the hair on Ike's arms rose, feeling like a soft caress. It gave him such a chill that he shook.

Oh, great. You damn sissy.

He tried like hell to make the sensation go away, but it wouldn't. And he looked up, half expecting the creature to open the door. To his surprise, it turned away.

Footsteps clomped across the floor above.

"Downstairs," a raspy man said. "I think I saw it go downstairs."

Ike squatted, feeling like he was sinking into the darkness of the crawlspace. He could still see through that gap above the plywood door, though. And that was unfortunate.

The creature intercepted both soldiers when they reached the bottom of the stairs. The sounds that followed sickened him: gunshots riddling the area, a spray of blood splattering against a wall, the sound of Ike throwing up when the creature tore off one soldier's arm, the screams, the begging, the silence that followed. Even worse, he'd seen most of it. Then something hit the door, and it rattled open a little more. What hit the door rolled into the open, and Ike struggled not to scream when he saw the severed leg, fresh blood seeping out of the torn end, making it look like ground beef.

When it was over, chunks of flesh lay scattered across what little of the basement Ike could see. Bright red covered the stone walls. But Ike didn't see the creature. And until he knew he was safe, he'd stay back in that crawlspace. Fuck everything else. But, as it often did, Ike could only stand so much. Despite all his wishes to stay put, he creeped forward on his hands and knees, wanting to make sure the creature had left, hoping he was safe.

As he neared the door, he saw the thing he least wanted to see, the puckered flesh of a single ruined eye peering back at him. Fresh blood dripped down its horrid face. The creature's mouth, looking like a frown, almost seemed to smile in that moment. And although Ike believed it couldn't see him, it appeared to sense his presence.

Right then, Ike's bowels released.

Well, you've fucked yourself now.

Then, with a sudden disregard for Ike, the creature turned, as if sensing something else approaching. It retreated up the stairs, leaving Ike there on all fours, unable to move. Ike stayed in that crawlspace for six more hours, pants soiled and shivering.

Chapter 34

By the time Ike worked up the nerve to head for the door, Marty had just commanded the beast to stop and then leave.

What the Sam Hill does he think he's doing?

When he got there, it looked as though Marty was backing himself into a crawlspace of his own creation. And Ike, against everything he'd ever known or felt, suddenly liked the damned fool. He couldn't explain it and wouldn't if asked, but this guy seemed to have a good heart. And he also was a special crazy, and Ike liked that, too.

Thinking about his change of heart made Ike feel a little sick. He wasn't used to liking anyone. But if not for that pause, reflecting on his feelings, he might not have seen the gun lying there. Lord knew why he went after it, because it was all he could do to keep standing the way his legs were shaking.

The creature took a step toward Marty. He couldn't believe the idiot was just standing there, daring the creature to tear him limb from limb. And it would, too. Ike had seen that much.

Legs like jelly, Ike bent for the gun. He picked it up and leveled it on the creature. That was when he remembered Marty's story, how he'd gotten away after shooting it. But Ike also knew that wouldn't be enough. Heck, a bomb hadn't even been enough to kill that fucker.

But it might give us enough time to escape.

As the creature took one more step, Ike pulled the trigger.

Nothing happened.

What the—

Then he saw the safety and made sure he had it off. This time when he took aim and fired, he unloaded five shots into the creature's side. Two hit, only one pierced the tender flesh Marty had described.

He waited to see the sac expand with air, only to hiss like a balloon, but something was off. This creature's abdomen didn't expand with air at all. Only then did Ike realize his boldness had come in error as the creature turned on him.

When it did, Private Masterson took the opportunity and jumped on its back. She withdrew a bowie knife from her belt and stabbed deep into the creature's eye, perhaps having heard Marty's story.

The creature wailed, trying to throw Sandy off its back. When it didn't succeed, it stumbled backward, arms flailing. Dark green oozed from the eye socket as its wings flapped wildly, revealing its confusion.

Marty watched, a grimace across his flushed face. Right then Ike felt bad for the guy. This had to remind him of his brother.

Finally, the creature threw Sandy to the side. Without hesitation and screeching in pain, the creature lifted into the air and flew off.

Ike couldn't help but feel glad it had left.

"We need to leave. Now!" There was a sense of urgency in Marty's tone.

"What? Why?" Sheila asked. "We beat it."

As if to answer her, a chorus of roars arose in the night air as many creatures realized what had transpired. In that split second of indecision, that same urge to crap himself washed over Ike again. Somehow, he held it in.

"They'll be coming," Marty said. "We best not be anywhere nearby when they get here."

Chapter 35

Bernard ran but wounded himself when he stepped on a little league baseball trophy, of all things. The tiny bat drove into the arch of his foot, not penetrating the skin but hurting him enough that he had to stop. When he did, the bat snapped in half beneath his foot, the remnant puncturing his skin. That hurt so bad he almost screamed.

Once he got going again, he had to half-hop down the corridors, leaving behind a fresh trail of blood that would reveal his escape route. More odd objects presented themselves as obstacles to him, scattered throughout the corridors. He saw things he wouldn't have imagined being here. Some of these items he recognized as clothing, much of it stained with blood, appearing torn. Other objects might have been whatever the people were holding at the time of their abduction. He also saw two of those floating carts, only one supporting a cauldron full of unidentifiable slime. Both just sat there, with no creature present to tote them about.

Bernard suddenly realized trouble was brewing, elsewhere. It was as if he could sense this, still connected to the others in some strange way, to that pod where he'd been a prisoner. Whatever caused this, the trouble didn't seem to involve him. As a result, the creature he'd seen in his thoughts had either forgotten Bernard or was more concerned with this new matter—something involving a group of people and a...brother. Bernard's only concern was to see Nancy safe. He prayed to God she still was.

He glanced over his shoulder as he ran but saw no adversaries. Upon spinning back around, he ran into a wall which he believed would have knocked him on his rear if it had been a normal wall. But this wall was more like a padded cell, cushioning his hands and arms as he stopped, his face pressing against the strange substrate.

Something inside the wall caught his eye, and he took a moment to examine it closer. There were people inside the wall, each within their own pod. He couldn't discern whether they were male or female, but the thought this had been his state only moments earlier made him feel sick.

Each body started trembling, slightly at first, and then shaking violently as some unseen force passed through them. They were neither alive nor dead, but part of some biological network, both receiving and transmitting information simultaneously. That was when he realized they didn't need to worry about Bernard because he was already part of this network. They would always know where he was, as he would know everything about them. Some cosmic thread bound them together, all of them sewn into some greater tapestry.

With that thought firmly in place, he no longer felt any need to run. He took his time, looked down the path to the right and to the left, seeing nothing of consequence in either direction. Behind him he saw a flurry of shadows heading his way. He tried to hide, looking for anywhere, anything to hide behind. There was nothing.

A dozen alien-like monsters fluttered by without so much as a sideways glance. When they went right, he followed, but didn't think he was off the hook yet by any means. So he kept his distance, certain they'd deal with him in good time, no matter where he went or hid.

Bernard followed them left, along a long stretch of amber walled corridors that spun in a wide circle. He tried not to look at the convulsing bodies as he rushed by, but that was becoming more and more difficult, as he could sense their thoughts. The idea he might know one of these people bothered him and intensified his concern for Nancy's safety. But the worst part was this sense that he'd changed inside, maybe not fully one of these creatures but a part of them for sure.

Still, he glanced at his skin to make sure. His eyes traced the contours of his naked body, thankful to see the same old out-of-shape form he'd grown accustomed to over the years. To his surprise, the gun wound had completely healed, a blister-like scar marking the point of entry. He was positive he'd died, beyond all doubt, which meant someone had reanimated him somehow. Having seen several movies on the subject, he didn't want to think about the consequences of this truth. Instead, he focused only on Nancy.

He loved her. So why had he been afraid of telling her? He supposed he'd never thought himself worthy of her love. She deserved better than him, a mere gas station attendant. He could never provide for her the way he thought she should be, not with his meager salary. Now, after rising out of death, he longed to tell her his true feelings. He would, too. Even if doing so led to a second death.

The path came to a Y and, caught in his thoughts, he'd lost track of the creatures. He scanned both sides for movement but saw none. Part of him wanted to go left, but he didn't know why. What he knew was that he didn't want to stay stationary for too long. Unsure whether to trust his instincts, he believed he could find his way back to this point as long as he didn't take too many more turns. So, after a quick decision, he headed left and took the next right a short way down the corridor.

He came to a large circular room, scattered with clothes, wallets, purses, and other belongings. He imagined this a trash receptacle, where all the odds and ends from the corridors ended up, eventually. He scanned the outermost layer, realizing only then he was looking for signs of Nancy. That seemed like a hopeless task given the sheer quantity of attire in this area. It would be like finding a needle in a haystack. Instead, he dug through the pile of clothes, searching for something relatively clean and undamaged that fit him.

Shoes weren't an issue. The first men's sneakers he found were a size eleven, even if they were two different brands, one black and the other white. The biggest jeans he found were a forty-two waist, which was slightly too big. And the inseam was thirty-two, so given Bernard's size, these pants gave new meaning to the word "floods" once he had them on. He dug through, looking for a belt, and found a torn length of rope, which he used to help keep the pants up. He tied it off with a double knot.

The biggest shirt he could find was a large, and it was hideous. Not only was it bright pink, but it had some unidentifiable stain on the back about the size of a basketball. Even though Bernard wasn't overweight—he had a beer belly. But he slid on the T-shirt, which felt more like a layer of skin than clothing. The shirt offered a peek at his gut, and he desperately kept tugging it down every few seconds, which did little good.

There. Dressed for success.

Bernard doubled back, but a strange sense of being lost overcame him. When he reached the first intersection, he couldn't remember where he'd come from. This was strange given his innate ability for such things, having been a Marine. But something about the path had…changed.

You've gotta be kidding me?

Alive or dead, lost or not, they were trying to keep him here. And they weren't playing fair, either.

Bernard took the right path, venturing into the darkness of the amber-lit hallways, writhing bodies lighting his way.

Chapter 36

Sandy led them to the only place she could think of, her thoughts still scattered.

"Where the hell we going?" Ike asked.

"This way," Sandy said. "There's a laboratory nearby."

"A lab? What kind of lab?" Nancy asked, her tone accusatory.

Sandy didn't bother answering. She knew it would only make Nancy angrier with her, not that she didn't have every right to be furious with her. Nancy held her accountable for Bernard, and there was no getting away from that fact. Her special ops training allowed Sandy to identify such things, to monitor them, and when the time came, she could fend for herself if need be. But she didn't want to. And she loathed herself for knowing it no longer mattered in this case. She'd killed the man this woman loved. How could Nancy ever forgive her for that?

A greater concern underlined Sandy's thoughts. They headed to the place where this all started. She remembered how they all went through the training and could almost see herself standing there in line that first day, unsure of what to expect. She remembered leaning to one side, seeing the faces of a dozen soldiers, most of whom she'd trained with all along. How could she have known then she that before long she'd never see them alive again?

It gave her this odd sense of déjà vu, considering the days back in this facility and these people she now traveled with. Her mission would have spelled death for her. There had been nothing diplomatic about her mission to lead these people right into the hive, to see what chaos they could bring, to shake things up. It was all about taking those who were most expendable and raising some hell in their final hours. The goal had been to discern the nature of what was happening on the inside and end it. That was a death sentence if she'd ever heard one.

Sandy knew things she hadn't shared yet and maybe never would. Like Cooley, how he was the first to change and not Marty's brother like he believed. Marty had hit on this to a degree, his suspicions almost right on the nose. Why they'd attempted to change Cooley and the others, Sandy knew bits and pieces. But none of it had been right then or now.

"This way," Sandy said.

No one questioned her. It occurred to her she could have used that trust to her advantage if she opted to. She might have even been able to lead them straight into the front door of that hive if she wanted.

Why do they still trust me?

She'd already killed one of them. Who was to say she wouldn't kill again?

Lucky for them, Sandy had enough of playing soldier for now. She didn't have it in her to go on any suicide mission. Nor had she ever wanted to become one of those creatures. They'd forced her to do all of it. And she'd had enough. Killing Bernard had been a mistake. She'd been a trained killer, but she hadn't planned for things to play out that way. Sandy was certain she'd had the safety on.

None of this mattered now, anyway. Death was death. Sandy had seen so much of it and had grown desensitized and resentful of the time it stole away from people that she no longer even batted an eye upon seeing it. She'd experienced loss firsthand. There was no mistaking it now; she saw defeat in Nancy's eyes. This woman would kill her if she ever got the chance. That meant Sandy had to make sure she remained alert.

They reached a shallow embankment of large stones, constructed in a way to form a wide ledge. Tall grass hung half-dead, draped over the side. Sandy stopped for a brief second to observe the scenery, remembering everything that happened here, how irrational it had been. The others watched, confused by her hesitation, but she couldn't explain any of that yet. She had a lot of bad memories associated with this place.

"Why—" Marty started.

Sandy cut him off, holding up a hand. "Over here." She waved him over. Together they shifted a large stone to one side. Doing so revealed the large metallic tunnel. Inside, the shaft diminished into complete darkness.

Sandy kneeled, Marty squatting beside her. They both stared into the belly of the hole.

"Where does it lead?" Marty asked.

"Down," Sandy said. "Right now, it's our best shot at finding some useful gear."

"Gear?" Sheila said. "We don't need gear."

Sandy stood, doing her best to show some restraint. "Gear. Weapons. That's exactly what we need right now. Trust me." She showed her gun to Sheila. "This and a knife are all I have. I don't think anyone else has anything more. And I doubt I need to remind you what we're up against, how effective these weapons are against those creatures?"

Sheila shook her head.

Ike pushed his way through and bent to look in the tunnel. He inspected it for a moment, then crawled inside. Sandy went in next. The others followed.

The smell was something awful, and Sandy did not know why.

"Sorry," Ike said. "My stomach doesn't agree with all this fucking stress."

Sandy's eyes burned. "Fart again and I shoot, get it?"

She'd meant that as a joke and immediately worried how the others would take it. Looking back, Nancy was right behind her. Now she really regretted the comment.

Nancy just stared at her, looking numb to everything, her eyes cool and calm, likely plotting.

Sandy turned and kept moving forward, though now more mindful of the woman close at her haunches. At any moment, if Sandy let her guard down even the slightest bit, Nancy could try something.

"Marty," Sandy said. "Try to pull that rock back over best you can." She watched as he pulled at the rock. "We don't want one of those creatures following us in here."

He struggled for a moment. The rock fell back into place with a solid thunk. Her concern dissipated, knowing it had blocked their escape. What lay ahead in this facility, though, was another matter altogether. It was possible that Cooley and the others were still here. Sandy doubted that would be the case, but she wanted to be ready for them just in case.

Chapter 37

Something about this didn't feel right to Marty. He wondered how much of that resulted from what had happened and his level of trust in Private Sandy Masterson. She'd already broken that trust once. Might she not do it again?

He did his best to present a calm outward appearance, paying close attention to every decision she made. But something about this shaft didn't feel right. He knew what it was right away, an exhaust of some sort, likely leading to an underground shelter. He remembered when they closed up this old mine shaft years ago, declaring it unsafe for the public. It was the kind of news that scrolled across the television, and everyone forgot seconds later. They'd put up signs and barriers over the years, marking the area as government property and detailing the penalties for trespassing. No one ever came out here, not anymore, not even the teenagers to drink their swill. This shaft was directly above that old coalmine.

Who knew what waited for them at the end of this tunnel? Without doubt, there would be a fan casing. Marty was sure they could either break through that, or, judging by the size of this tunnel, squeeze between the blades. Also, Sandy appeared to know the place well, and he doubted she'd lead them to a dead end. He suspected she knew more about what might be waiting for them than she let on, though. For now, they had few better options than to come here.

"Sandy," Marty asked, trying to pry at her tight-lipped nature some. "What is this place?"

All she did was press her forefinger to her lips, followed by a "Shh."

She even took the time to make sure the others saw the

gesture, holding her other hand to her ear, showing they should listen closely. To what he did not know. And he was trying to—

Marty heard something big clunk against something else. He couldn't tell what it was, but it had come from the end of this tunnel.

As if seeing that he'd heard it, Sandy nodded.

Now that he'd heard it, he could identify every clunk, clank, and thud. And Nancy appeared to hear them, too, her fear visible. Her lips trembled, evidence she might scream.

He held his finger to his lips, doing the same thing Sandy had in hopes Nancy wouldn't. She seemed to see him and settled some, but Marty understood what she was going through. He, too, worried some creature was waiting for them at the end of this tunnel, that it might hear them coming and come after them. And he wasn't so sure another standoff would be as successful.

Marty had grown to expect Ike's boisterous responses. It was his way of dealing with it all, and truth told, he'd even come to enjoy them to a degree. He anticipated Ike's question before he asked it.

"What the fuck was that?" Ike said.

Sandy hushed him and waved them forward. Then she held up a hand to let them know to take it slow. They all did, listening, being careful not to make too much noise.

When they got to the end of the shaft, Sandy looked down. The crashing sounds he'd heard were louder now, what sounded like something being thrown below them.

Sheila frowned, exhibiting her doubt that this would lead to anything good. Marty responded with a wink, hoping to reassure her and let her know he concurred with her assessment. He needed Sheila to remain strong in case Sandy led them astray, and a quick nod to Sandy, who wasn't looking his way, was all he had to do to convey this message. Sheila nodded.

Sandy waved Marty forward, and, with some effort, he squeezed by the others and made his way to the front. There, Sandy showed him what waited for them below.

He saw a fan which he'd expected. But he saw something else, too. An odd-looking man in a white coat frantically stacked whatever furniture he could find up against the door. The big question was: what was he trying to keep out?

She spun around on her rear and dropped her legs down to the fan. If it had been moving at full speed, it could have taken her legs. As it was, the fan's rotation seemed a more gravitational pull than electric. There was plenty of room to squeeze between the blades, but Sandy hopped and thrust her feet down against the blades. One blade broke free, and she disappeared between the remaining blades, collapsing into the room below.

Surprised by this, Marty hurried down after her, his only thought to keep her from getting any significant advantage over them in case she was being disingenuous. Upon landing on the floor, hunched over, he saw the man dressed in a white coat, back into the corner of the room, covering his face, startled by their intrusion.

"Who—?" he said. "What do you want? Are you infected?"

His sideburns ran down along his jawline. But the hairs there barely covered his chin. This made him appear like a cheap Elvis impersonator. He had buggy eyes that looked bigger through his thick glasses. And though he had brown skin, possibly a Middle Eastern man, his face had a pasty quality to the cheeks and around his eyes. This was someone who'd spent far too long locked away inside of this place, playing with computers and crunching numbers.

He slid down the wall to another corner, far away from them. There, he sank to the floor, his feet skidding against the tiled floor, leaving dark streaks from the rubber soles. Marty always hated that back when he was a teacher. Students used to get such a kick out of scuffing up the floor.

"Easy," Marty said, shifting closer to the man. "We're on your side."

The guy held up both hands. "Were you infected?"

Sandy hurried forward, meeting his gaze. "No infections here Dr. Deradis."

The odd man stared at her. "Masterson?" His expression went from troubled to puzzled. Feeling better about his company, he turned his attention back to stacking items against the door, anything he could find. "You're not supposed to be here." He shook a finger at Marty and then pointed up into the shaft, showing he had seen those who were still up in the shaft. "They shouldn't be here."

"None of that matters anymore, Doc."

He stopped, facing her. He looked away each time another jumped down, seeming to contemplate what it meant. "You mean—"

"Yes," Sandy said.

The doctor stopped working on the door.

"What aren't you telling us, Sandy?" Sheila asked.

"Spill it, dame," Ike added.

The doctor approached Sheila, then faced Sandy. Turning back to the others, he said, "It means there's been a breach."

Marty believed he knew what this meant, recalling the child he'd seen sneaking across the border. It was more than probable there had been several breaches. The others didn't come by this knowledge as easy, so Marty explained it to them. "It's not just here anymore."

Sheila took his hand. "How far?"

Ike's face scrunched up with a discouraged scowl.

Nancy lowered her head into her hands and cried.

Sandy remained cold as ever.

"Who knows," the doctor said, reaching into his jacket pocket. He pulled out a pack of cigarettes and lit one. He huffed at the cigarette, as if trying to get the full effect of the nicotine in mere seconds. "Hope you don't mind. I tried to quit, but it hasn't taken."

Marty shook his head.

"What's out there?" Sandy said, thumbing to the door.

The doctor spoke out the side of his mouth. "I don't know."

Sandy had her hands on her hips, perhaps having her own thoughts on that matter. She was considering something. And Marty believed she full well knew what sorts of things were beyond the door.

"So, if you don't know, then why?" She motioned to the desk, chair, and other junk piled in front of the door.

"The power went out and the containment cells failed."

"So, they are out?"

"Maybe. I'm not sure," the doctor said. "Better safe than sorry."

"Why the fuck wouldn't you check, idiot?" Ike said.

The doctor eyed him with obvious annoyance.

Sandy said, "If they got out and are on the other side, it won't be easy getting out of here."

"Who?" Sheila asked.

Sandy's eyes appeared to well up a little right then. "Well, Cooley for one."

"They aren't connected yet." The doctor stood frozen for a second. "But they'll be looking to get out, and, once that happens, they'll be able to relay this location to the others."

Sandy's fists tightened at her side.

"What the fuck does that mean?" Ike asked.

"If they get out, they'll come for us," Sandy said.

Marty regarded the doctor first, then Sandy. He bent over and pulled a chair away from the door. Sandy helped him.

"What are you doing?" The doctor dropped the cigarette and squished it out with his foot. He appeared so nervous and seized the back of the chair in Marty's hands, trying to hold it in place. "Stop. They'll get in."

"It won't matter," Sandy said.

"Listen," Marty said, taking a calm approach, "if we don't get out of here and they manage to get out of this facility, it won't matter how much junk you stack in front of that door."

The doctor's eyes widened with realization.

"We don't have much time," Marty said. "You need to tell us everything while we clear this mess."

"Okay, okay." The doctor spun away from them. "But don't shoot the messenger."

Ike groaned, which seemed to annoy the doctor. Marty thought Ike might be useful in squeezing every detail out of the doctor.

"It started fifteen years ago in New Mexico," the doctor said.

"Holy Jesus Christ, they got fucking aliens," Ike said, throwing his hands up in the air.

Marty smiled, trying to disguise his amusement.

And perhaps Ike saw that, because he grinned right then,

too, slight but there all the same. "What else, Doc? What else you bastards been hiding from us?"

Yes, Marty thought, *very useful.*

Chapter 38

Dr. Xavier Deradis rolled a chair over to the one they called Marty. There, he sat, watching them break down the barrier he'd only just built. He stayed out of the way of the others, especially the scruffy-looking skinny man named Ike. He didn't like the way Ike stared at him, tapping his foot, as if Xavier wasn't doing his best to recount all the details fast enough. He was well aware there was a need to hurry, but this intimidation wasn't helping. No, Xavier didn't care for that foul-mouthed man one bit.

"Well, we're waiting, Doc," Ike said.

Xavier thought Spike would have been a more appropriate name, given his personality and how it pricked at him like a large needle.

"Yes," Xavier said, "well...the first thing to remember is that none of this was our idea." He was referring to both Sandy and he, wanting to make sure they were at least somewhat absolved from the mayhem having ensued because of government meddling. To make sure, he thumbed to himself and Sandy. "That all came down from a higher authority."

"Yeah, yeah, Doc...we've heard all that 'don't blame me' shit before. Get on with it."

"Ike, let him tell the story, will you?" Nancy said.

"Yes, well." Xavier adjusted his thin-rimmed glasses and tried to clear his throat. Even then his voice felt raspy, what he worried might be the beginning of a cold. "In layman's terms, you've heard of exchange programs? Like those in the educational institutions, where one school sends a student to another country in exchange for one from that nation?"

"Yes," Marty said.

He rather liked Marty. He seemed far more intelligent than his modest clothes suggested.

Xavier cleared his throat again. "Our government took part in an exchange program of sorts."

"Wait, what the fuck?" Ike asked.

"Not literally, of course, but we have been in contact with extraterrestrials for over forty years now. At least that's what I've heard. I have no empirical data to prove that hypothesis." He reflected on this for a moment, considering whether he could prove it. Then he refocused his thoughts on the immediate issues. "Anyway, our exchange program wasn't one of students, although we have done something similar to that, but this exchange focused more on technology."

"Doc...I ain't buying whatever load of crap you're selling here."

"Please, Ike," Xavier said, wishing the guy would just back down. "Let me finish. Yes, they might be far more advanced than we are, but they've always lacked the primal nature of our existence."

"Primal?" Sheila said. "You mean war?"

"Of sorts, yes. Mankind has been, and always will be, obsessed with war. We gave them technologies to aid them in that area. Not weapons, mind you, but intelligence. An understanding of how war works."

"For Christ's fucking sake," Ike said, interrupting the doctor. "We taught them how to fight? What the hell were you ignoramuses thinking?"

Xavier examined Ike, disrupted by his tone. In part, he didn't like this because deep down, Ike was right. He was ashamed for what they'd given them, even if it wasn't his doing. But whatever they'd done, he'd been complicit, and that bothered him. What they got in exchange, though, made it all worthwhile. Or at least it seemed so.

Xavier directed this part to Ike. "You've heard of the Fountain of Youth?"

"All you got was a frigging fountain for that shit?"

"Not exactly, Ike, but something of that nature, yes. You see...they have technology to repair our bodies. We've known about this ability for some time, having witness accounts from the abducted. We exchanged what boils down to a series of strategies for a complex link to a means of repairing our bodies."

"So they couldn't just give the technology to you?" Nancy asked.

"No. That isn't how this exchange worked. This was information only. How-to manuals, if that makes sense. Humans must produce this technology for it to be effective on humans. What we really got was a microbial sample. One we could study and figure out how it functioned, and we could then build our own machine to repair humankind. That technology would have made war obsolete, so we all deemed it valuable."

Marty stopped working, turned toward Xavier, and stared at him for a moment. Xavier could see the understanding register in Marty's expression. He stood there, tugging at the hairs on his chin.

"We turned whoever is on the other side of this door into monsters?" Marty asked.

Sheila put her arm around him.

But Marty looked angered by all this. "Is that what happened?" He was yelling now.

"Of sorts. We created a breed of creature that could produce the chambers we needed to achieve that end. It's similar to how a spider creates a web, how they entomb their victims. Only in this case, the patients aren't victims. They're—"

"You mean to say, my brother died so the rest of us might live forever," Marty said.

"Please, Marty," Sandy said, using both hands to remind him something bad might wait for them on the other side of this door, and yelling would only attract them.

"Damn it, I don't care." Marty stormed away from the door.

Sheila tried to grab his hand, but he pulled away. Xavier felt anxious about the way he was acting.

"This," Marty said, looking around, "this place.... You killed my brother?"

Xavier pushed his glasses up on his nose. This wasn't the entire truth, but it was close enough he supposed. "I'm afraid so."

Marty screamed loud enough the others winced. Then Marty turned to the door, throwing objects aside in haste.

"Marty, please," Sheila said.

"No!" He kept working. "These people killed my brother. He was all I had left."

The others had stopped working, all of them watching Marty exert himself upon the pile until he had almost cleared it. Xavier stood and joined them, worried about what might wait for them once he opened the door. Marty worked tirelessly, pulling a desk away, hurling a chair aside, throwing all his weight against another desk. Spent, Marty dropped to his knees. There, he withdrew into himself and cried.

Sheila kneeled beside him and wrapped her arms around him. And he let her this time.

Xavier didn't know what to say. But he felt he must say something. "I'm terribly sorry—"

Marty held up a hand to the doctor. He waved off the apology. "Tell me. What else?"

"It didn't work," Sandy said, breaking her silence. "We failed."

"Yes, and badly," Xavier said. "We produced several new discoveries as a result, but very little toward our original goals. We came close several times, but eventually, when the bacteria got outside of our control, the rest of this...well, you know."

"So, you didn't plan the mosquito?" Sheila asked.

"No. That was mere coincidence." Xavier looked up to the shaft. "It likely came in and escaped through the very means you used to enter this room. Once it was out, though, it was only a matter of time."

"Discoveries? What discoveries?" Marty asked, his voice sounding weak and defeated.

"A weapon or two. That's all us Earthlings have ever been good at...destruction. The first was an enhanced electroshock weapon, which at the very least has been effective against the aliens."

"Oh, I've got to fucking get me one of those," Ike said.

"Yes, maybe all of us should have something." Sandy added.

"The other is a bomb of sorts. It could theoretically interrupt their internal network, which could allow enough time for one assault, whatever that might be."

"Network?" Marty said. "I think we saw something like that."

"Yes, they can communicate with each other, seemingly through telepathy."

"And this bomb, it works?" Marty asked.

Xavier hated looking him in the eyes. "Well, it's not been tested, but yes, I believe it would."

"What good is that," Ike said. "You saw that thing. I shot it at least twice and that didn't even phase the bastard."

Xavier knew what they were talking about. He'd seen their resilience firsthand. "You have to severe the head from the body. That's the only way to execute them."

"The only way?" Sandy asked.

"Well, maybe not." Xavier was uncomfortable with this next part, though. Not only was it untested, but their findings had been inconsistent. "In theory, we could administer a high dosage of the same serum we used to seed the transformation, and that could terminate them."

"Fucking overdose those asshats," Ike said.

"Why, that's exactly right, Ike. The point is to overdose the alien to the point their internal infrastructure could no longer function properly, similar to a heroin addict overdosing."

"How is this a bad fucking thing, Doc?" Ike asked.

"Well, it's only a theory. It was scheduled for testing, but we never got that far."

"Of frigging course," Ike said.

Marty stood and took Sheila's arm. He pulled her close, thanking her for the comfort by patting her shoulder, offering her a brief smile before letting her go. Xavier envied Marty right then, seeing that something more than a friendship was brewing there.

"I need to go," Marty said.

"Where?" Nancy asked.

"To your brother?" Sandy asked.

Marty nodded.

Ike sighed. "Well, shit."

Xavier, though, would be going nowhere near that thing. He would hide out here as long as he could, despite their feelings on the matter. He knew just how bad things could get. He also knew there was a stash of rations and other supplies that could keep him alive for a year, maybe longer. He didn't plan on sharing, either.

"Marty," Sheila said, "there must be another—"

But he turned to the pile obstructing the door, pushed the few remaining items out of the way, and opened the door.

Chapter 39

Marty opened the door and stood facing near dark, trying to reel in his anger but failing. In the background, the ductwork rattled, air still being pushed through at a high intensity. Though he could see little, Marty marched into the room.

His foot fell upon a puddle of water, what he thought might be condensation from the cooling system. He bent and touched it with his fingertips, making sure it wasn't blood. Only when he felt somewhat certain it wasn't, did he stand and continue onward.

He took another step into the darkness, the sound of water splashing beneath his shoes. Nothing appeared to move within the room, but down the hall he could hear a rumble, which could have been machinery of some sort or possibly a creature. He couldn't be sure if they'd escaped their containment or not and really didn't want to check. If they were out, they were out, and that was it.

Above all, Marty wanted out. Out of this bunker. Out of this state. Maybe even out altogether. He was so tired of losing people. So much that it had drained him mentally and physically. Knowing the government had been instrumental in the loss of his brother infuriated him, which defied how he'd lived his meager life. He'd had enough, and he no longer believed in anything. Call it Atheism, label him a heretic, accuse him of treason, he couldn't care less. He felt betrayed by both God and his country.

Behind him, he heard the others following him in silence. He couldn't fathom why they still bothered; he was anything but their leader. Nor did he care that they followed. If they were to walk away, he'd be fine. This was the end of the line. He felt that more than anything right now.

Sheila hurried up behind him, but he did his best to keep ahead of her. He couldn't stand another loss.

"Marty, slow down," she said.

But he didn't. Each deliberate step came with a splash of water. Behind him, the others tread more lightly. They did so because they still cared. Realizing this, Marty sped up, almost stomping in the water. The noise he made echoed in the darkness.

"Marty?" Ike said. "You want to cut that crap?"

Marty ignored him.

Ike grumbled something under his breath. "If you don't and one of those fuckers are free, we'll be toast."

They asked so much of him. He was so tired of being careful his entire life. Look where that got him. More than anything, he just wanted to not have to worry.

From the corner of his eye, Sandy peeled off into the darkness of this cavernous room. He didn't know where she was going, nor did he care. It made him glad to have one less person following him.

Then, as if fate was rewarding Marty's insolence, he came face to face with a creature. Seeing it reminded him so much of Jake. And that, too, angered him.

Marty shoved the creature back, then went at it again with both hands raised and shoved it in the chest again. The creature stumbled back each time, appearing stunned by his anger. Marty shoved the creature aside and kept on walking. Behind him, the creature bellowed a complaint, a low grumble. But Marty never even flinched. He kept on walking, even when that grumble turned to a roar.

He had this coming. He'd cheated death one too many times. It was time to go to his family. He stopped, letting the creature catch up, and met it face to face.

A burst of light flashed, bringing the entire room into clarity for a split second. The light shot out in every direction behind the creature like tendrils of lightning. Marty saw all the stunned faces in this instant. They were afraid for him, but they were also afraid of him.

The creature dropped to the floor, water splashing against Marty's pants up to his thighs. Seeing the creature drop like that shocked him.

Sandy stepped out of the shadows, holding a long staff. Its end glowed like a giant sparkler. She handed the staff to Nancy, went into the dark again and returned with an axe. She hoisted it over her head and brought it down hard and accurate on the creature's neck. The snap echoed down unseen hallways.

Still stunned, Marty allowed Sheila to get closer. Her hands warmed his cheeks as she pulled his face down to hers. She stood on her tippy-toes and leaned into him, their foreheads touching. Tears sprinkled her cheeks as their eyes met, and Marty cried, too. She hugged him, and Marty fell into her embrace.

When she pulled away, her eyes never left his. "Marty, let ghosts be ghosts."

The guilt he experienced every time she got close to him was overwhelming. He was a married man. He'd dedicated himself to his wife. But Sheila was right. What good was living in the past like this? All it ever achieved was more misery.

He looked over Sheila's shoulder and saw most of the others watching. Sandy handed a large sparkler-like weapon to Ike, and kept two more, apparently waiting for them to finish. That woman didn't have a soft side that he'd seen, but she was kind enough to know he needed the moment. And he wanted to savor this one.

When he finally pulled away from Sheila, Sandy handed one staff to him and another to Sheila. She picked up the axe and placed it in a long duffle bag.

"So, what's in the bag, Toots?" Ike asked.

"Whatever bombs I could find and a case of vials containing the bacteria," she said.

Marty put his hand on Sheila's shoulders, thanked her with a smile. They turned together, him taking her hand. They began walking again, this time with more apprehension of their surroundings. Each step brought them closer to freedom.

When they reached the exit door, Marty looked back. None of them, including himself, knew what to expect. But they all knew what must be done.

With that, Marty opened the door. When he saw the man standing outside, he recoiled, both surprised and full of joy all at once.

He regained his footing, checked again, and then acknowledged the man. "Bernard?"

Chapter 40

Nancy pushed by Ike and the rest of them and ran right straight into Bernard, arms wide, wrapping them around him. Bernard just stood there, looking as though he hadn't slept in days, even when she pulled his cheek down to kiss him.

Ike knew then something wasn't right, and it wasn't just the goofy clothes. A quick glance to Sandy confirmed this thought. He could see it on her face. They were too much alike, her and him. It bothered him when she telegraphed this thought by turning up the corner of her mouth, as if about to smile.

He knew a lot about tells. He'd learned how to pick them up during a long stint in Vegas. While he'd never been a great poker player, that never kept him from betting. And that meant he spent a lot of money losing, which was why he'd had to borrow money. That's what got him in the hole, how he'd gotten himself into trouble with the loan sharks. That's also what landed him here in Illinois, looking to start a new life, one that didn't require a steady fucking diet of gambling.

A quick glance left or right confirmed one thing. *Some good that did.*

He often wondered why he hadn't chosen Florida. What wasn't to love about the ocean? Hell, they had their own oranges for Christ's sake. Florida also had a longer baseball season, and Ike loved baseball. That was a game full of tells. When he was younger, his mom was always going on about it, Florida this and Florida that. Maybe that was why he didn't go there, because she loved the area so much. And that made him wonder if she was still alive, maybe somewhere in Tallahassee. But why on God's green Earth did he ever choose the Midwest?

The tell on Bernard's face right now let Ike know something

had gone wrong in that guy's noggin. His body was too damn stiff, like someone had shoved a pole right up his ass. That big oaf had an issue with his back, one that didn't allow for him to walk so straight, despite what he might have learned as a Marine. What Ike saw now was an uncomfortable-looking man, and that always spelled trouble with a capital T.

"What's with the clothes?" Nancy asked.

Well, that was a relief. Ike hadn't wanted to say it himself.

"I escaped." Bernard said, his face riddled with confusion. "I'm not sure how, but I did."

"Are you all right, bud?" Marty asked, taking a step toward Bernard.

"I...I'm not sure." And right then, as he answered, Ike could see he wasn't lying. "Truth is, I'm not even sure how I got here."

"Us either," Ike said, finding his words. "We left you for worm food."

Nancy shot Ike a glance, but it was true. They were all thinking it. He'd only given words to the concern that this guy had come back from the dead.

"Well, I did die." Bernard spoke as if it were an everyday occurrence.

Ike couldn't believe what he was hearing. Was anyone buying this crap? And how could he be so nonchalant about it, as if it were such a small thing to come back from the dead?

This made Ike recall something the doctor had said, about living forever. He couldn't help but wonder if there was something more to this infection, some kind of chemical alteration that brought people back from the dead. Maybe they'd all come back.

When he looked around at the others, Bernard was the only face that wasn't pale with shock.

"Do tell," Marty said, encouraging Bernard. He took two more steps closer to the man, letting go of Sheila.

What's he doing?

"I'm connected in somehow," Bernard said.

Sandy's eyes widened. So did Marty's. Ike thought for different reasons.

"When I woke up and got loose, I found myself trapped in

that thing back there." Bernard motioned to the hive.

"The hive?" Marty asked.

Bernard nodded. "Then, out of nowhere, I saw their leader. He was in my head, talking to me, but he wasn't using any words."

Bernard faltered, and Marty got closer, his hands ready to help.

Still wrapped around Bernard's torso, Nancy looked like she would never let go. Bernard was rubbing something between his fingers, but Ike saw nothing, so he thought it was just nerves. Marty seemed to see this, too.

"What happened next?" Marty asked.

Ike thought Marty looked concerned for both Bernard and Nancy. Again, it was for different reasons. Ike was also aware Sandy was moving in behind Bernard.

"He told me to come and get you," Bernard said.

At this, Marty stopped closing in on the guy. "All of us?"

"No," Bernard said, "just you."

"Why Marty?" Sheila asked.

Ike could see a growing understanding on Marty's face. He wished he understood, too.

"What if I say no," Marty asked in a calm voice.

Bernard's face gave away nothing now. "He said you would say that."

Nancy looked confused, more so when Bernard pulled away from her. Still, she clung to him as Bernard walked ten paces to the left and pried her off him. "He said you should talk in private."

"How are we supposed to do that?" Marty asked.

Bernard's eyes fixated on him. Marty took another step toward Bernard. Ike saw then the big guy had stopped rubbing the invisible object in his hand. Bernard's arms shot straight out to his sides, and that was when Ike backed the hell up. This shit was right out of Marty's story, like some bolt of energy was shooting up through Bernard's body and out his extremities.

Marty ran to Bernard's side, but before he got there, Bernard settled. It took a moment before everyone else did. When the big guy spoke again, everyone heard him.

"Hello, brother," Bernard said. Only it wasn't his voice.

Chapter 41

This latest development gravely concerned Sandy. It was unlike anything she'd ever witnessed, and her eyes had taken in more than most. She'd observed things she shouldn't have, much more than she'd ever reveal to this group of people she'd only just met. And she liked these people, so that meant she trusted them enough to let them in on a secret here and there.

There was something about Ike, too, more than his hard exterior. She could see he'd also seen things, most of which he'd likely kept to himself. She was good at reading people, as the ability had been a focus during her training. And she could tell he was reading her right back. People like that smelled their own in a crowd, able to spot each other from a distance, always offering a knowing glance. But that didn't mean she had to like it.

Marty was too educated for a farmer. She suspected he'd gone to college, maybe even a quality school. He'd also seen things beyond his quaint farm in Illinois, much thanks to his brother.

The woman, Sheila, seemed to have taken a liking to Marty, which was understandable. He was a born leader and somewhat easy on the eyes. Sandy didn't think the woman lived around these parts anymore, substantiated by the clothes she wore. Having spent the last several years in the area, Sandy knew the local fashion trends well enough. Sheila was a city girl if she'd ever seen one. Maybe she'd lived around here at one point but not anymore. She'd likely just been passing through or visiting family when the bombs dropped.

Nancy was the closest thing to farm folk in this group. She

had a knack for lying, which Sandy learned over the last few hours whenever anyone asked if she was all right. Of course, she wasn't. And Nancy was astute at hiding her anger. Sandy had killed before, too many times in fact, and she'd encountered no one so calculating, so patient in seeking revenge. But she could tell it was coming.

All these secrets made Sandy feel like a monster at heart, and she supposed that was what she really was. She remembered killing three civilians recently, after one of her superiors came across one of Marty's letters. Her orders had been simple: to find them, blend in, and wait for the right opportunity. When that time came, she was to put her plan in action. The first two parts of the mission had been easy; an amicable Marty let her right in and even shared details with her they shouldn't have. He treated her like he'd known her for years, and she supposed that was the reason she'd scrapped her plan when that time came. But deep inside, part of her couldn't shake the urge to finish the mission. And since she doubted that need would ever go away, she would have to get used to her thoughts nagging away at her. It was an addiction of sorts, like the cotton candy aroma she always got from cigarettes now, six years after she quit smoking.

Her training was a part of her now, tattooed onto her soul. And now, after proclaiming her willingness to give up on her mission, the hive called to her still. The urge to charge in overcame her. It too had a sweet candy-like smell that only an addict could sense.

She cast away the thoughts of her duty, taking a moment to consider the latest member of their group. He'd died. She'd seen it herself. Yet, here he was, brought back to life by who knew what force, possessed by some engineered alien dictator. Well, that rubbed her over twenty ways wrong. She hadn't trusted the man before, and she trusted him even less now that she knew some outside entity could influence him.

Glancing around their group, apparently she wasn't alone in this sentiment.

Chapter 42

Somewhere deep within the corridors of the hive, he sat, considering what he needed to say. The amber glow emanating from the walls reminded him of the dried cornhusks come fall, of stoking a fire in the barrel they kept outside. He remembered all those things well, everything he'd seen and done as Jake. But that wasn't who he was anymore.

Now, he was two. He was still the displaced brother—Jake was what Marty had called him—a being who stood out from his new race as being unlike any other because of that human past. And then there was the part of him that been so tightly weaved into this alien race, that they accepted him as their leader. And why shouldn't he be their leader? After all, he'd created every one of them in his image, fixed their flaws, added a means of transport. This brought back another memory, that of his mother reading Marty and him the scripture when they were younger.

This new race referred to him as the Infinite, for his mighty ways were endless. His knowledge was great. And he was godly, even if that sounded like blasphemy. Even his human half, the part of him that had retained all those sermons, knew that if a God existed, he or she could no longer help the people of Earth. The Infinite was their only salvation now.

He rather liked the moniker, too—the Infinite. He much preferred it to Jake, which sounded so much less intimidating. And when he gave orders to his followers, he did so with few words, such as "The Infinite wants Marty." And they would do as commanded, all of them, without question. That was the sole reason he'd let Bernard escape. Even though the man wasn't part of his race yet, he'd been useful for this purpose, especially regarding their primitive form of communication. When he finished with the man, he'd send his kind to hunt the man down, and he'd decide what to do with him later. Bernard would either return to the hive's grid or undergo the transformation. The Infinite hadn't decided which, as it much depended on how things went with Marty. But either would be an improvement.

He rested his mind, pushing away all troubles, and prepared for the moment. Arranging his thoughts, the Infinite relaxed his mind and gazed through a mental eye, as his brother had destroyed his physical one. Once he was inside of Bernard's conscience, he could think of only one thing, how much he wanted his brother to join him.

Chapter 43

Once again, Marty recalled the childhood game they played, where they would each pretend to be leaders of various countries' armed forces. As the younger of the two, Marty always ended up representing the weaker of the two choices. Jake was the tyrannical leader, commander of a brutal force that attacked Marty when he least expected it. At first, Marty would fight back, doing his best to protect his imaginary homeland. The two of them would duel, using sticks like swords instead of guns. When their sword snapped in half, they'd grapple with each other. But eventually, as if predetermined, the larger more formidable Jake got the upper hand.

Marty would yell, "Stop, Jakey!"

And he would…sometimes. But most of the time he'd continue until Marty cried. His big brother could be so cruel, no matter how much Marty loved him over those years.

Afterward, they'd sit and negotiate the surrender of Marty's army, much like they'd seen many times in the movies. The terms were never fair, usually requiring Marty to perform some awful tasks or take over one of Jake's chores for a day. Whatever the case, the details were never fun. Marty often wondered why he'd ever agreed to play. Yet he always did, every time.

Now, here they were, Jake the leader of some alien race, Marty the leader of what—a small group of unlikely heroes? And that was exactly what they were, one of the smaller more insignificant countries. One his brother could roll right over if he wanted to. But that never had been Jake's strategy. He liked to tease, to torture, to make Marty cry.

"Brother?" the voice of Jake said.

"I'm not your brother." Marty's tone sounded defiant. He'd

meant it. Sheila had been right after all; his brother was dead.

"I assure you, I'm still your brother. Say, does this remind you of anything?"

Right then Marty wondered if Jake had read his thoughts, as he'd been visualizing that precise image of the two of them playing as kids.

If so, read this.

In his mind, Marty gave Jake the finger.

"No," Marty said, finally.

"Come on, really? You got nothing?" The creature speaking through Bernard either didn't read his thoughts or would not respond to the gesture.

Bernard's mouth moved almost like a marionette, as if some invisible puppeteer was throwing his voice. It cast an awkward light on how much Bernard reminded him of Jake. They were about the same size. Even their voice had a similar quality, especially now that Jake had lost his accent. This made it hard not to see Bernard as his brother. That was likely what the creature had planned, to make Marty feel somewhat normal again, and that was something he very much doubted he'd ever feel again.

Marty had trusted Bernard right from the start. So anything the creature said through Bernard was definitely easier to listen to than it would be from the source.

"Well, one thing's for certain. You always were such an astute fellow."

"Why are you here?" Marty asked, raising his voice. "Why are you doing this to my friend?" He motioned at Bernard's limp body.

"All in good time, brother. All in good time."

"So, what then?"

"I've come to proposition you."

"What is it already?"

The urge to walk away from this summit of sorts was wearing Marty down. But he had greater concerns than his own feelings, and that was why he stayed. He wasn't sure whether Bernard would live through this if he left, especially if he angered the creature, which was a fine line he was already stomping all over. Uncertain how far this control went, whether the creature could use Bernard to kill one of them, perhaps an act that was already set into motion without Marty's knowledge. He needed to see this through and pay close attention to every detail.

"I need to have my brother by my side," the creature said.

"You aren't my brother. Not anymore."

"Please, Marty," the creature said, his tone suggestive. "Let me prove that I still am."

Marty didn't respond.

"We can rule this world together, brothers until the end of time."

Marty felt his eyes widen. This wasn't at all how Jake thought. Maybe he'd said things like this as a kid playing games but not as an adult. The real Jake would never—

Marty felt his head swirling with dizziness. Images were being pushed into his thoughts, visions of the creature and Marty side-by-side. In the background, there were fires and bombs, explosions, legions of alien forces, hives everywhere. The worse part was Marty suddenly started grinning slightly. Somehow the creature had entered his head and made him desire this outcome.

No, that isn't me.

This was too much power for anyone. Even before Marty answered, he knew what he had to do. He also realized he couldn't let so much as a hint of it into his thoughts for fear the creature might see. Instead, the images he focused on were those of he and his brother throughout their lives. With each image, he attached a sentiment of love, of adoration and their brotherly bond. If nothing else, hopefully the creature would see how much he missed his brother, and think he was considering this absurd proposal.

"Would it be okay if I gave this some thought?" Marty asked. He looked over at the others, standing there. They stared back.

Marty hadn't realized the conversation had stalled until he looked back to Bernard. For a few seconds the creature appeared to be trying to read Marty's thoughts, searching for deceptions. Marty worried the creature might have seen more than he wished, that he might have uncovered Marty's sham. And Marty prayed that wasn't true.

"You think on it, brother," the creature said. "Let Bernard here know when I can talk to you again." Marty saw a vision of a large, wounded eye winking in his mind. "It's big, Marty. Big, big stuff. I want my brother by my side."

With that, Bernard's body went limp and collapsed to the ground. Marty went to him, wanting to help, but remained cautious of his thoughts because he knew at least part of Bernard remained networked to that creature. He wouldn't risk giving away any details.

With his help, Bernard sat up. Marty stood, looking down at him, and offered his hand.

Bernard looked up at him. "What happened?"

"Nothing," Marty said. He helped Bernard to his feet. "Nancy, why don't you take care of Bernard?"

Marty didn't need to ask Nancy twice. She ran to Bernard's side, and this time Bernard was much more receptive of her affection.

Marty used the opportunity to hurry the others back inside fast. When he went to speak, Sandy put up her hand. She grabbed his collar and pulled him deeper into the shelter, the others following them. Scanning the ceiling, she didn't stop until they all passed beyond a red line painted across the ceiling.

She pointed to the line. "No network."

"I see," Marty said, wondering how they'd blocked the signal. Marty also wasn't sure he cared.

"Static," Sandy said, as if sensing his thoughts.

"Ah." Marty shook his head. "Well, here's the thing. We have little time." The others moved in closer, so he didn't have to speak any louder. "I didn't want to say anything in front of Bernard for obvious reasons, and knowing that, above all else, keep your thoughts clear or he might find out. Understand?"

"Good fucking plan," Ike agreed.

Marty grinned. "And keep Nancy out of the loop, too. She'll be susceptible to Bernard's suggestion." Marty thought about it for a second. "I mean Jake."

"That's a better idea," Sandy said.

Ike winked at her. She grimaced in response.

"What the fuck did I do?" Ike asked.

"We'll go through all the details later," Marty said, ignoring Ike. "Soon. But for now, this is all you need to know, and this will sound strange. I'm going into that hive."

"What?" Sheila looked surprised. "Marty, no!"

"I have to," Marty said. "There's no way around it."

"He'll frigging kill you, Marty," Ike said. "You know that."

Marty shook his head. "Maybe not."

"What do you have in mind," Sandy asked.

Marty noted her interest. "Well, first…" Marty pointed back to the small room they'd been in earlier. "We need to convince the good doctor there to do something for us, which I assume he's capable of?"

Marty saw the look in Sandy's eyes. An idea occurred to him just then, and his eyes drifted to the ceiling.

"What is it?" she said.

"Tell me the doctor knows about these bombs."

"Oh, he knows all about those fucking bombs," Ike said. "I guaran-damn-tee it."

Sandy shot Ike another look. "Yes, he does. In fact, he helped create them."

"Great." Marty pulled at the hairs of his chin. "I have something for him to do that I hope isn't too problematic." He looked up at the red line again. "And maybe something else, too. We need to pick his brain a bit."

"I can help," Sandy said. "I know a lot about the weapons."

"Good," Marty said. "We need to get started on this right—"

"Marty?" It was Nancy, the panic in her voice clear. "I need you." She hurried off outside.

His gut told him either Bernard hadn't been able to endure this second chance at life or worse, being networked in with that creature had ignited some irreversible change in Bernard.

Marty rushed outside. The others followed close behind. When he got there, Nancy was kneeling, Bernard lying in her arms. He was breathing normally and otherwise looked fine. But Nancy wasn't looking at Bernard. Her eyes stared up at the dark sky, to a place far above the hive. He traced her line of vision and what he saw sent him stumbling backward into the others. They were all too stunned to notice, their bodies like a rigid wall deflecting him.

Marty saw Ike, readying to say something. He waited for it.

"What the fuck is that goddamned thing?"

"It's a ship," Nancy mumbled.

"A mammoth spaceship?" Sheila said.

"It's them," Sandy said, confirming Marty's deepest fears.

The giant saucer took up a large amount of the sky over the hive. This complicated matters. But he couldn't think about this now, not in front of Bernard.

"They've come to take their children home," Bernard said.

Marty considered Bernard's words and thought he should be able to connect the dots right then as to what bothered him about those words. But it wasn't registering. He was too shocked to think straight.

Everything would change. Everything already had changed.

Chapter 44

To Sandy's surprise, they hadn't needed to coax the doctor out of the back room at all. He came of his own freewill after detecting the ship on a monitoring device. When he walked up behind them, they were unaware of his presence and thus startled when he spoke. Except for Bernard, who was staring up at the ship with wide eyes. He might as well have been drooling.

"This is bad," the doctor said.

Sandy knew he was right. She could see he was trying to formulate some conclusion why they'd come. He liked to take his time pondering such matters. Nothing was worse than people flying off the handle over nothing. But she wanted to know what this was now, because there was no time to contemplate.

"What? Why is this so fucking bad?" Ike asked before she could. "Is there more to this shit than what we see?"

"Why yes," the doctor responded.

"What then?" Sandy asked.

"There's no opposition," Marty said, mumbling, which made him difficult to hear.

Sandy scanned the horizon. He was right. No fighter jets screamed through the air. Not a single helicopter loomed, preparing to fire missiles at the ship. Not one bomb exploded against the ship's hull. There weren't even any ground troops.

"Jesus Christ," Ike said.

"Yes, I wonder just how far this has spread," the doctor said.

Sandy walked over to Bernard and looked into his eyes with determination. She looked him up and down, found it hard to ignore the goofy, too small, tight clothes he wore. "What do you know?"

"Leave him alone," Nancy said, splitting the distance between them.

Her hand smacked against Sandy's chest a little too hard. There were men who'd committed this mistake and paid a far steeper price. "Move. Your. Hand."

"No. I won't." Sandy could see the anger boiling behind her eyes. "And you will leave Bernard alone. Haven't you done enough already?"

"Move it or lose it, sister," Sandy said.

Then, with that same starry gaze in his eyes, Bernard wrapped his arms around Nancy and drew her back, protecting her. He looked down at her, and for a split-second Sandy saw that old Bernard. Even when he bent down and kissed her forehead.

Nancy smiled, moving to his side where she glared at Sandy. He put a long, heavy arm over her shoulders, pulling her in close.

"It's what they wanted all along," Bernard said, sounding disorientated.

"What?" Sandy asked. "What do they want?"

Nancy's face wrinkled with anger. But stuff like that never bothered Sandy.

"They never wanted tactics," Bernard said. "They wanted a technology they didn't have. That they couldn't make themselves." That dazed look clouded his eyes again, as they shifted back to the ship.

"Of course," the doctor said. Sandy hadn't even noticed he was still standing there. "They never wanted to learn how to fight, or even know about our weapons and how to use them. They never intended for us to keep our so-called, fabled Fountain of Youth."

"So what?" Sheila asked. "It was a ruse?"

"Not at all." Now the doctor was looking at the ship. "They merely wanted a way to disable our forces, or rather to incapacitate them. That way no one could stop them from taking what they *really* wanted."

"Energy," Bernard said.

"Well, not really. Close, though. What they wanted was fuel."

Ike sighed. "I don't fucking get it."

"Well, we've known for some time now how their technology works. It's a pod of sorts, spun out of their special spidery silk. And you need at least one soldier to create that pod. Those pods, they have incredible healing powers. So, in a way, we found what we were looking for. We just weren't able to sustain those pods long enough to use them in the way we'd hoped."

"So, these pods can cure cancer?" Sheila asked.

"They can raise the dead," Sandy said, raising an eyebrow to Bernard. "But let there be no mistake—he's more one of them now than he is us."

Nancy sneered at Sandy. "That isn't true!"

Bernard stared at Sandy as if she'd seen something she shouldn't have. He looked as though he was about to respond but couldn't find the proper words to explain his thoughts. "That isn't how it works."

"Enlighten us then, genius." Ike said.

"There's two of me now. The Bernard tied to them." He looked at Nancy. "And the Bernard who can't live without her."

Nancy smiled, snuggling into his chest. Seeing it made Sandy want to puke.

"You see," the doctor said, "the individual pods would only remain functional for a limited time without a human inside of them. This was the setback we always ran into. We managed to heal but were unable to bottle this technology up as an injectable cure—as Sheila suggested—to fight cancer."

"So, without a human constantly inside the pod, there is no pod?" Marty asked.

"Yes, eventually that is the case. And it seems probable this is the same manner in which the alien hives work, only perhaps they feed off other life forms from other planets, possibly even their own. And when there isn't a being inside one pod, the other pods support it until there is. So, you see their quandary?"

"We aren't food. But we are the fuel that keeps their hives running?" Marty asked the doctor.

"I believe so. What better fuel than one that is disposable, and yet, renewable."

"Frigging hell," Ike said.

"And that isn't all, either." The doc wrung his hands together. "We only put the infected into those pods. So, they're no better off than your Bernard."

Sandy found she was staring at the doctor and looked away.

"Are there more of those creatures inside?" Marty asked.

"I believe so."

"Sandy?" Marty grabbed her shoulder, shaking her out of her memories. "Do you think you can rig one of those explosives halfway down the corridor that leads to their cells?"

"Sure Marty, but it hasn't—"

"Don't worry about it. If nothing else, it will alert us if they're coming. We can deal with them from that point."

"Okay."

Marty looked at Bernard. "Nancy?"

She looked up at him for a second.

"I need you to take Bernard inside, into the main room there, far past the red line on the ceiling. Do you understand? Find a place way back in there and take care of Bernard. But no matter what, don't come out until I or someone else tells you to."

"You don't trust me, Marty?" Bernard asked.

Marty didn't answer.

Sandy watched Nancy usher the big man inside. Bernard kept looking back over his shoulder, staring at Marty with a sad face. Sandy waited to make sure they were well beyond that line. Once they were, she returned to the group.

"The rest of us, we need to get back to that room." Marty looked deep in thought. "Doctor, I need you to make some revisions to one of these bombs if you will."

"Sure, what did you have in mind?"

"Let's get inside first. We must make quick work of it and get right back on guard."

Marty led the way down the short hall, past Bernard and his moping eyes. Sandy didn't like the way Bernard's eyes followed Marty. Nancy appeared to notice, too, her eyes evidence of the hatred she had for Sandy.

They went into the room, one by one. Sandy entered last, right before Marty. Once they were all in, Marty pulled the door shut.

Chapter 45

In the morning, Sheila saw Marty standing in the doorway, looking out. Bernard was watching him with what looked like an expression of envy. But Sheila believed he was busy planning to go to the hive, which concerned her very much. She was trying to understand best she could.

Marty's brother had told him to let Bernard know once he was ready to talk again. Once Marty let Bernard know his decision, he informed them that also was as expected. This bothered Sheila, because Marty's brother seemed to be one step ahead of Marty.

The bags sitting by the door, just behind Marty, worried her, too. The night before, as the doctor and Sandy worked, all of them save for Nancy and Bernard, had listened to Marty detail his plan. There was agreement that the idea was a sound one, but Sheila still wasn't so sure. But she hadn't been able to come up with a better plan, either.

As the sun stretched its tired self over the horizon, the light glowed around Marty, illuminating his silhouette. The slight morning breeze teased at his hair, flickering as Marty tugged at his chin hairs. He was still thinking on it, and that was a good thing.

Someone walked up behind her, Bernard approaching Marty. She looked up to the red line on the ceiling, realizing he was about to cross it and intercepted him.

"Bernard," she said, grabbing his hand and pulling him back, "how are you this morning?"

"I'm fine."

He wore a dull expression and kept looking at Marty. She didn't know which part of him was doing the staring, either.

Was it the caring lug of a man or the networked receptor of all things bad? Looking into his displaced eyes—eyes she hadn't seen in Bernard before—she wasn't sure.

"If you're planning what I think you are, don't," Bernard said.

Marty turned to Bernard and closed in on him, leaving the vest and two bags by the door.

"What's that, my friend?" Marty said.

"That place, it isn't right. And he...your brother is an evil monster." Bernard looked at each of them, then back to Marty. "He means to turn you into one of them."

"I'm aware of that possibility."

"But he can read minds. He can see right inside of you. He'll do it, Marty. He won't even—"

"No!" Sheila said. "No, he won't!"

Bernard patted the air. "Sheila, you don't know—"

"But I do, Bernard. I know," Marty said.

They both stared at him.

"I'm going with you." Sandy said, entering the room.

Sheila considered it, staying behind or the possibility of going with, thus increasing the odds of someone not coming back. "Me, too," she finally said.

Marty pushed his fingers back through his hair. "Sheila, I—"

"I don't want to hear it. I'm going."

He stared at her for a long moment, considering this, tugging at the hairs on his chin again, likely working out the odds. Bernard was rubbing his fingers together. Marty's plan was already changing. She hoped for the better.

"Fine." Frustrated, he swung around back to the door.

"Well shit," Ike said. "I guess I have to fucking go now, too."

Marty smiled at Ike over his shoulder. Sheila had to admit, the guy had a way of growing on people, kind of like a fungus. Ike seemed to have affected Marty in the same manner.

"Me, too," Bernard said.

This request Marty had to consider for a long moment. Sheila knew just by Sandy's reaction she didn't approve. Ike seemed to echo this concern. The longer it took for Marty to answer, the more their unease seemed to grow.

"I know things," Bernard said.

Marty stared at Bernard's twiddling fingers, still tugging away at his scruff. "Okay then. You're in." Marty flashed him a smile, almost as if he'd planned on Bernard tagging along right from the start.

This also meant Nancy would go. Sheila couldn't help but worry about Marty's decision, sharing both Sandy's and Ike's concerns. Bernard would give the alien a direct connection, allowing them to know where Marty was, and God forbid anyone give up anything about the plan.

"Marty—" Sandy started.

He stopped her right there, holding up a hand. He smiled at her just then, and she seemed content enough with that. Marty turned his attention to the doctor.

"Don't look at me," the doctor said. "I think you're all crazy. I'm not leaving this place."

With that, Marty laughed. But Sheila saw something then, Marty's eyes looking beyond the doctor. She saw a map on the wall where he looked, a few photos pinned around it. One of those pictures was of a small farm. Marty stared at the photo dreamily.

Sheila went to him and took his hand in both of hers, pulling him close. He looked into her eyes, and for a brief second she could see his sadness. Then, with the others watching, she leaned in closer.

"Thank you," he whispered.

It almost felt like electricity passing through his hand, through her fingertips, surging into her veins. And though she'd been cold, she felt warm now. Her heart pounded in her chest, forcing a quick breath from her lips. She peered deeply into his eyes and stood on her tippy-toes, leaning in to kiss his neck.

"You're very much welcome," she whispered back.

Chapter 46

The explosion was louder than Ike expected. The flash of light temporarily blinded him, unable to see the cause, though he thought he knew.

"Sandy, no!" Marty said.

Ike tried to find her through the bright spot engraved across his vision. Someone, a female by smell, pushed her way around him. He heard someone struggling, several strikes with a staff, and someone fell into the water with a splash. Ike tried to find the wall, tripped over something big, unable to identify it.

"Marty, come back," Sheila said.

Someone else ran by Ike. He heard a door slam, chairs and such being thrown to brace it shut. It had to be the good doctor. That idiot was a weakling, but Ike sort of envied him, wishing he, too, had sought the safety of that back room given his inability to see anything.

"Marty, get that side," Sandy said.

Ike could almost make out her silhouette. She had nice curves for an army chick.

"I got it, I got it," Bernard said.

More blasts came from the staffs, and something thumped to the floor. This time the water wet Ike's shins. He tripped over whatever was on the floor, stumbled away, and bumped into the wall.

A gunshot near deafened him. It didn't sound like it had hit its target.

Ike felt along the wall and found something leaning against it. When he picked it up and let his hands explore the item, he realized this was the axe.

"Ike," Marty said. "Do it! Do it now!"

Ike turned to them, seeing only hazy silhouettes. There were too many, and while some might have been larger than others, they were all too close to each other. He couldn't make out who was who. Then, someone gurgled, sounding like they were being choked.

"Now, Ike!" Marty said.

Ike swung the axe back over his shoulder and hesitated, trying to bring clarity to what he was seeing.

"Damn it, Ike. Swing," Bernard said, sounding panicked.

He didn't hear Sandy, though. That meant she was likely the one being choked out.

Ike squinted, blinked, and shook his head. The images improved only slightly. He traced the outlines in his mind, trying to fit the pieces of the puzzle. Only he couldn't make enough sense out of what he was seeing, so he chose the target in the middle on a hunch.

He lifted the head of the axe, easing it back. Tightening his grip on the handle, he brought his weight around, his target still blurred. The axe went forward with ease. It was a clean swing, its weight carrying the axe on a true path. Right before it struck, Ike's eyes cleared enough for him to see their faces. His target, her flesh almost purple now, looked at him with wide eyes, her mouth hanging open, trying to suck in air.

Ike saw the creature, too, and pushed the axe out, trying to keep from hitting Sandy. Still, the axe grazed her shoulder but didn't do much damage. The creature dropped her when the axe sank into its chest, then it staggered back, pulling the axe out of Ike's hand.

Sandy dropped to the ground coughing, holding her throat. If she could have said anything right then, Ike was sure she would have a few words for him.

"What the hell are you doing, Ike?" Bernard asked.

Ike couldn't respond, still somewhat dazed by it all, how close he'd come to killing her. And she just sat there staring up at him, her color coming back. But as Ike's eyes finally cleared, he saw her grin, and was thankful she wasn't mad.

Bernard moved to the creature and pulled the axe free of its chest.

Ike went to help Sandy but tripped over something. One creature lay on the floor, its head severed from its body. Ike kneeled beside Sandy, checked her throat, but found nothing a little time wouldn't heal.

The sound of a staff alerted him to some action from behind. Marty thrust one of the electroshock staffs at a creature again. This time it struck the creature's neck, forcing it to its knees. Bernard moved in fast, swinging the axe hard enough to slice the head right off. It rolled to Ike's feet, and he stared into its ominous eye.

Bernard rested on the axe, heaving, trying to catch his breath.

"Any more?" Marty said, struggling against his shortness of breath.

Sandy shook her head, winded. "No. I don't think so."

"Well then," Marty said, taking a knee. "I suggest we get out of here just in case."

Sandy nodded.

Nancy ran to Bernard, took the axe and slid it toward the others. Bernard smiled. Seeing this made Ike feel like puking. Then he felt a soft kiss on his cheek, saw Sandy, and his cheeks flushed.

Chapter 47

Though all remained silent on the way to the hive, Sandy knew they were thinking the same thing; this could be the end. It relieved her some that they were doing this. Either way, it meant she'd served her country to the best of her ability. That she would complete her mission, whether they succeeded or failed.

But she also felt sorry for these people, which was an unexpected emotion. Most of all, she felt bad for Marty. While she suspected that if caught, most of them would become the fuel the doctor spoke of, she believed Marty would undergo the transformation. She knew just how awful that process would be, the memories, the madness, all of it. She thought it a fate worse than death.

Having heard Marty's story while standing guard outside the barn, every detail reminded her of her fellow soldiers, how each of them had fallen to this transformation. How the man she loved had become something unrecognizable. Sandy knew well how this must have been wreaking havoc on Marty's thoughts.

She also knew of the temptation. It would be so easy to surrender to it all, to rejoin with his brother. And though she believed giving up would be a difficult pill to swallow for Marty, she could understand if he ended up doing just that. She'd been there herself at one point. But seeing what Cooley had become, how much of his humanity he'd lost, that helped maintain her sanity. She hoped, for Marty's sake, it would do the same for him.

But she also noticed the starry look in his eyes, back in the bunker, when he was looking at that picture on the wall. How he seemed to get lost within it. Who wouldn't want their old life back? Even if it were only a small slice of that past. Even if he ended up being strong enough to fight off his brother's will, she didn't hold much hope for herself or the others. They had so few weapons among them, and the creatures would outnumber them.

Marty was holding Sheila's hand. They made a cute couple, although she'd never reveal that fact. She no longer gave in to such vices—couldn't bear it. Seeing them like this brought back memories of Greg Cooley. Although they'd only recently killed him, Cooley had passed long ago in her eyes.

He'd tried to kill her, and she would have let him if not for Ike driving the axe in Cooley's chest. Then she let Bernard cut off Cooley's head. She still felt guilty after all this time, for being the reason Cooley went first. She was lucky they hadn't slapped her with a dishonorable discharge. Even that would have been better than this, walking into this hive, which was likely a guaranteed death. At least she'd be with Cooley.

She cast her eyes up to the sky, trying to find the edges of the saucer. The cloud cover made that difficult. Still, it was a stark reminder of everything they'd done, how they'd cemented this fate for humanity. She wondered if the world would ever be the same again. She doubted it. Yet, much like the cockroaches, humanity always seemed to find a way.

Entering the hive with the ship hovering over it made her nervous. What did the aliens intend to do now? She couldn't imagine any scenario of them conquering Earth. They might have disabled Earth's war machines, but even with their strategies, they didn't seem capable of war. Their race seemed more a race of thinkers than anything else. Even then, they wouldn't have the numbers for such an assault if they attacked, especially if this was worldwide. Still, they came for a reason, and whatever that was, it dismayed her.

"You okay, Sandy?" Marty asked, looking over his shoulder.

"Yes. It's just—" She wasn't sure of how to describe what she was feeling.

"Good," Marty said, relieving her of any need to explain herself.

Marty stopped, eyeing her up. Something in his eyes

revealed his knowledge of what she was going through. The others kept walking, except for Sheila.

"Don't worry," Marty said. "Everything will work out."

Tears welled in Sandy's eyes, but she choked them back. Big girls don't cry, especially big girls on a mission. She bit her tongue, her cheek. The feeling swelled behind her eyes, worsening the longer she looked at him. She diverted her gaze elsewhere, to the ground, off in the distance, but she could feel his gaze penetrating her even then. He seemed to see right into her soul, the young woman she was under that impenetrable shell. He was beginning to crack her exterior.

Marty stepped closer, slung the bag over his shoulder and passed his electroshock staff to Sheila. Sandy carried the other bag and wouldn't part with it until she'd completed what Marty asked of her. This was her responsibility, and she would not fail him. He extended a hand to her.

After a moment, she took his extended hand, and that was when all those memories came flooding back. A few tears wet her cheeks as the three of them walked hand in hand. For the first time since this all started, Sandy felt relieved.

Chapter 48

Nancy had watched the man she loved die, and now he was back. As a result, she had her doubts whether him being dead or alive was real or not. It had felt real, and she'd seen that bitch pull the trigger, so it had to be real. Deep inside she resented Sandy because of it. But that death had also changed Bernard.

Before, he hadn't been able to show his love for Nancy. Now, back from the dead, he was affectionate. Did that make Nancy uncomfortable? Not one bit. In fact, it was all she ever wanted. Things weren't perfect, she guessed, considering their plan and that giant ship in the sky. But it was as close as she would get, it seemed.

"You okay, Sandy?" Marty asked.

She didn't know why he even cared after what she'd done to Bernard.

"Yes. It's just—"

Just what, bitch?

"Good." All three of them stopped. "Don't worry. Everything will work out."

Perhaps, Nancy had been wrong about Marty. She'd tried to peek inside Sandy's bag more than once but hadn't been able to tell what she had in there. They hadn't included Bernard and her in whatever plans they made the night before. They'd even closed the door. She resented them for that. At least they let her take care of Bernard.

Marty took Sandy's hand and right then, Nancy wanted to curse him up and down. Had he forgotten so quick what this woman was capable of? She squeezed Bernard's hand, looking at him to make sure he was really there. He didn't seem to notice, not even that she was squeezing tighter than she meant. His face looked empty, and that worried her.

She couldn't help but wonder if that alien had possessed Bernard again. He didn't seem himself, the way he kept looking up at the saucer, seemingly unafraid of it all. A hint of a smile formed at the corners of his mouth and seeing that made her shiver.

With that, he looked at her. He grinned, and she smiled back, such an odd thing to do given where they were heading.

It's him, she told herself, forcing those thoughts out. *So what if he's part alien?*

She continued staring at Bernard, searching for any clue whether it was him or the alien, either good or bad, but perceived nothing. As far as she could tell this was the man she loved, sprinkled with a hint of madness in his eyes.

Nancy looked at the hive. The thought of going inside revolted her. She knew only one truth; at some point, once they were inside, she'd exact her revenge on Sandy. This she felt in her heart, and she was sure Bernard knew it, too.

When that time came, they'd find out what was in that bag. Then Bernard could decide what to do with it.

Chapter 49

Ike had spent most of his life alone. Now, in what he thought would be his darkest hour, he found himself surrounded by company.

A quick glance to Sandy, and he saw her glaring gaze. He didn't think she hated him. He read her actions, and he thought it more a form of respect.

That's right, honey. I got your number.

And he believed himself correct, too. Until Marty took her hand, and she started to cry. Then he wasn't sure about anything.

She'd proven herself to be one tough cookie. Now, that reputation was tarnished. And he didn't enjoy feeling uncomfortable, so he diverted his gaze up to the ship. That was when he saw something he wasn't sure the others had. Mostly because he wasn't sure if his eyes were playing tricks on him or not, maybe there was a faint orange beam between the top of the hive and the ship and maybe there wasn't. He couldn't be sure yet, so he kept a watchful eye. Until he could be sure, he thought it best to keep this detail to himself. Then he saw something else.

At least one creature was up there, flapping its fucking wings high above them. It didn't look like it was planning to attack them, though. Instead, he thought it might check on their progress, which, if nothing else, meant those bastards knew they were coming.

Damn it, Bernard.

He expected the creature to fly back into the hive, but it flew to the ship. And now he saw at least two others up there.

What the fu—

He heard something. Maybe a slight giggle and maybe not.

Whatever the case, Bernard was smiling. Even if it was only slight, he saw it all the same.

Nancy appeared enamored by the big lug, too. He doubted she saw any of this. Did she even know this wasn't Bernard anymore? He didn't think so.

Ike wasn't about to get snowed over like that. He kept a close eye on Bernard and his lovesick girlfriend. That's how he noticed the way Nancy kept looking at the bag Sandy carried. Did that mean Bernard had gotten to her? He didn't know, but he didn't like it one bit.

He gripped his staff tighter, realizing his expression might give him away. He composed himself and decided then he had to be more careful.

A quick glance to Bernard's fingers gave everything away. His hand was at his side, inactive as the calmest seas.

Chapter 50

As far as it concerned Sheila, she thought they would die. Not all of them maybe. Likely not Marty, but he'd probably become one of them. For everything they'd been through in their short time together, if they ended up dead, she wanted to hurt this alien race. Despite her doubts, she hoped Marty succeeded even if she didn't.

She spent a lot of time studying him and thought she knew him better than the others. If nothing else, she'd gotten closer to him, and wished with all her heart they'd have time later to explore those feelings. He could be such a stoic figure, especially when he was considering his options. The way he tugged at his goatee was cute. But once he decided, that was it. There was no turning back. And that worried her.

From what she'd seen, Marty was a smart man. But was he smarter than his brother? His brother had an advantage given his outlandish abilities, but Marty was a keen thinker. He would have thought this through, every outcome, every possibility, and he'd have planned accordingly. It was there her faith in him faltered, though.

How could he trick a monster that could read minds? How could he keep that monster from uncovering his plan when Bernard was but a window to this alien, allowing it to spy upon them? And even worse, Marty had said he wanted the creature to know he was coming. Was he insane?

She didn't think so. There was hardly any sweat in his palm. He wasn't nervously twitching. Nor did he squeeze her hand any harder than he had to. Without a hint of fear, did that give him the upper hand? She didn't know.

Had he merely accepted the fact he would die? Or did he

have this confidence because he knew his plan was flawless? Sheila prayed it was the latter.

As far as she knew, Marty had lost plenty. He'd told her he couldn't stand losing anyone else—not now, not ever again. She wondered what that meant.

Then, looking at him, she realized something about him she hadn't felt before. She was falling for him big time. And she wanted to be with him, right now and afterward. But how could she tell him?

He looked at her then, and she almost melted. His smile warmed her heart. She gave his hand a little squeeze, and he winked at her. And that was when she knew he'd do anything to make this plan work, no matter the cost.

Chapter 51

"Tell me what you know, Bernard?" Marty said, suddenly, as they neared the hive which confused the Infinite.

He wasn't sure how to respond.

"You said you know things." Marty was looking at him. Well, looking at Bernard. And he kept looking at his hands.

The Infinite looked through his eyes, staring at Bernard's hands. Everything appeared in order. He tried to remember saying this but couldn't place it.

"Come on," Ike said. "What do you know, fucko?"

When he looked at Nancy, he saw her glaring at Ike. But he didn't think she'd be able to save him from this. He had to say something. But what did Bernard know?

The Infinite stopped, not realizing he'd done so. He searched his thoughts, trying to recall every single thing he'd said to any of them. No, he definitely did not say that. This was a trick. They were hoping to get him to say the wrong thing. So maybe he was better off saying nothing. Maybe he could fake fainting again.

Besides, all he cared about was his plan. He would lead Marty right into his chamber. There, his brother would join him. The rest were expendable. Maybe he'd keep one as a pet, perhaps Marty's girlfriend. He'd seen them holding hands, and Marty seemed to acknowledge Bernard was looking at this now. But there was something about the way Marty looked back at him that made him feel uneasy.

There was no real reason to worry. His strategy was sound. He'd considered the memories of those childhood games, how Marty had been so weak. They always ended the same way. Because of that, he couldn't figure out why he believed an existence without Marty wouldn't be fruitful. It would. But in some odd way, a small part of the Infinite needed Marty. He couldn't say why.

For now, playing things safe was for the best. He let the real Bernard back in, pushing himself away, pushing himself out. As he did, for the briefest of seconds he sensed Bernard's confused state. Then all of it vanished.

Chapter 52

"Well, answer the man, you dolt," Ike said.

Bernard saw the way they all looked at him. "Huh?"

"Marty asked you a question, Bernard honey," Nancy said, stroking the hair on his arm.

With that, he felt reality creeping back in. "I...I—"

"It's okay, Bernard," Marty said. "I know."

"What?" Bernard asked.

"Never mind. We have little time." Marty was grinning. "I need to know everything you can tell me about this hive before we go in. And fast."

"Anything you want Marty, you know that."

Nancy stopped rubbing his arm, as if suddenly aware he hadn't been himself. Regretful, shame washed over him. When she saw this, she returned her hand to his arm.

Marty patted Bernard on the shoulder. "I know, my friend. I know. Tell me fast, though. And if you feel him coming back, let me know right away."

"Sure," he said, looking around, feeling queasy.

"Nancy," Marty said. She acknowledged him. "When that happens, no matter what you do, don't stop rubbing Bernard's arm. Can you do that?"

She nodded, her unease of this clear in her eyes.

Bernard told them about the corridors, how they changed, and what they looked like. He told them about the room he'd found and how the Infinite had brought him to the main chamber by changing the walls. The pods took the most time to explain. He explained what the leader looked like. Before he finished, though, the numbing sensation returned to him. He alerted Marty.

They continued walking. Bernard felt the wooziness, like he might pass out. And then he felt nothing.

Chapter 53

Directly outside the entrance to the hive, Marty gathered himself, preparing to go in. He knew what he believed would happen, that he would end up separated from the group. This knowledge gave him only a slight advantage, if any.

He didn't ask Sheila for the staff back. Ike had one, and Sandy had the other. Nancy had Sandy's gun, which no one loaded. Marty had instructed her to remove the bullets before handing it over. He'd known she wouldn't check, given Bernard had come back. They had equipped Bernard with Sandy's knife, and that seemed to appease them both, knowing everyone had a weapon. They questioned none of it.

Marty removed the axe from his bag and handed the bag to Ike. "Take care of this, please."

Ike nodded.

Bernard's eyes were on the axe. And Marty knew it wasn't Bernard in there. He did not know where the real Bernard went, only that he went somewhere else. His brother was spying on them, trying to decipher Marty's actions. For certain, the creature had full access Jake's memories, but he didn't think the creature had thought to access Bernard's most recent memories. And with Marty entering the hive, why would he? The creature was getting what it wanted, and that was why it was so important to wait for the very last second before they entered. Marty had to know what they were in for, but he wanted the creature to have as little opportunity to discover this as possible.

The creature seemed enamored by the axe. He studied Bernard, watching how his eyes shifted to the bag Ike now carried. In those eyes, Marty saw a curiosity that needed satisfaction. It desired answers, to reveal the secret of what was inside the bag Marty had carried. That was what Marty hoped for above all else.

Bernard's eyes danced on the fabric of the bag, tracing every stitch, as if trying to see inside the bag. Marty had instructed everyone to talk as little as possible if it got to this point. That had gone well. He couldn't be sure about the other instruction, though, asking them to think only of memories from their distant past and nothing of the present when around Bernard. Whatever the case, it went as planned so far.

He hadn't expected Sandy's brief outburst. Whatever she'd been thinking of had been too haunting. Those had been real tears brought on by some ghost.

Letting go of Sheila's hand, he separated himself from the group by twenty feet. The rest of the group stayed together, including Bernard, his eyes still fixated on Ike's bag.

"Are we ready?" Marty said.

One by one they nodded. Even Bernard, a hint of a smile formed on his lips. As a group, they turned and entered the hive.

An unusual orange glow illuminated the corridor. Coffin-like pods lined the walls, humans struggling within the confined spaces. They reminded him of back when the mosquito bit Jake, their bodies jolting as if an electrical charge was passing through them to the next. Then, as expected, the walls started to move, each cell moving like the pieces of a slide puzzle.

Sheila was the first cut off from the group. She'd been standing in the entry corridor by herself when the door closed, and the wall quickly sectioned her off. "Marty!" she yelled, seconds before he could no longer see her. Her being alone concerned him, but he supposed it was best to keep her separated from the others anyway, for fear she might get hurt.

Another wall began to shift, sectioning off Bernard and Ike. Last Marty saw of them, Bernard was still staring at that bag.

The walls sectioned off Sandy and Nancy next. Anger appeared on Nancy's face, and then they were gone.

Alone in a bright corridor with a sickening glow lighting his way, Marty moved along, taking his time, and letting the walls lead him where they would. Sorrow filled him for each lost soul he passed. He wished he could free them but couldn't risk losing sight of his endgame.

Gripping the axe tight, he pawed at his chest, hoping what Sandy and the doctor made for him would be effective. He also hoped he would survive.

As if hearing his thoughts, the wall to his left shifted. And Marty found himself eye to eye with the last person he wanted to see.

"Marty," Sheila said. She ran forward and embraced him. The game had changed.

Chapter 54

Ike led the way, but he knew it would be Bernard directing each of them to where he wanted them to end up. Marty had assured them of this, and Ike had no way of knowing where that was, so he needed to keep on his toes. If nothing else, that damn creature had taken the bait: hook, line, and fucking sinker. Better yet, the big lug hadn't taken his eyes off the prize. Whatever was behind Bernard's eyes, it was staring at that bag like a drunk would a liquor store.

They came to an intersection, and Bernard pushed Ike to the left. When Bernard tried to see in the bag, Ike moved it out in front of him, holding it tight against his chest. He wrapped both arms around the bag, holding it like a football. When he did, a frown appeared on Bernard's face. He could tell it annoyed him at this point.

"What's in the bag?" Bernard asked.

"Nunya."

Bernard seemed perplexed by this answer, as if he didn't get the reference.

Ike chuckled. "Nunya goddamn business, fucko." He let a shit-eating grin spread across his face, hoping it would achieve the reaction he wanted.

Now he saw frustration.

"Just tell me, Ike." Bernard said, both hands on Ike's back.

Ike didn't. He kept walking faster, a hurried Bernard nudging him one way or the other, leading him somewhere.

"Listen, Bernard," Ike said. "Marty told me not to tell anyone. Does that sound like he wanted you to know what was in the fucking bag?"

He fully believed this would stir things up. The emotions

were pouring out of Bernard, the roundabout answers only intensifying his obvious anger.

Bernard shoved Ike. Not a gentle push, either.

Ike stumbled into a wall. The wall of pods stretched. A horrified face stared up at him and screamed an unheard shriek. He saw others, too, each human form wakening to acknowledge him, all of them screaming.

"Geez, dickhead," Ike said. "I know you're in a real fucking hurry, but you didn't have to—"

"Shut up!" Bernard said.

He grabbed the back of Ike's collar, and Ike lost his grip on the staff. That hadn't been part of the plan. Bernard dragged Ike down a short corridor, waited for the wall to shift, and pulled him into a large room. As they entered, the path they left closed off. Now they were alone, and it wasn't nearly as bad as Ike expected.

Perfect.

"Show me what's in the bag," Bernard said. He shoved Ike across the room and thrust a finger at the bag Ike clutched against his chest.

"Fuck you, nut sack."

"Show me or I swear—" Bernard drew the knife from his belt.

"You fucking pansy. Bring it!"

Knife or not, Ike wasn't about to give in. He'd taken plenty of beatings before. He'd take one again if he had to. But he'd not go down without a fight. Not only did Bernard have a weapon, but he outweighed Ike by at least hundred pounds, and most of that was pure muscle. He was about a foot taller, too. Ike had to get rid of that knife or he wouldn't stand a chance. But, in Ike's favor, he didn't think the creature had the same killer instinct Bernard had from his days as a grunt.

At least he wasn't in Marty's shoes. He didn't envy that guy one bit.

"Fuck me?" Bernard moved in on Ike, holding the knife weakly. "Fuck me? Is that what you want, Ike?"

He did not know what this creature meant by any of that, but when Bernard tossed the knife aside and raised his fists,

Ike felt like laughing. And when a grin pressed upon Ike's face, Bernard's outrage intensified.

Bernard's lips snarled. A line of spit dribbled out of the corner of his mouth. He ran forward and brought his fists down on Ike's shoulders, but Ike still refused to surrender the bag.

Forced down to his knees, Ike tried to get back to his feet. "That's right, moron. Did I stutter? You can go fuck yourself."

With Ike still on his knees, Bernard brought a knee up into his mid-section. It drove all the air out, and it was all he could do to keep hold of the bag at that point. With him out of air, gasping to refill his lungs, Bernard shook him back and forth. Finally, the bag came loose with Ike flinging it across the room at last second. It landed near the wall.

Bernard shoved Ike to the ground and kicked him in the stomach. While Ike wheezed, rolling on the floor, Bernard made a break for the bag.

Before he got there, Ike jumped for him. He grabbed Bernard's shoe and pulled him back with all he had left. Bernard stumbled, tried to turn, and tripped. He fell just short of the bag, and Ike climbed up his back and tried to pin the big guy there.

Bernard glanced back, Ike saw the smile and despite the burning sensation in his lungs, said, "Fuck you and your goddamned hive."

The elbow came so fast Ike couldn't dodge it. It struck Ike squarely in the nose with a crack, knocking his head back. Blood gushed as a bolt of pain shot across Ike's mouth as the elbow came again. Now Ike could barely see thanks to the pain ringing in his skull.

Bernard army crawled over to the bag, pulling himself on top of it. Frantically trying to open it, he couldn't manage the zipper. Finding the knife close by, Bernard stabbed the bag and tore it open and lifted himself to see inside.

Though it hurt like hell to do so, Ike laughed so hard, he fell flat on the ground. Swimming in pain, his world spun out of control as Bernard got to his feet. Before Bernard could get to him, Ike passed out.

Chapter 55

Nancy didn't waste any time. As soon as they were out of sight, she rushed Sandy with the butt of the gun. Both the bag and staff Sandy carried dropped.

Sandy was shorter and thinner than her, but in much better shape. Nancy thought she might be stronger. She had her on street smarts. That's what came of having three brothers that taught her how to fight dirty. Plus, she still had this gun.

"Nancy—" Sandy pleaded.

But Nancy wasn't listening. She grabbed Sandy's hair and yanked a clump right out, strands of the dirty blonde hair clenched in her fist. She went back for more.

Sandy held up both hands. "You don't understand."

"That's right," Nancy said. "I don't. I don't understand why you had to kill Bernard."

"I didn't mean to."

Nancy ripped another clump of Sandy's hair out. This was satisfying. If she kept this pace up, the bitch would be bald in minutes.

Sandy kicked back, twisting her body loose of Nancy. It sent Nancy stumbling to one side. Sandy kicked up to her feet fast, too much so for Nancy. Before Nancy could do the same, Sandy had her knees in Nancy's chest, driving the air out.

Nancy lifted the gun, aiming it at Sandy's head. She wasn't sure if she had the strength to kill. The trigger was a sin begging to happen. Her finger teased it, and then, before Sandy could say anything else, Nancy pulled the trigger.

She heard a click and nothing more.

Sandy grabbed her hand and twisted the gun away. "Listen. Please. We have to do something for Marty."

Nancy felt like crying. She'd failed. Then she saw the large figure looming in the background. And Sandy saw this, too, relieved the pressure and tried to spin out of the way.

The creature threw Sandy. She collapsed in the corner like a sack of beans, sucking in air. But it was close to the staff. Sandy reached for it, her fingers missing it a couple times. When she found it, she swung it around in a dizzying pattern. The weapon struck the creature, but only knocked it back.

Sandy shot a glance to Nancy. "Take the bag."

Nancy remained where she was.

"Nancy, if you ever want to see Bernard again, if there's any hope at all, take the fucking bag!" She ran at the creature, forcing it against the wall. "Go! You'll know what to do."

Nancy got to her feet and ran to the bag. Sliding on her knees, she reached the bag and looked inside. Now she knew why they'd come.

She picked up the bag, looked at Sandy one last time. A confused array of emotions overwhelmed her.

"Go," Sandy said.

Nancy ran. Behind her, she saw a flash of light. The terrible growl revealed the fact Sandy might have hurt the creature. Nancy headed down the corridor. When she came to an intersection, she heard a voice deep in her mind previously hidden from them. This was someone who'd learned how to control this ability, trained to do so right from the start. It was Sandy. And she told her to go right.

Chapter 56

Marty pulled her behind him.

"Where are we going?" she asked.

"I'm not sure."

He wasn't, either. The walls were shifting so fast. They moved left and the wall behind them closed off. Forced to take a right, they lunged forward just in time, as the wall behind them shifted. Faster and faster the turns came, some up, some down, others left and right, until it stopped all at once. Marty was almost dizzy from it. Even then, he fully recognized the creature in front of them.

It looked different now. It still had that puckered skin on the one side of the torso and the blistered eye with the black sludge-like tears of blood surrounding it. This was Jake, but not the Jake Marty had grown up with. Jake had taken on yet another form, by far the worst incarnation of all.

The creature's head was larger now, swollen and fat. The frown above the one eye drooled endlessly, as if hungry. This newest form still had arms, six of them now, but the legs were missing, having formed into something terrifying. Jutting out from behind the monster was a long, intestine looking body at least four feet wide. It glowed with a yellowish-orange hue, the ribbed body pulsing off and on, almost mesmerizing to watch. This extension of Jake's new body was part of the wall behind it.

He could feel the creature searching his thoughts and feelings, pushing its way in deeper. Marty tried to keep him out, but he was persistent, and far stronger than he'd expected. Marty kept his thoughts only on those early days, back when Jake and he used to play war.

The creature's strange body writhed against itself like a

snake. The glow brightened, intensified, and then, with a sick sucking sound, something exited the end. Marty identified it right away—a cocoon. Dozens of them lined the walls of the hive. Beyond them, where the walls glowed the brightest, was what Marty believed to be the core of the hive. Jake was using the captured humans as a power source to mass-produce Earth-born aliens.

Sheila's hand tightened on his. He turned to look at her. But she was staring at Jake. By the time he looked, it was too late. A large, pale, scorpion-like tail rose into the sky, the tip dripping with some greenish fluid. It came down so fast, far too fast for Marty to do anything. It struck Sheila in the chest, and she collapsed, screaming in pain.

Marty kneeled beside her, letting go of the axe. "Why?" Marty screamed at the creature. "Why, Jake?"

The voice came in his head. It was calm and subtle. *Because I need you, brother.*

"Haven't I lost enough?"

You don't have to lose her. She can be with us.

"Sheila," Marty said, holding her hand.

He undid her shirt and examined the wound. Something squirmed there, trying to get out. Her body trembled, and her arms and legs shot out straight as some unknown energy passed through them. He knew what was happening all too well. He was losing her.

"No!" Marty said. "You aren't my brother! We won't go with you!"

The creature's frustration flashed in Marty's mind. He'd angered the creature. It raised its tail into the air, taunting Marty.

"Go ahead, damn it!" Marty picked up the axe. "You'll never be my brother again. You're dead to me, Jakey. Do you hear me?"

Again, flashes came to his thoughts, flooded with color this time: reds, oranges, yellows, blues, greens. Marty grabbed the axe and rose. The creature growled, and the tail came down, missing Marty by inches.

Marty swung around, bringing the axe around hard as he could, and severed the tip from the tail. Green fluid splattered the orange-colored walls. More colors, popped into Marty's thoughts, and the feeling of pain, each color bringing with it a different agony.

The tail darted back and forth behind the creature and Marty.

"You are dead to me, Jakey. Dead!"

Then, out of nowhere, Marty heard another voice, one he hadn't expected. It sounded familiar although he had some difficulty placing it.

Her voice said only one thing. "Now!"

Marty produced the device from his jacket pocket and pulled the pin. He lobbed it at Jake and retrieved the axe.

Chapter 57

Nancy stopped, unloaded the device, and sat beside it. A key stuck out of the side. They had fastened several vials of liquid to the outside, making the device menacing looking. She was unsure what it was or what it would do, but the device looked like a bomb similar to those Sandy collected back in the shelter. Only this one was different, larger, modified.

She waited, for what she didn't know. All she knew was she needed to set this bomb off. And, after doing so, she would need to find cover.

Nancy looked around, seeing very few places she could hide. Although unsure of where to go after she set off the bomb, suddenly she knew what to do when a single word popped into her thoughts.

"Now!" Sandy said.

Nancy turned the key and ran down the corridor. She ran as fast as she could, as far away from the bomb as she could get. By the time it exploded, she had gotten just out of reach. But she didn't stop there. She needed to find an exit.

Chapter 58

Bernard tore the bag open with the knife. Through his eyes, the Infinite saw what lay inside of the bag. A toolbox.

He studied it for a moment, trying to decipher its purpose in this. He used Bernard's hands to open the box, careful not to trip any explosives, which he expected to find rigged inside. But upon opening the toolbox, he saw a hammer, a drill, several screwdrivers, a few boxes of nails, and nothing else.

Before he could scream in frustration, the Infinite heard another voice, albeit it a faint one. This voice was unfamiliar to him, and to his network. He searched it out, unable to zero in on the source. Somehow this voice pushed a thought through the Infinite's network, and he could do nothing to stop it.

The faint cry said only one thing, "Now!"

And the Infinite felt himself forced out of Bernard's consciousness, stunned and unable to process what had happened.

Chapter 59

"Bernard, wake up, big guy," Ike said.

Bernard shook his head. "Ike? What's going on?"

The explosion had freed Bernard. Ike felt like he'd been right in the blast zone. He helped Bernard to his feet.

Bernard looked as though he might fall, so Ike helped steady him. "You're all right, buddy."

"Where are we?"

"Later, Bernie, old pal. Right now, we have to get the fuck out of Dodge. Got me?"

Bernard nodded.

Using each other for support, they ran, searching for a way out.

Chapter 60

The flash of light would have blinded Marty if not for his hand shielding his face. Something popped, leaving Marty's ears numb, unable to hear well. For a moment, time stood still as Marty combatted the odd sensation. A wave of electricity rolled over the creature, enveloping the Jake monster and intensifying.

Getting some sense of himself back, Marty raised the axe and didn't think twice about it. He brought it around and sank it into the creature's neck. It struck deep, more than halfway through, sending the creature into a fit of convulsions. Marty wanted that axe back so he could strike again. He needed to make sure he succeeded.

When the corridor behind him opened, though, it offered an unexpected opportunity. He saw Sheila lying there, unable to move, dying. He couldn't lose her, too.

Running to Sheila, Marty bent over and picked her up. She went limp in his arms as he carried her out into the darkening corridor of the hive, the orange glow flickering. The paths shifted and Marty found he had to hurdle a wall here and jump through a closing passage there, leaping over the next without hesitation. There was no pattern, the randomness of it all making it difficult to find any escape.

He ducked left, darted down the corridor, then dashed right. When he felt out of breath, he ran harder, doing his best to protect Sheila. She'd become almost weightless in his arms, both appendages almost feeling like leather straps holding her to his body. Then he found the thing he'd been searching for, an empty pod. Beside it sat an unattended cart, floating there with a large barrel of orange goop, just like Bernard had described.

Marty placed Sheila in the pod and used his hand to seal

the side. Before he could finish, she said something. He moved closer, trying to hear her words.

"I love you," she said, her voice so weak now.

"Me, too. Now hush. Let's get you fixed up."

He did not know if he was doing this right, but he followed Bernard's vague description best he could. Once he had it sealed off, a fluid filled the tank, running over her body and plunging into her lungs. She convulsed, her body surging with energy. Marty felt helpless to it all, destined to watch her endure this struggle.

The pod flickered. Would it be enough? With the network disabled, could the pod even heal her? He didn't know, but he remained determined to see this through.

An instant later, she grew still, her wide eyes staring out at him. He felt his heart melt right then, and leaned against the wall, certain she'd stopped breathing. While the wound on her chest seemed to heal over, her lungs weren't filling. He saw no movement. And when he was certain he'd done all he could, he waited longer, hoping she would breathe. She didn't, and the wall he'd created to seal her in began to crumble apart.

Orange liquid spilled onto the floor, surrounding him in a thick pool. He couldn't stand seeing her like this and started tearing sections of the wall away. The coat of slime still covered her when he picked her up and started on his way. He paused only when she went into a fit of coughing, hacking up whatever fluid was still in her lungs. Once she finished, he started running again, intent on freeing them both.

The wall to his right faltered, and daylight filled his eyes with brightness. He ran toward it. As he closed in on the exit, he saw his friends: Bernard, Ike, and Nancy. But not all of them.

Where's Sandy?

He didn't see her.

A mere five feet from freedom, the exit to the outside world closed off to them as a wall rose out of nowhere, perhaps his dying brother's last-ditch effort to keep him from leaving.

The hive started tearing itself apart, a searing cut as if someone had taken a giant blowtorch to it. Most of the hive started sliding, a gap forming at the side no larger than a foot. Marty believed the hive would soon collapse on them, but it didn't. It rose, suspended in the sky, the gap growing. More significant, though, the tear seemed to further interrupt the network.

An explosion behind them blasted a huge section of the hive to pieces. Whatever people had been in those pods were surely dead. Others far enough away from the explosion found themselves freed, naked and struggling to regain some sense of control as they floundered about on the floor, writhing over one another.

Sheila looked stronger now, and Marty helped her down to her feet. Hand in hand, they hobbled for the large opening in the hive's side, the sun feeling almost too bright to Marty. He dodged flying mucus, chunks of hard plastic-like debris, and human viscera. Upon reaching the opening, Marty lifted Sheila again and carried her through.

On the outside, he set her down and led her away from the hive as fast as he could. She stumbled along behind him, looking over her shoulder as if still connected to the hive despite it falling to pieces. Around them, others gathered—not their group, but survivors all the same. Marty didn't know their stories, but the aliens had held these unclothed people captive inside the hive.

After several minutes of searching, they once more found Ike, Bernard, and Nancy in the field some hundred yards away. Sadly, Sandy still wasn't there.

They looked back together, watching as the small portion of the hive left on the ground burned. Above it, though, a larger section rose, supported by a red glow. A portion of the hive remained connected by some tissue, pods that were likely still filled with humans. A beam of light shot out from the bottom bubble of ship to the core of the hive, severing the larger half from its Earthly bind. With that, the bottom half burst into fiery red flames.

They heard screams, and more than anything Marty wanted to help. But perhaps sensing Marty's lack of strength, Ike offered to go instead.

"Who knows," Ike said. "Maybe I'll find someone I like." And with that, he left.

Bernard looked at Nancy, and she back at him. He looked so much better now, and Marty was thankful for that. He walked over and gave the big man a pat on the back.

Bernard only shook his head.

For a moment, Marty wasn't sure how to interpret that. Then he realized, Bernard remained plugged in. And though he was some sense of his old self, the growing detachment likely left him with that same ravenous longing of an addict. He just kept staring at the hive, even as the bottom of the ship began to open.

Another realization dawned on Marty. "Is it my brother?"

"I'm sorry," Bernard replied.

"What?" Nancy asked

Marty couldn't respond.

Neither did Sheila who was also staring up at the ship as if it were calling to her. "I...I—"

Marty hushed her. She still wobbled weakly but looking up at that ship gave her some inner strength. And that worried Marty. He knew then he'd need to monitor her, to make sure the slightest hint of what his brother had gone through never happened to her. If it ever did, he'd end matters quickly—never let it get this far again. But most of all, he wanted to stay with her because he had feelings for her.

After some time, Bernard also went to help the survivors, as did many others. Nancy helped care for those who'd already escaped, along with Marty. Mostly, though, Marty couldn't stop looking over at Sheila. She hadn't stopped looking up at that ship, even once they had fully loaded the hive and the doors closed for good.

He wondered if Sandy had made it. He prayed she had.

For a moment, everyone seemed to stop what they were doing, many looking up at the ship as if expecting something more. But nothing else came. Then, as suddenly as it appeared, the ship vanished into the crisp blue sky.

To be continued in:

GRAVE REVELATIONS

Book Two of the Infinite Cycle

Eggs in the Attic

Something woke Alberta Jones, and she rolled over to look at her clock. Anson and she were long retired, so she didn't need the clock anymore, but she kept it there for the sake of aesthetics. Looking at it now, seeing it was just after four in the morning, she wished she hadn't kept it. They typically relied on the rooster to wake them, but having seen those glowing blue numbers, she couldn't ignore them. She sat up in bed, then heard...

Bam bam bam!

She rolled over to her husband. "Hey." She shook his arm. "Wake up, Anson."

"Okay, okay." He sat up on his elbows. "I'm up already." He looked around, focusing on the window, how dark it was outside. "What time is it?"

"It's early, but never mind that. I heard something."

"Heard what?"

Bang bam!

"There! Did you hear that?" she whispered.

"Well, yeah. Sure did."

"What do you think that is?"

"I don't have the slightest—"

Anson scratched his balls. He had been complaining a lot lately about how they always stuck to his leg, so the image of him peeling them off his skin popped into her thoughts. Despite her trepidation and worry over the noises, she couldn't help but grin.

"Something funny?" he asked.

"No. It's nothing." She elbowed him in the ribs. "Aren't you gonna go check out the house?"

"Dear, it's probably just a squirrel or a racoon. Something that's gotten into the attic. I'll call an exterminator after I get up...later."

"Get *up*. I'd rather you check it out now."

Wham! Bang bang.

"See," she said. "There it is again. Please, Anson, won't you check it out for me?"

She batted her eyelashes, which used to work on him when she was both younger and more attractive. Now, it warranted a sigh, but at least it got him out of bed.

"All right. All right. I'll go."

She watched him grab a flashlight out of his end table drawer and leave the room before getting out of bed herself. Before she followed, she grabbed her robe and slid it on. It was cold this time of year in the mornings, though it warmed up fast. Now, given the situation, it felt twice as cold as usual. Anson was right, too. She could tell the noises were coming from the attic, and like him, she was certain it was nothing. But, in her experience, it was better to be safe than sorry. Besides, if there was some rodent up there making all that noise, she wouldn't sleep, anyway. And if she couldn't sleep, she wasn't about to let him rest without her. Not while she was up and about, seeing to chores.

Anson struggled to find the rope in the dark. Alberta considered flicking on the light but decided not to, as it would likely startle anything in the attic. That might cause more trouble. Finding the rope, he pulled. A chorus of creaks and pops preceded the lowering of the ladder, accompanied by a cloud of dust that made Anson wave his hands back and forth. Even then, she could see he was about to sneeze.

"Choooooo!" his eyes looked puffy in the glow of moonlight that stole in through the window at the end of the hallway.

Well, if anything was up to no good in the attic, if it didn't skedaddle when it heard the ladder come down, Anson's sneeze surely scared the living daylights out of it.

"Yuck," she said.

"Must be decades of dust up there. Heck, think the last time I set foot up there Nixon was still in office."

"Yeah, well—"

Boom! Bang bang!

"What the hell was that?" she said, moving back a little. Even from this far away, she could feel a cool draft. Worse yet, she could see a swirl of dust moving about up there, appearing almost ghost-like the way it moved. The dust ebbed down through the opening, though it quickly dispersed before reaching the ground.

Anson pinched his nostrils and braved the first step of the ladder.

"Honey, be care—"

"I know. I know." He waved a dismissive hand at her. "I've heard it a million tim—"

Alberta couldn't believe her eyes. It was almost like magic. One moment Anson was there and the next, he wasn't. It was like he had vanished, only he hadn't. What she had seen was slightly different, a hand, large and muscular, reached down and yanked Anson up into the attic so quick, it only looked as though he had vanished.

"No! Stop!" he screamed.

Wham! Boom boom bang! Slam!

"Ahhhh!" She heard clawing at the wooden floorboards. "Help! Help me! Jesus, Alb!"

She wanted to call out to him, to let him know she would go get help, but she couldn't. In fact, she couldn't do anything, too stunned by what she had just seen, terrified out of her wits. It was a wonder she was still standing, as faint as she now felt. The sensation overwhelmed her, making her woozy. Worse yet, whatever had taken Anson was now beating the living shit out of him up there. She knew that, yet did nothing but stand there, shivering, staring up into that opening, seeing the occasional shadow and something...else.

"Help!"

Thump thump bam!

"Ow ow, fuck fuck fuck!"

And then she heard something most disturbing, the sound of human flesh being torn, followed by a spray of blood.

"Raaaarrrrr!" the creature said.

But her husband said nothing. Evidently, whatever had happened was too much for him, so he had either passed out or—

She stared at the opening, praying to Jesus, to God, to anyone who would listen. *No! Please don't let it be true.*

Thump!

The first thing she saw was his ring. That was how she knew it was her Anson. Something had torn his arm off and flung down into the hallway. She didn't know what to do, who to call, where to run. So many things were running through her head, she couldn't make sense of it all. A small pool of blood began to form under the severed limb. And then something came into view through that opening, briefly, just a glimpse of what it was, and all she could think was it must be some kind of monster.

Dear Lord, what is that thing?

Unable to break her gaze, she couldn't see much. She felt guilty about not getting help in time, but truth told, even if it had been her up there, she doubted Anson could have done better. They were simple folk with basic needs, and they had each other, which was more than enough for either of them. Simple people didn't go around being brave. They had to work up to it. Judging by what little she had seen so far, she had not wanted to draw any attention to herself.

Whatever was up there, it was big, maybe the size of a dog or larger. It was big enough to yank Anson up with just one hand, so that meant it was likely bigger than she could imagine. Although Anson was well into his seventies, he was no slouch in a brawl. Her husband had been a hard worker, up at five every morning and straight to the gardens, where he would spend all day tending to them by hand without modern machinery. He'd had muscles like knots in a thick rope for as long as she could remember. Being wrapped up in those arms never made her feel the slightest bit susceptible to anything, but she felt vulnerable standing here, caught in her thoughts.

Looking around, she sought refuge before it caught her. She saw the half-opened door to the bedroom and backed into the room. From there, she quickly slid behind the door and stared out through the gap between the door and the trim. What she saw made her shiver.

A figure larger than any man was up in their attic. If she had to guess, the man—for she believed it a man—was at least seven foot tall. Every nightmare she had picked up while watching the evening news came to her. Just thinking about what could happen bothered her. Here she was, a good Christian woman, and their house was being broken into? Weren't there more deserving people out there? Wealthier people? What could anyone possibly want up in that attic? All they kept up there were old pictures and dry-rotted luggage, stuff like that. All her concerns tripled when the figure lowered its head below the ceiling of the hallway, and she saw what it was. Or rather, what it wasn't...

What she saw now was...something inhuman.

Its face was larger than a human, and its features appeared reversed from what she'd expected. So, with it looking around upside down, its expression looked correct to her. Although she didn't see any fangs, the mouth was large and drooling, large globules of spit dropping to the floor every few seconds. Overall, its alien-like face was enough to make her piss herself. Even as she felt the warmth trickle down her leg, she could see the creature's nostrils flaring, smelling something aromatic and taking interest. Realizing this, there behind the door she trembled.

Stop it! Stop shaking. You're going to—

The creature looked her way.

Now you've done it.

The creature's lone giant eye stared her way, and she might have escaped, not drawn attention to herself—if she had stopped herself from shuddering. She could be out the front door and in the truck in seconds, driving to the neighbor's house. Marty and Jake were still young, and they were good men. They would help her. But first she needed to—

Eeeerrrrrrrr.

The door creaked open slightly. She cursed herself for shaking so much.

Thump bump bam!

She returned her eye to the gap behind the door and saw it, the creature standing there. It looked almost insect-like with its segmented body. It had two arms and legs like a human, but there was a secondary limb hidden behind each, slightly smaller than the original. Together, the fists at the end of each hand opened and closed. Its clawed feet grabbed at the carpeted floor. Large sacs at its sides expanded as it breathed in, its nostrils working as if trying to find her.

Terrified by what she was seeing, she moved away from the gap, trying to disappear into the shadows behind the door. But even as she slinked back into the room, the creature approached, and she had to look for somewhere else to hide. Quickly, panicked, she tiptoed across the room, ducked behind the bed, and wriggled underneath the bedframe.

From there, she could see much. One of the creature's feet crossed before the other, coming her way. As the creature neared her position, she felt like screaming. Inside, she was a complete and utter mess. Here she had already wet herself, and now, she felt closer than ever to fainting. The pressure behind her eyes, the overwhelming trembling, all of it worked against her. Her throat had gotten so dry, feeling almost like someone had stuffed a cloth in her gaping hole, which made it difficult to breathe let alone scream. With her ears attuned to the slightest sound, she heard the bones within the creature's body crick and crack as it came closer. Now that it was so close, the strange sound of the creature's breathing alarmed her.

The creature stood there for a long moment. Bracing herself against the floor helped to steady her. She was still trembling and feeling woozy, but at least she had the floor, something to ground her to reality, one in which creatures like this didn't exist. As the seconds wound away and her hope dissipated, the creature finally retreated, moving to and climbing the attic ladder in bounding steps. But it did not withdraw the ladder, and instead left it there, perhaps knowing she was hiding and trying to lure her out. Thinking this, she waited, and eventually, as time passed, she fell asleep.

When she woke, it was light out. She hesitated to slide out from under the bed, but upon realizing how quiet it was in the house, she got to her feet. Slowly, she crept across the floor, doing her best not to make any sound, and came to the ladder.

"Anson?" she said, quietly.

No response. No nothing.

"Hon, you up there?" She spoke a little louder. "Are you okay?"

Still no answer. If the creature was still here, it wasn't making any sound. She would have expected it to attack her like it had Anson, so she was certain it wasn't in the house...yet. That didn't mean it wouldn't come back, though.

Wait a minute. Something's missing.

She identified it right away. There was a bloodstain on the carpet, but the arm itself was no longer there. Instantly, she felt like purging her stomach, convinced the creature had eaten not only the severed arm but also her husband. Knowing this, she considered skipping what came to mind, but she had to see for herself. She had to know.

Cautiously, she placed her foot on the first rung and pulled herself up. A waft of warm air found her, the smell of something rancid. She could barely contain herself, thinking the smell must emanate from Anson's rotting corpse. Almost positive that was the case, she felt slightly weakened by the thought. Yet, she continued climbing, another rung up the ladder every few seconds until only her head was in the attic. She glanced about, trying to make sense of what she was seeing. When she could not, but had confirmed the creature wasn't there, she climbed the rest of the way up and tried to discern what these things were. Kneeling beside one, she examined the pods more closely.

The object was a grayish-brown color, with ridges that ran up and down its egg-like shape. Just thinking about that word brought on a whole new realization, only she didn't think that was what they were, not entirely. They appeared more like a chrysalis, a cocoon of sorts. What hatched from them, she couldn't be sure, but she had an idea it would be one of the creature's young. They were too squat and thin for an adult creature. That much, she could see.

She stood and walked among them, counting. There were eleven total among the clutter of the attic. Apparently, all that bumping around had been the creature creating a nest. Broken wooden furniture, chairs she had long forgotten about, all of it sat broken into shards among cardboard boxes and trees and shrubs and dirt. There was so much refuse, she almost forgot about all the belongings the creature had just shoved to one end of the attic in one heaping pile.

Bang!

The sound alerted her to the broken gable vent, the wooden slats popped out, making for a portal. Without hesitation, Alberta made her way to the pile of past belongings and hid, watching from the shadowy corner of the attic as the creature appeared in the round opening.

Trembling, she had to grab hold of an old wooden chair to steady herself. She leaned in against the Christmas tree box and watched as the creature pulled itself into the attic. Once it plopped down on the floor, she could see it was carrying something. Without her glasses on, she couldn't identify what those objects were until the creature came closer.

Human body parts!

It had them cradled in its arms like a bundle of firewood. Seeing this made her want to scream. The urge to do so crept up her throat, deadened by the steady beating of her heart, rapping against the cardboard box like a base drum. She tried to calm herself but found it impossible. Worried the creature would hear her, and then, as if hearing her thoughts, the creature looked her way. It took a step closer, and when it did, she nearly fell back as she quietly took a step deeper into the shadows. The creature stood there for a long moment, staring her way while she panicked, wanted to scream and run, to do anything but just stand around waiting.

A second later, the creature turned, sat the body parts in a pile on the floor and squatted over them. To her amazement, the creature had a stinger-like appendage which it used to secrete some strange orange goo over the body parts. As it did, its secondary arms and legs worked to shape and manipulate the goop along with the body parts to form a cocoon similar to the others. And as the goo began to harden, she could see that in fact, this was the same as the others.

Did that mean Anson was inside one of those cocoons? Perhaps torn to pieces but becoming something new, something horrible? Would her Anson become one of *them*?

The process took less than twenty minutes, but she felt like she couldn't breathe the entire time. She'd been holding her breath without even knowing it, so when the creature finally left through the gable vent, she let it out in one loud gasp. Knowing the creature had left, though, did nothing to steady her nerves.

She ran to the opening, staring out into the daylight, trying to spot the creature. But she saw no signs of the thing. Thinking of what she had just witnessed, she turned and observed the cocoons. She couldn't help but wonder if Anson might still be alive.

Alberta ran to them, got to her knees, and moved her head close to one. "Anson? You in there?"

No answer.

She quickly made her way to another and did the same, with the same response. One after another, she moved through them, calling Anson's name, seeing if there would be a response. And so far, there hadn't been, and already she was at the last of them.

"Anson?"

No answer.

Then, she heard something. At first, she thought it a whisper, but now she could hear that it was a whimper.

She got closer, moved her head right beside the cocoon. The whimper was louder now, not crying so much as straining, she thought. And then another sound, something like what she imagined it would sound like of someone tore leather. And that was when she saw it, the hole in the cocoon, just large enough to catch a glimpse inside. A red-fleshed fist opening and closing upon the edge, prying away little bits of the cocoon's shell. Whatever was inside, it was hatching.

Without hesitation, she made her way back to the refuse pile and began digging through old books and decorations and clothing, searching for anything she could use as a weapon. Anson never had been too fond of guns—a fact she now cursed him for—so they didn't own one, but he had been a civil war fanatic. Somewhere up here in this mess, he had a few replica swords. They might not do much damage, but it was her best option in a pinch. And after digging through a few boxes, she found some of Anson's period clothes and soon found one of his swords. She wielded the thing like a baseball bat and waited. Then, thinking better of her situation, she tried to make a break for it before the thing hatched.

Alberta backed toward the ladder, cautious of the cocoons and the hole in the attic wall where the creature might appear at any moment. Each step she took came with a wave of emotion, realizing that not only had she lost her Anson, but she was also fighting for her own survival. Yet, the moment and came and went, and before she knew it, she was halfway down the ladder, sword in hand. Once she hit the floor, she was off and running, heading for the front door.

She grabbed the keys off the hook and threw open the door. The glimmer of sun on the horizon assaulted her eyes. Fighting through the brightness, she quickly made her way to the truck and fumbled through the keys until she found the right one. Even then, it was a struggle to get the key in. But, within a matter of seconds, she sat in the driver's seat and turned the key in the ignition.

Rah-rah-rah-rah-rah-runh.

"Don't do this!"

Rah-rah-runh.

"Please! Start, damn you!"

Rah-rah-rah-runh.

"Jesus!"

She checked the gauge. There was plenty of gas. So, what was the issue?

Then, she saw it. In front of the truck, the creature from every nightmare she'd ever had was standing there, and she knew it had done something to the engine to keep her from fleeing. When the creature made its move, shifting from the front of the truck to the driver's side, she slid across the bench seat and hurried out the passenger door. With nowhere to hide, she did the only thing she could think of, and took off running through the neighbor's cornfield.

There were enough stalks of corn to get lost, yet, as she ran through them, the stalks swung and swayed behind her. She caught glimpses of crimson red now and then in the distant background. She knew it was chasing her, and that if it caught her, she, too, would end up in one of its cocoons. The only way to survive was to lose it, which she believed difficult given its obvious determination. And she didn't think she could get within yelling distance of the neighbor's house. Now more than ever, she wished she had taken a moment to call the neighbor's first. The fact it hadn't even occurred to her while still in the house bothered her.

As she wriggled her way through several rows of stalks, she came to an opening and ran down the length of the row. She'd not gotten but thirty yards and had seen nothing but corn yet. When she risked a split-second to look behind her, she saw nothing of concern. She realized that didn't mean much, so she didn't slow down, and she kept running for whatever came at the end of this gap. The further she ran, the more hopeless that seemed, as row after row of endless corn shouldered the path. And then, she saw someone, though they were still very far away, and she was too out of breath to scream. She ran for him, what appeared to be Marty Sanderson.

He didn't see her, and she wished he had. As she made her way toward him, she waved her arms, trying to get his attention, but he was too busy staring off to her left to notice her. She tried to call out to him, but all that came out was a gurgling sound along with some squeaks and pops. There was a hope he would hear that, but she was still too far away for him to hear anything so quiet. And, even if he saw her, he likely wouldn't think anything wrong...at first.

When Marty finally did her look her way, he still didn't see her. But in that instant, hope filled her. Waving her arms like a mad person, jumping up and down, she began to tire. Especially at her age. The more she did it, the weaker she felt. Her heart hammered in her chest, and she felt faint again, as though she were dying. And because of all these distractions, she had forgotten about the creature chasing her.

The ambush came from her left. It felt like a truck had hit her. Flying through the stalks of corn, she lost sight of Marty.

No way she could recover from this. The creature would be on her within seconds. It would tear her limb from limb and then turn her into one of those cocoons. While the thought of that terrified her, there was a certain peace in knowing she wouldn't have to run anymore. In knowing her lungs wouldn't continue to burn, feeling like they would explode. Her legs wouldn't feel like toothpicks on the verge of snapping, and her eyes wouldn't water, making it so hard to see. And most of all, she would be with Anson, the love of her life.

Before she knew it, the creature was standing over her. She closed her eyes, shielding herself with trembling arms, as she prepared for the worst. When that moment didn't come, she dared a peek through prison bars made from her fingers.

Where is it?

She glanced to her left. Then to her right, and found it standing there, staring off into the distance, at Marty.

You should warn him.

Did she dare?

She got to her feet, having to fight just to stay afoot. Bruised and battered, she stared off in the direction where Marty had been, worried, wondering if he was still okay. She couldn't hear much of anything, and worse yet, she hated herself for not wanting to say anything to warn him. She couldn't risk it.

What can you risk?

She crept back through the corn until she reached the clearing once more. From there, she saw Marty. Her didn't see her, but that was okay. He was safe. Then she saw something move, faster than she could believe. The crimson figure sped through the corn, a wake of stalks behind it. Within a second, the creature leaped out of the corn and confronted Marty. Only, oddly, Marty didn't appear so surprised. Scared, yes, but he looked as though he had expected this. Whatever the case, the creature wasn't attacking Marty, and that meant he was okay.

Without further delay, she turned and hurried a few rows over, then continued her path toward freedom. Even with the creature being preoccupied with Marty, she had to hurry. There would be no hope unless—

That was when she saw it, a small shed out in the middle of

the corn. It was only big enough for a few hand tools, nothing of much significance. But she was sure she could fit inside, enough so she could stay there until it got dark and maybe slip away in the night. Surely the creature wouldn't wait around all day and night for her. It would have moved on to easier prey by then.

She opened the door and began removing the tools, hiding them in heavy patches of stalks so as not to arouse any suspicion. It wasn't much, a rake and a couple shovels. The smaller hand tools, she left, and she squeezed inside. After pulling the door closed, the intense warmth overwhelmed her. But she tolerated it, knowing she could heal up and rest for later. She would be safe.

After a few hours of that heat though, she felt like pulling her thinning hair out. And even when it started to cool down, it was unbearable. Sweat poured down her face. Her eyes were red from crying and the sting of the sweat. The skin on her face and arms felt blistered, as though her skin was melting. But she stayed long and quiet in her little hidey-hole the entire time, until she could crack the door and see it was well into the night hours. Only then did she move to escape.

She opened the door and slid out on her butt. With some difficulty, she got to her feet, a chorus of pops and cracks escorting her up. She stood and observed the field, finding nothing out of the ordinary, so she listened, trying to pick up the slightest sound.

When she finally thought it safe to leave, she did so slowly and with care, mindful of every step. She didn't want to make any noise because that would alert the creature to her presence, and she did not know how keen its senses were. All she knew was that it could kill and what it did with the human body parts.

After several minutes of walking, she saw an opening. She couldn't tell what it was but thought it a road. If she could get there and figure out where she was, maybe she could follow the road into town. Maybe hitch a ride even, if she were lucky. From town, she could send help for Marty and then get as far away from this place as possible.

Overwhelmed by this notion, she hobbled along, faster and faster. As she closed in on the road, she saw a street sign in the distance, one that was familiar to her. This was route 81. All she had to do was stick to her plan. Hope filled her, more and more, as she neared the road, and she was almost there, when something dropped with a thump before her eyes. She couldn't make out what it was, but she didn't have to because she knew right away. Maybe it wasn't *the* creature, but it was one of them.

When she lifted her eyes to it, she saw wings. She turned to run, but it was too late. Something grabbed her from behind. She closed her eyes, waiting for the pain, but that didn't come. Instead, she felt herself being lifted into the air and carried away. When she opened her eyes again, she was staring down at the ground, her yard, her house.

The creature dropped her off at the door where two others greeted her. They forcibly escorted her inside. From there, they went to the attic. She knew the way. In the attic, she stood before the wingless creature and observed the hatched cocoons. She didn't know what to do; feeling too old, too tired, too weak to care anymore. This thing had already taken her husband. How was she going to defeat something like this? She couldn't even take her own life as she'd seen firsthand what these creatures could do with dismembered humans. It would bring her back, make her one of them.

Would that be so bad? You'd be with Anson again.

She got down on her knees, giving herself willingly to the creature. One of the winged creatures moved in on her, seizing her hands. The non-winged one stared at her with its large eye. She didn't know what to think, what to say or do that she hadn't. But she sensed a certain conflict in the creature, something that wasn't entirely evil—a struggle.

The creature behind her let her go. All of them took a step back, except for their leader, the non-winged creature. She saw the opportunity and stood, began inching away. They only watched, and she did not know wh—

A twinge in her chest alerted her. The pain brought her to her knees once more, and the creatures moved in right away. Was that it? Were they showing her she would die, anyway? What an awful trick. And that was just it, if she had to die, she would put up a fight. Maybe she could take one of these things with her.

She scanned the attic, saw the boxes, a lamp, some clothes, the hilt of another one of Anson's swords. This was her chance. She took off for the pile, diving and seizing the handle. Bringing the sword around fast, the tip met flesh, and she thrust the sword deep into one creature's neck. It flapped its wings madly, the air bringing up years of dust. But all Alberta felt was the pain, her heart literally being wrung like a dishtowel inside her chest.

Standing, she withdrew the sword. She leaped forward and swung wildly. Having spent years and years farming, she had muscles unlike most women, so she could do some damage, even if by accident. She made contact here and there, taking out a chunk of flesh or causing a nasty gash. But none of the creatures were going down. And the pain in her chest was becoming unbearable.

You're dying, girl. Give up.

No, she wasn't about to go out unless she finished this. She had an idea how to take one of these things out, but it would take everything she had left. Heading for the closest one, she swung cleanly, swiftly, and with all her might. She saw the blade make contact, saw it slice through the creature's neck, then felt a pain so sharp it took her down. And the darkness that followed ate her alive, but at least she'd gotten one of them before they got to her.

Please let it be Anson.

Only that didn't matter, did it? Because even as she was dying, part of her already dead, she could sense what they were doing. She couldn't feel or see it, but she knew she was being torn limb from limb and formed into one of these cocoons. They were making her one of—

Everything went orange. She felt more alive than ever, her body already healing, becoming whole again. Her heart beat like it had when she was in her twenties. And there were dozens of them out there, other voices like her own, calling to her, convincing her. Most of all, she heard one voice in particular, that of her husband, calling her home.

About the Author

Kenneth W. Cain is the prolific author of *A Season in Hell*, *Darker Days*, *Embers*, and several other books, short stories, poems, and articles. He is also the editor of the well-known anthologies *Tales From The Lake Volume 5*, *When the Clock Strikes 13*, and *Midnight in the Graveyard*. As an Active member of the Horror Writers Association, he is chair for the membership committee, heads the Pennsylvania chapter, and was given the 2017 Silver Hammer Award for his service. Currently, Cain helps several publishers with their editing, formatting, book cover, and graphic design needs. Cain resides in Chester County, Pennsylvania with his wife and two children.

Curious about other Crossroad Press books?
Stop by our site:
http://store.crossroadpress.com
We offer quality writing
in digital, audio, and print formats.